LIFE OR DEATH

ALSO BY ANDREA KANE

Forensic Instincts Novels:
THE GIRL WHO DISAPPEARED TWICE
THE LINE BETWEEN HERE AND GONE
THE STRANGER YOU KNOW
THE SILENCE THAT SPEAKS
THE MURDER THAT NEVER WAS
A FACE TO DIE FOR
DEAD IN A WEEK
NO STONE UNTURNED
AT ANY COST
STRUCK DEAD

Other Suspense Thrillers:
RUN FOR YOUR LIFE
NO WAY OUT
SCENT OF DANGER
I'LL BE WATCHING YOU
WRONG PLACE, WRONG TIME
DARK ROOM
TWISTED
DRAWN IN BLOOD

Historical Romances:
MY HEART'S DESIRE
DREAM CASTLE
MASQUE OF BETRAYAL
ECHOES IN THE MIST
SAMANTHA
THE LAST DUKE
EMERALD GARDEN
WISHES IN THE WIND
LEGACY OF THE DIAMOND
THE BLACK DIAMOND
THE MUSIC BOX
THE THEFT
THE GOLD COIN
THE SILVER COIN

LIFE OR DEATH

ANDREA KANE

ISBN-13: 9781682320686 (Hardcover)
9781682320693 (ePub)
9781682320709 (Kindle)

LCCN: 2025934585

LIFE or DEATH

For questions and comments about the quality of this book, please contact us at: CustomerService@bonniemeadowpublishing.com.

BonnieMeadowPublishing.com

Printed in USA

Publisher's Cataloging-In-Publication Data
(Prepared by The Donohue Group, Inc.)

Names: Kane, Andrea, author.
Title: Life or death / Andrea Kane.
Description: Warren, NJ : Bonnie Meadow Publishing, [2026] | Series: Kane, Andrea. Forensic Instincts novel.
Identifiers: LCCN: 2025934585 | ISBN: 9781682320686 (hardcover) | 9781682320693 (ePub) | 9781682320709 (Kindle)
Subjects: LCSH: Detectives--New York (State)--New York--Fiction. | Irish--Fiction. | Murder--Investigation--Fiction. | Forensic sciences--Fiction. | LCGFT: Thrillers (Fiction) | Detective and mystery fiction. | Psychological fiction. | BISAC: FICTION / Thrillers / Suspense. | FICTION / Thrillers / Psychological. | CULTURAL HERITAGE / Irish.
Classification: LCC: PS3561.A463 L54 2026 | DDC: 813/.54--dc23

LIFE OR DEATH is dedicated to all the beloved people like this novel's Maureen McKay—the grandparents, great-aunts and great-uncles who are such an integral part of their little ones' lives, who help care for them, carpool them, share the ups and downs of child rearing with the moms and dads; who do projects with them, share stories of the past with them, and bring a layer of love to their lives that are indescribably meaningful. These special family members are precious and they are irreplaceable.

1

The McKay Residence
Woodlawn, Bronx, New York
Friday, March 10, 2:18 p.m.

Maureen McKay carried her bags of groceries into the house, smiling as she contemplated her menu for that Sunday's dinner. It would be the first family meal in ages where all four of her adult children would be there with her and Colin, sitting around the dining room table, eating, bantering, and laughing.

Just like old times, with the welcome addition of significant others.

The past decade of being an empty-nester had been hard on Maureen. Despite filling her time volunteering at the local library, she was still first and foremost a mother. She'd longed for that role ever since she and Colin were married thirty-five years ago. Their first son, Nolan, had been born one year later, followed by Garret, then Ryan, and finally Fiona. And now, even though all four kids had left the nest, Maureen's commitment to them remained strong.

On that thought, Maureen slid out of her coat and began putting away the perishables. Mentally reviewing what she planned to serve, she applauded herself for choosing Shepherd's pie as a main course. Everyone loved it, and the boys devoured huge portions, with Colin not far behind.

Her cheery thoughts were interrupted by the bing of her cell phone, alerting her to the fact that she'd received a text message.

She scowled, hoping none of her kids were cancelling. If they were, she'd certainly be giving them a piece of her mind.

Plucking her iPhone out of her handbag, she glanced at it with a blank expression. She didn't recognize the phone number. Probably an obnoxious scam.

She was about to simply delete the message, when a little voice inside her made her change her mind. She had no idea what prompted that little voice, but she heeded it and clicked into the text.

Her brows rose when she realized the message was from Shane. Her nephew worked for the FBI, and wasn't in the habit of contacting her in the middle of the day. Certainly not from a strange phone number.

As she read, her chest tightened:

Aunt Maureen. Urgent. Get Kennedy at school. Only you. NOW. Do NOT let her go home. Shane

Maureen's grip tightened around the iPhone, a hundred unanswered questions crowding her mind. She couldn't help herself; she texted back, holding her breath as she did:

Shane. I'm frightened. What's the emergency? Where's Caitlin? Please answer.

One second. Two seconds.

No received confirmation. And no response.

Desperate, she called the number. An automated voice answered, "The number you have reached is not in service at this time. This is a recording."

Maureen hung up, her breath coming faster, as panic seized her. Explanations would have to wait. A quick glance at the time told her there was no wiggle room. Kennedy would be getting out of her fourth grade class in under an hour. Clearly, her mother wasn't picking her up, which was unprecedented and unnerving. The implication was that no other arrangements had been made.

Still clutching her cell phone, Maureen considered using the Uber app that Ryan had installed for her. But she'd never tried it, not even set up an account. That would take time—time she didn't have. Not to mention, it would take the driver who knows how long to get here.

The local taxi service, just two blocks away, made much more sense.

She called them, stressed that this was an emergency, and was told the cab would be on its way in moments. She grabbed her purse, locked the front door, and waited outside.

Four minutes later, the cab pulled up to her house. She climbed in and gave the driver the address of Kennedy's elementary school.

Moments later, the cab was flying up the Bronx River Parkway to its destination-- and Maureen was praying.

***

Offices of Forensic Instincts
Tribeca, Manhattan, New York
2:40 p.m.

The Forensic Instincts brownstone was pulsing with energy.

The company president, Casey Woods—now Casey Woods-Hutchinson—had just returned to work, after a near-fatal shooting and months of rehab and recovery. Then, in joyous contrast and just weeks ago, had come an elegant wedding to her now-husband, high-level FBI BAU coordinator and head of all New York City violent crimes, Kyle "Hutch" Hutchinson.

Hutch had escorted her into the office at two-thirty this afternoon and planned on taking her home by five. Casey's surgeon had firmly stated that building up her stamina with shortened work days of just a few hours at a time were essential to her complete recovery. She didn't like it. But she'd agreed. Anything to return to the investigative company she'd founded and headed up, as well as to the employees who had long since become her dear friends.

Marc Devereaux, former Navy Seal, former FBI, and former FBI Behavioral Analysis Unit—and now Casey's right-hand man since Forensic Instincts' inception—was first to give her a warm hug and a broad, relieved grin when she and Hutch walked through the front door.

"Welcome back, Case," he said. "No matter how incredible the wedding was, it's even better to see you return to FI as commander-in-chief."

Casey hugged him back, grateful to no longer have need of her cane. "I can't tell you how much I've missed this place—and all of you." She smiled as she saw the group of people waiting to greet her. They all hung back, making sure to keep enough of a distance so as not to impede her entry.

"I'm fine," Casey assured them, steadily making her way in, and hugging each of them in turn.

"It's been a tomb here without you," Emma Stirling announced. A former pickpocket, now one of FI's official investigators, Emma looked deceptively like the storybook Alice in Wonderland and always blurted out her uncensored thoughts—at least to the team. To the world she was all pro, a chameleon who changed hues as the case required.

"Not *quite* a tomb," Patrick Lynch corrected, as he, too, hugged Casey. After thirty-five years with the FBI's violent crimes division, Patrick was FI's head of security and the father figure of the team—not to mention the person who kept them from toppling too far over the sharp edge that separated legal from illegal. "We've hardly been idle."

"Indeed we have not." Yoda, the FI team's invisible but close-to-omniscient AI system, concurred, his voice reverberating through the halls of the brownstone. "We wrapped up one solid case, which Casey was able to assist with from home. In addition, we closed the enormous case prior to that, the one we all recall that came a hair's breadth away from claiming Casey's life."

Everyone fell silent for a moment, remembering that nightmarish time right before Christmas.

Yoda broke the pained silence. "Given that this is an awkward and emotional moment, let me speak up by also welcoming you back, Casey, and assuring you that you were missed. However," he added, reverting back to his more scientific self, "I can report that all day-to-day operations ran smoothly here during your absence."

"Thank you, Yoda," Casey replied fondly. "That's good news, although I never doubted it."

"Yoda's operating on a whole new level." Ryan McKay, Yoda's creator and the team's techno-genius and creative problem-solver announced, after hugging Casey. Ryan was quite the antithesis of a tech-geek, with drop-dead Black Irish good looks and a boatload of sexual magnetism. He also had an ego to match his skills.

"Just this morning, I installed Yoda's latest update, which will make him faster, broader in scope, and better than ever—if that's even possible," Ryan added like a proud papa. "I've even enhanced his emotional capabilities."

"Okay, I'm impressed." Casey gave him a high-five. Despite his brilliant IT skills and his equally brilliant spycraft—which helped him produce robotic creations that were capable of doing just about everything—Ryan still regarded Yoda as his greatest achievement—one he'd created at the formation of Forensic Instincts and continually updated to be the most multi-faceted and sophisticated of inventions.

Ryan had one weakness, and that was the lovely, blonde-haired woman who was now kissing Casey's cheek and squeezing her hands—the FI team's own claircognizant, Claire Hedgleigh. She was a rare and accomplished intuitive, whose insights were crucial to solving their cases. She and Ryan were quite the couple—he, the diehard facts guy, she the believer in the metaphysical and the intangible.

At work, their differences resulted in many a sizzling argument. At home and in bed, they also sizzled.

Right now, Claire's eyes were damp with tears. "Casey, I can't tell you what it means to have you back, healing and strong."

Casey squeezed Claire's hands in return. "I'm so thankful to be here where I belong."

Hutch spoke up in that authoritative voice of his. "Let's get Casey seated and comfortable." He glanced to his right, at the warm, inviting FI library, and gently urged his wife in that direction. As the BAU coordinator and squad supervisor of the FBI New York field office's NCAVC—the National Center for the Analysis of Violent Crimes—Hutch was innately a take-charge guy. "This is ideal," he said, easing Casey onto the settee. "No stairs. A soft settee. And lots of room for everyone to gather round."

Casey's lips curved as she got settled. "I feel like King Arthur surrounded by my Knights of the Round Table."

"Good," Hutch replied. "Then go ahead and hold court. As long as you follow the surgeon's instructions."

"Yes, sir."

Hutch leaned over and gave her a quick kiss. "Agreement without a battle. I could get used to that."

"Don't," Casey advised. "It won't happen often."

The whole team laughed.

"I presume Hero stayed behind at your place?" Marc asked, referring to the team's human scent evidence dog who was now retired from the FBI and an integral part of FI—not to mention Casey's loving pet and a gift from Hutch.

"Yes." Hutch nodded. "Bringing an energetic bloodhound in was too much for Casey on her first trip back—"

"But he'll be coming in with me next week," Casey interrupted. "He belongs with the team, and with me."

Hutch's lips twitched. His wife might be a force to be reckoned with, but it felt so good to see her coming back to herself. "Let's make sure…"

"I'll be fine," Casey replied, meeting Hutch's concerned gaze. "Things need to get back to normal. Please, Hutch."

He wavered, never immune to that persuasive look of Casey's. "If you're up to it," he said.

"I will be."

Marc grinned. "So we'll have Hero back with us on Monday. And the team will be reunited."

Emma held up one index finger. “Hold that thought.” With that, she went up to the kitchen and returned in minutes with a cold bottle of champagne and a tray of flutes. “Celebration time,” she announced, popping the cork. “Casey was cleared weeks ago to have a drink, as she demonstrated at her wedding. So it’s time for a toast.”

Casey gratefully took her glass of bubbly from Emma. “You guys are the best. By the way, I spoke to Angela this morning. She’ll be starting here full-time on Monday. And I, for one, can’t wait. A whole new challenge and a whole new—and much-needed—area of expertise.”

Angela King, a barracuda of a defense attorney who had been a frenemy to FI during their last big case, was leaving her prestigious law practice to come on board with FI, after a unanimous vote of yes by the team. She was a powerhouse, and having her on their side was going to be a great asset—not to mention she’d be able to finagle things with the NYPD in order to keep the FI team out of jail.

“To Casey’s return,” Ryan said, lifting his glass in a toast. “Finally our captain is back at the helm.”

The entire team echoed the toast and drank.

As he took a healthy swallow of champagne, Ryan’s cell phone buzzed.

He saw the number and took the call, angling himself away from the group. “Hey, Mom. Everything’s on track for Sunday night’s dinner. No lecture required. Claire and I will be there, as promised.”

Maureen’s response was anything but what he’d expected. “Ryan…” Her voice was shaking… “Something bad is happening. I need your help.”

Ryan’s good humor vanished. His mother might be a worrier, but she wasn’t one to panic for no reason. “What is it? Where are you?”

"I'm in a taxi, heading for Kennedy's school."

"Why?"

In a choked voice, Maureen managed to fill Ryan in on Shane's message. If anyone could make sense of it, Ryan could. Even though Shane was older than Ryan, the two had been tight cousins since they were kids. And, regardless of how seldom they got together, that closeness had lasted. In addition, Shane's nine-year-old daughter, Kennedy, worshipped the ground that Ryan walked on.

Ryan left the library and went out to the entranceway, needing privacy for this call, and trying to digest what he was hearing. "Shane's never cryptic," he told his mother. "And he certainly doesn't call you from burner phones, which I'm sure this was. As for Kennedy—where's Caitlin?" Ryan asked, referring to Shane's wife and Kennedy's mom. "She picks Kennedy up every day except Wednesday, when she's not working virtually—and even then she has one of Kennedy's friend's mother pick her up. Besides, today is Friday."

Gripping the phone more tightly, Ryan forced himself not to overreact. There could be a logical explanation for this. But, in his gut, he knew otherwise.

His mind shifted into fix-it mode. "Try to stay calm, Mom," he said. "Pick up Kennedy. Bring her to your house. She'll love that. I'm going to New Rochelle, to check out Shane's place. Whatever it is that he wants to keep Kennedy from is obviously there."

"What could it be?" Maureen asked, frightened beyond words.

"I don't know." Ryan swallowed, trying not to further freak out his mother. "But I'm going to find out."

2

Offices of Forensic Instincts
Library
Friday, 2:55 p.m.

Ryan walked back into the library, standing at the threshold and making eye contact with Casey.

"I'm sorry, boss. I have to go," he said. "A family crisis. It could be dangerous. I need to be there."

Casey and the whole team caught Ryan's uncharacteristically frozen stance and white-faced fear.

"Go." Casey's response was instantaneous and unquestioning.

Ryan turned to Marc. "I need you to drive me. I'm not dealing with mass transit."

"Done." Marc turned and loped up the stairs to his office. There, he grabbed his Glock and two pairs of latex gloves, all of which he shoved into his pocket. That done, he headed back downstairs, ready to roll.

During Marc's absence, Ryan turned to Hutch, grappling with what to say, yet determined to do this on his own—for now. "I may need to reach out to you. I don't have the facts yet."

"No problem." Hutch didn't know the connection Ryan's situation had to him, but he didn't ask for clarification. "Call my cell."

"Thanks." Ryan was already retracing his steps, heading for the entranceway.

Marc joined him there, car keys in hand. "Let's go."

***

Bronx River Parkway
Friday, 3:55 p.m.

It wasn't rush hour—not quite yet. So the drive was an hour plus away. That now left a short distance to go.

Ryan remained quiet and tense, staring out the passenger window as he had throughout the trip to Westchester County.

"Where are we going in New Rochelle?" Marc finally asked, glancing at his GPS, aware that he didn't recognize the address Ryan had given him.

"To my cousin, Shane Walsh's, house," Ryan replied.

Marc nodded as they reached their exit and he eased his car around a loop and off the parkway. "Tell me only what I need to know. I'm not going to pry."

"You're not prying. I'm just really freaking out." Ryan cleared his throat and relayed the entire situation to Marc.

Marc took it all in. "You've mentioned that you had a cousin with the Bureau. But that's about all you've said, other than the fact that he has a wife and a young daughter."

Ryan shrugged. "Shane's a private guy, so I don't talk about him much. He's a Special Agent, Violent Crimes division, at the New York field office. He's been there since he joined the FBI about eight years ago."

"Does Hutch know him?"

"I never asked. But I doubt it. Hutch is in charge of all the Violent Crimes divisions. That's too high up to know every agent who works under him." Ryan pointed, shifting to the edge of his seat, and reiterating what the GPS was already showing them. "Make your next right. Two blocks down and make a left. Go through a few lights. You'll see a cul-de-sac on your right. Marigold Terrace. Shane's house is number 15."

Marc understood that Ryan's redundant supply of information was a manifestation of his anxiety. He just nodded again, then pressed his foot a little harder on the gas pedal to speed them up without accelerating too much. Suburban cops lived for speed traps.

Four minutes later, Marc turned onto Marigold Terrace and eased slowly around the curvy road.

"Three down on your left," Ryan instructed. "White clapboard house, blue shutters." His tension intensified as Marc reached Shane's home. "That's Caitlin's car parked in the driveway. And Shane's parked in his usual spot on the street. If they're both home…but they don't want Kennedy there… Shit."

Ryan flung open the passenger door before Marc had brought the car to a complete stop. He was halfway to the front door, digging in his pocket for the key Shane had given him long ago, when Marc reached his side.

"Ryan, wait." Marc grabbed his arm, stopping him in his tracks.

"Why?"

Marc tugged out the two pairs of latex gloves and shoved one pair into Ryan's hand. "Put these on."

Ryan gritted his teeth, while he and Marc worked their hands into the gloves. "Can't leave any new fingerprints," he muttered. "In case this is a crime scene." He sounded ill.

"Is the door unlocked?" Marc asked, quickly assessing the garage door, which was up. He might have suggested accessing the house through there, but Ryan was already in motion. And time was precious.

Ryan jiggled the doorknob. "No."

"Okay, use the key. I've got my Glock. Let's go."

Ryan's hands were shaking as he turned the key and pushed open the door.

He and Marc stepped inside. The foyer was empty and quiet. In fact, the whole house was silent in a way that suggested no one was home.

"Shane?" Ryan called. A pause. "Caitlin?"

No response. No sound of footsteps. Nothing.

Marc eased his way in front of Ryan, then crept ahead, sweeping the area with his gun.

Ryan followed behind him, aware that, not only was Marc armed, he was former FBI. He was trained at this. Ryan was not.

They'd barely gone fifteen feet, when Marc caught something in his peripheral vision, and swerved to his right. "Shit," he muttered.

Ryan peered around him and gasped. Just outside the bathroom was a crumpled body, unmoving and lying in a pool of blood. Beside it, were two shell casings and a cell phone that had been crushed. On the other side of the cell phone was a jagged line of blood.

The inconsistency of the blood pattern struck Marc at once. Reflexively, he whipped out his cell phone and took a few quick photos.

Ryan was in a whole different headspace. Pushing past Marc, he strode over, squatting as he reached the body. "Shane," he managed. "Oh my God. Shane."

Marc was beside Ryan in a heartbeat, restraining him from doing anything that would contaminate the scene. He leaned over Shane's body, checking for a pulse, a breath—any sign of life.

There were none.

Marc gripped Ryan's arm, standing and pulling him to his feet. Ryan's entire body was stiff with shock, but Marc knew that consolation would have to wait.

"Ryan, we've got to get out of the house," he said, visually sweeping as much of the ground floor as he could. "The killer might still be inside. He might have Caitlin." A hard swallow, as Marc considered the possibility that she might also be dead. That additional jagged line of blood didn't bode well. "I'll call 911 as soon as we're on the front lawn."

Ryan didn't budge. He was staring, wild-eyed, down at Shane's lifeless form. It was only when Marc tugged insistently at his forearm that he regained some semblance of awareness. "No, Marc." He gave a firm shake of his head. "I have to stay with him."

"He's gone," Marc stated simply, placing a supportive hand on Ryan's shoulder. "But Caitlin might not be. Let's get the EMTs and the cops here. We might be saving her life."

Slowly, Ryan turned, allowing Marc to lead him outside the house and to the front lawn, where he sank down on the grass, still unable to process this horrific occurrence.

Marc kept his Glock at the ready—just in case it was needed. "I'll watch the windows and the doorways to block any attempt at escape," he told Ryan. When there was no response, Marc glanced down, giving Ryan a worried look. The poor guy was staring off into space and wasn't even hearing him.

Stationing himself close to his friend's side, Marc took out his iPhone and called 911.

"What is your emergency?" was the immediate response.

Marc supplied his name, the address of the crime scene, and then, in staccato phrases, the necessary information.

He disconnected the call, knowing that it would be two minutes, at the most, before the ambulance showed up. He used the time wisely, pressing the button to Hutch's private cell phone line.

One ring. Then, "Marc?"

"We're in New Rochelle," Marc said. "Ryan's cousin, Shane Walsh, has been killed at his home. He worked for the Bureau, New York field office, Violent Crimes. I called 911, so the locals must already have been dispatched."

Not even a heartbeat of a pause. "Text me the address."

"Already done."

"Then I'm on my way."

***

McKay residence
Woodlawn, Bronx, New York
Friday, 5:15 p.m.

Maureen was sitting alone in Fiona's empty childhood bedroom, her heart hammering, her hands clasped in her lap.

It had been almost two hours since she'd picked Kennedy up at school. Given that both sets of Kennedy's grandparents were gone, Maureen and Colin were, not only next of kin, but authorized for Kennedy's drop-off and pick-up. So Maureen had just stepped outside the cab, waved at the security guard, and called out to her great-niece.

A bright smile, along with a tinge of puzzlement, had shot across Kennedy's face, and she'd rushed over to hug Maureen and jump into the taxi. Maureen had hugged her back, saying only that Caitlin had an unexpected late-day work conflict, and had asked Maureen to pick her up. She then went on to tell Kennedy how much fun they'd have on this impromptu get-together, chatting and watching a "girls' choice" movie with her great-uncle Colin.

An exuberant child by nature, Kennedy had been super-excited, and not at all alarmed by the explanation Maureen provided. Her daddy's being at work till dinnertime was the norm. Her mommy worked virtually all days but Wednesdays, but it wasn't the first time she'd been called into the office for a last-minute meeting on a different day.

So the ride from school to the Bronx was filled with fun chatter, along with Kennedy's proud announcement that she'd gotten an A on her social studies project.

She had no way of knowing how hard Maureen's heart was pounding, nor how lost she felt being totally in the dark.

They'd been halfway home, when Fiona called her mother from the subway.

"Hey, Mom," she'd said, keeping it short and sweet, since she obviously knew that Kennedy was in the taxi, all-ears. "Claire thought you might need some help getting ready for Sunday's family dinner. So we're on our way to your place." A pause. "Hi, Kennedy," she called out, loud enough for Kennedy to hear.

"Fiona! Are you coming to Aunt Maureen's house, too?" Kennedy asked eagerly.

"Sure am. Be there soon." Fiona made a kissing sound, and then disconnected the call.

Maureen's chest had constricted. She understood Fiona's implicit meaning only too well, as well as what had prompted it. Or rather, *who*. It was Claire, God bless her. She was more attuned to Ryan than anyone else in his life. Given that fact, combined with her metaphysical gift, she'd clearly picked up on the dark energy surrounding him—maybe even sensed filaments of what had happened. She was on her way to help, and she knew that bringing Fiona would help distract Kennedy from whatever anxiety she might start feeling.

Shortly after they arrived home, Colin had walked in the door, brow furrowed with worry. He'd received his wife's terrified text at the Bronx School of Science, where he taught, and had left for home the instant he'd read it.

Seeing his wife's drawn expression, he'd kissed her forehead, and then joined Fiona and Claire, who were sprawled on the living room rug, beginning a competitive game of Monopoly with Kennedy. Claire met Maureen's gaze only long enough to give a sensitive shake of her head, meaning she knew nothing definitive.

They'd have to wait to hear from Ryan.

Maureen had needed some space to deal with her emotions before Kennedy could pick up on them. She also wanted to be alone when Ryan's call did come, so Kennedy couldn't overhear it. As a result, she'd excused herself, then retreated to Fiona's childhood bedroom.

There, she'd braced herself for the worst.

***

Not ten minutes later, it came.

Maureen's cell phone rang. Seeing the number, she simultaneously accepted it and pressed the phone to her ear. "Ryan. Tell me what's happening. Please."

"I will." Ryan's voice was hoarse and ragged. "Are you alone?"

Maureen squeezed her eyes shut. Ryan never sounded so broken. Whatever he was about to say was going to be even more severe than she'd imagined.

"Yes," she said. "I'm in Fiona's old bedroom. Dad, Claire, and Fiona are playing a game with Kennedy in the living room."

A heartbeat of a pause. "Claire sensed something," Ryan realized aloud. "That's why she and Fee are there. Thank God for her insights. I'll text her now. Somehow she'll find a way to tell Dad and Fee what happened without alerting Kennedy." He swallowed, hard. "Mom, I need you to be strong. For me."

Maureen didn't hesitate. "I will be."

"Shane is dead," Ryan managed. "He was murdered in his house. Marc and I found the body. And Caitlin is missing—I have no idea where she is or who she's with. We tried calling and texting her, but no response."

"Oh, dear Lord, no." Tears welled up in Maureen's eyes. "You're sure Shane is…?"

"Yes." Ryan made a choked sound. "The paramedics and the ME were there. He was pronounced dead and taken away by ambulance. The local police showed up right away. But Marc also called Casey's husband, Hutch, who's the head of all violent crimes at the Bureau's New York field office. He jumped in his car and checked in with his Assistant Director in Charge during his drive to New Rochelle. This case is now under FBI jurisdiction, with Hutch at the helm."

Ryan took a sharp breath, words just tumbling out of his mouth. "Hutch showed up at the scene in less than an hour, and began running the show. The FBI is all over this, since Shane was one of their own. The Bureau's evidence response team sealed off the house, and did a full sweep, setting a perimeter that kept everyone else out.

Marc and I had already gotten a good look at most of the first floor, which was empty and undisturbed. My guess is the rest of the house was the same, given that this was no robbery. I'm sure the agents will question a slew of people, including members of the NYPD, since Shane was with them before he joined the Bureau. Between both organizations, who knows how many enemies he's made?"

Maureen absorbed the gist of what Ryan was saying, and she fought back her tears. "But to kill him? What kind of sick person would do that? And Caitlin—are we sure she's alive? Could Shane's killer have taken her?"

"I don't know, Mom. Both her car and Shane's car are parked outside the house. That's all I know." Ryan drew another shaky breath. "I'll get a copy of the locals' crime scene report later. Right now, I'm having a hard enough time accepting the fact that Shane is gone. I keep waiting for him to call and ask me to meet him somewhere to shoot hoops."

Ryan's voice broke. "But I know Shane. He'd order me to focus on Kennedy. Hutch instructed me that we shouldn't say anything to her. He's sending SA Darren Barkley, the case agent, along with an FBI victim specialist, Dr. Sheryl Abel, to your house. Dr. Abel has a lot of experience in this area. She and Special Agent Barkley will speak with you first, explain their procedure. I don't know the details, but I do know they'll want you to be with Kennedy when she's told. That will offer her the emotional support she needs." Ryan knew the answer to his next question even before he asked it. "Will you be able to handle that?"

Instantly, Maureen called on her stoic core, stemmed her tears. "Without question. I'll hold Kennedy's hand and give her my strength."

"She's going to be devastated." Ryan was a hair's-breath away from losing it entirely. "I don't see how she'll ever recover."

Maureen frowned, recognizing that her son was still in shock. "Where are you now?"

"In Marc's car. He's dropping me off at your house. We hit traffic. But I should be there in fifteen minutes."

"Good. You need to be with us. Plus, Kennedy will be thrilled to see you. You know how she adores you." Maureen paused again. "When will the FBI people be arriving?"

"Soon. They're already nearing your neighborhood. They'll wait until I get there and have a few normal minutes with Kennedy. Then I'll text them and they'll drive right over." Ryan swallowed. "Keeping myself together is killing me, Mom. But, I have to…"

"My poor Ryan," Maureen murmured. "I'm so sorry the weight is on your shoulders. But, remember that Dad, Claire, Fiona, and I are all waiting. We'll all be here for you. And, of course, for Kennedy. We're family. We stand together."

Ryan felt a rare surge of feeling come over him. Relief. Gratitude. Love.

"Thanks, Mom," was all he could manage to say.

3

McKay Residence
Woodlawn, Bronx, New York
5:50 p.m.

"Hey!" Ryan called out as the front door shut behind him. "Anybody home?"

Kennedy abandoned the Monopoly board and was on her feet and in motion all at once. "Ryan!" she squealed, racing straight from the living room to the foyer, and flinging her arms around him. "I didn't know you'd be here!"

Ryan hugged her back. "That's why it's called a surprise, sunshine," he replied, ruffling her hair. "Besides, did you think I'd miss out on seeing you? Or at trouncing Fee at Monopoly? Once I heard that you, she, and Claire were here, and the game you guys were playing with my Dad, I rushed right over to join in." He winked at her. "I know you'll wipe me out, but at least I'll come in second, right?"

"With a little luck, maybe." Kennedy's smile lit up her face, and it made Ryan ill to contemplate what she was about to go through.

Over Kennedy's head, Ryan's gaze locked with Claire's. A current of painful communication passed between them. Ryan had spoken about the Walshes to her—but not in detail. Still, she just knew. Ryan didn't have to elaborate, to say thank you, to or ask her to stay. She understood the state he was in. And she wasn't going anywhere.

"Fiona, your dad, and I are holding our own quite nicely," Claire said aloud, still holding Ryan's gaze. "But Kennedy's a pro. So the rest of us need time to join forces and discuss our strategies, so at least one of us is sure to beat her. You two go ahead into the kitchen and eat some of the brownies we brought. They're awesome."

Kennedy had already seized Ryan's hand and started to pull him in that direction.

"We've got the better end of this deal," she called over her shoulder. "We get brownies and catch-up. You get strategy-building time. And I'm still about to buy Broadway which will eventually wipe everyone out."

Still struggling valiantly to focus on the here and now, Ryan followed Kennedy to the kitchen, quickly punching in a text as he did, alerting the FBI agents that he'd arrived.

No matter what they did, would Kennedy ever be close to the same? To Ryan's way of thinking, that was an impossibility. Kennedy and her parents shared a special kind of closeness. So, no matter how good Dr. Abel was, how much love and support the rest of the family showered on Kennedy, the end result was the same.

Nothing could bring back Kennedy's daddy.

***

Still alone in Fiona's childhood bedroom, Maureen glanced out the window and saw the FBI's case agent and victim specialist's car pull up to the house.

As a result, she reappeared in the foyer just as the doorbell rang. With a pained expression, she greeted the two of them at the door.

"Agent Barkley, Dr. Abel," she said, her tone hollow. "I'm Maureen McKay, Kennedy's great-aunt. Her father Shane..." An agonized pause. "...was my nephew." She gestured for them to come in.

"Mrs. McKay, we're terribly sorry for your loss," SA Barkley said with genuine compassion. He was in his early forties, with a solid build, sandy hair, and a personable manner.

"You have our deepest sympathies," Dr. Abel echoed, her tone gentle. She was older than her counterpart, with fine lines around her eyes, a soothing demeanor, and an astute expression. "We're here to make this as painless for your great-niece—and for the entire family—as we can."

Maureen nodded. "Thank you. I don't know where you want to talk with me alone. I need to understand what I should expect and what you want me to do—both before, during, and after you speak with Kennedy."

"Where is Kennedy now?" Dr. Abel asked.

Maureen gestured, first at the living room, then at the kitchen. "She was playing Monopoly with the family. Right now, she's in the kitchen with my son, Ryan. She's very fond of him."

Barkley nodded, ingesting that fact, then glancing into the living room. "You obviously have a big, close family."

"We do."

"That will be of great comfort to Kennedy." Barkley gave a thoughtful pause. "Tell me, is there an empty room on this floor where Kennedy feels most comfortable? That would be my choice for our conversations—the one with you, and, afterwards the one with her. We'll have privacy but the rest of the family will be close by after our talk."

Maureen nodded, pointing. "We have a small den behind the living room. It's very cozy. Kennedy loves to read and do her homework in there."

"Good. Then I'd like for the three of us to go there while Kennedy is still in the kitchen. She doesn't need to know we're here just yet."

"Understood." Without pause, Maureen turned, leading SA Barkley and Dr. Abel to the lovely room she'd spoken of. It had a cushy sofa, tufted chairs, high-piled carpet, and family photos lining the shelves.

"This is ideal," Dr. Abel said.

Barkley nodded. "Let's sit. I'll explain what is going to happen, as well as guide you so you're prepared—as prepared as anyone can be in this situation. Once we've answered any questions you have, you'll get Kennedy and bring her in here to join us."

Maureen perched at the edge of a tufted chair, waiting as the others took their seats.

"When you bring Kennedy in, why don't you sit with her on the sofa?" Dr. Abel suggested. "You'll be right beside her."

"Good idea." Maureen understood at once. "That way, I can hold her, embrace her."

"Exactly," Dr. Abel said.

SA Barkley leaned forward and began. "I'll be the one who delivers the difficult news. As we term it, I'll be the talker, Dr. Abel will be the comforter. I'll be sure to keep eye contact with Kennedy so she feels connected throughout my entire explanation. I'm going to be very gentle, but very straightforward. Euphemisms don't work. They're confusing and ineffective. Kennedy needs to understand the truth and not feel patronized. I'll use her name and tell her that her dad is dead, that he was shot and killed. I know that sounds cruel, but she'll process that better than a longwinded sugarcoated explanation."

"I'll assure Kennedy that we're here to answer any questions she has and to help in any way that she needs," Dr. Abel added. "I'll be sure to ask Kennedy if she wants any more trusted adults present, or even a religious leader. We'll wait, if need be. After that, we'll hold a moment of silence while she's processing."

Once again, Maureen was fighting back tears. "I…that's very kind of you."

"Weeping is a natural reaction, Mrs. McKay," Dr. Abel said softly, studying Maureen's face. "Shane was your nephew. You're feeling his loss, as well. In addition, your emotional expression will encourage Kennedy to display hers. That will keep her from repressing her feelings, which is of vital importance. We don't want her to internalize. We want her to reach out to you and to share what she's experiencing."

You'll be assessing her, Maureen deduced, unable to say the words aloud. *A suicide assessment.*

She shuddered. "I understand," was all she said aloud.

Her gaze met Dr. Abel's, and the victim specialist saw her reaction and interpreted its cause. "You're a wise and strong woman, Mrs. McKay," she said. "And a caring one. Kennedy is fortunate to have you. With so much love surrounding her, she'll get through this. And we'll be here to help make that happen."

Maureen swallowed, understanding what Dr. Abel was telling her, and feeling a swell of relief at her words. Her mind raced on. "What about afterwards, once you've told Kennedy what she has to know. Will you leave immediately? Is there follow up of some kind?"

SA Barkley answered. "We'll stay as long as Kennedy wants us to. We'll ask how we can make her feel safe. We'll also reassure her that we'll keep an FBI presence at the house. Hopefully that will ease any fears she has."

Maureen paled. "I never even thought of that. Given that Shane was killed and Caitlin is missing, Kennedy herself could be in danger. The killer might think she knows something or that she overheard her parents talking..."

"I don't believe that's a strong possibility, but we are prepared for it," Barkley said. "The Bureau will ensure her safety. We'll have to shut down her social media and IT presence—laptop, cell phone, iPad—to minimize potential tracking by the offender."

"She has no social media presence," Maureen replied woodenly. "Plus her devices have strict parental controls on them. Being an FBI agent, Shane was very protective of Kennedy and her safety."

Agent Barkley nodded. "Good. That will make the process that much easier."

Dr. Abel spoke up. "I'll be giving Kennedy a Bureau-issued cell phone and my work cell number. She can call me anytime she needs to. In addition, before I leave this evening, I'll ask if I can call or visit tomorrow morning. Whichever makes you and Kennedy feel more comfortable, I'll do. At that time, you and I can discuss grief counseling, coping skills to mitigate Kennedy's anxiety, and all the other resources that are available to you, especially given that your nephew was FBI. We're not going anywhere. We're in this for the long haul."

Maureen's lips quivered as she looked from Dr. Abel to SA Barkley and back. "You're fine people. I can't tell you how grateful I am for all your support."

"You're very welcome." Barkley gave her a questioning look. "Are you ready to get Kennedy? Or do you need another moment or two?"

Slowly, Maureen came to her feet. "I'm ready."

***

Ryan looked up when his mother walked into the kitchen. He and Kennedy had been munching on brownies—brownies that tasted like sawdust in Ryan's mouth. He gently gripped Kennedy's shoulder as his mother spoke.

"Kennedy," she said softly. "There are two people from the FBI here to talk to you." She caressed Kennedy's face, making sure she felt loved and never alone. "I'll be with you the whole time."

Kennedy's eyes widened. "Talk to me about what?"

Maureen swallowed hard. "They'll explain."

As if sensing something bad was about to happen, Kennedy turned to Ryan, gave him a nervous look and then immediately began fiddling with her pendant necklace—a gift from her parents that was a silver heart with her initial K in the center.

"I'm right here, sunshine," Ryan told her. "I won't even finish my brownie."

Nodding, Kennedy gripped her great-aunt's hand, following her from the kitchen to the den.

The door shut behind them.

Ryan joined the others in the living room.

"We assume those are FBI agents," Fiona said, rising to her feet, even as Claire and Colin followed suit. "They were in with Mom for a long time."

Ryan nodded. “It’s the case agent and a victim specialist. They were prepping Mom. She’ll stay in there while they tell Kennedy about Shane.”

“Poor child,” Colin murmured. “My heart breaks for her.” He gave Ryan a questioning look. “Did you already speak to your brothers? Or should I call them now?”

“I called them both from Marc’s car,” Ryan replied. “Nolan should be here soon. Garret is cutting short a client meeting, and then heading straight over.”

Colin nodded.

No words were spoken after that. They just stood together as one, exchanging worried glances, and waiting. The clock ticked by. The time crept along, endless in its duration.

At last, the door opened, and the world shifted forever.

SA Barkley and Dr. Abel stepped out, gesturing for the family to go inside. “Be with her,” Dr. Abel said softly. “She wants and needs you all.”

Ryan shot a quick glance at Claire.

“I’ll be out here waiting,” she told him, her voice soft and caring.

He nodded, heading for the den. He could hear Kennedy’s hysterical sobbing long before he crossed the threshold with his dad and Fiona.

If hearing her tore out his guts, seeing her was worse. She was like a broken doll, collapsed against Maureen on the sofa, her body shaking with sobs as she clutched her pendant. She wept until she was gasping, repeatedly whispering “Daddy”, and clinging to Ryan’s mom like a lifeline. Tears were flowing down Maureen’s cheeks as she gazed at the rest of the family, and she held Kennedy tightly, rocking her like a baby to ease her pain.

Ryan squatted down beside them, taking Kennedy's quaking hand in his. Seeing him, Kennedy wept all the harder, tightening her fingers in his. Her great-uncle and Fiona gathered around her, as well, hugging her and giving her their strength.

Having issued a few quiet instructions to Maureen, SA Barkley and Dr. Abel went to disable all of Caitlin's devices and then respectfully departed, leaving Kennedy in her family's loving arms.

They all remained together, joined shortly thereafter by Nolan and Garret, who looked equally as pained and lost as the others.

A timeless time later, Fiona spoke up. "Sweetie, why don't you lie down on the living room couch?" She tenderly stroked Kennedy's hair. "I'll get you a little something to eat and we can all sit with you."

"I can't eat." Kennedy shook her head wildly, her voice barely audible.

"But you can lie down." Ryan added his suggestion to Fiona's. "I'll carry you in and sit right beside you. You don't have to sleep. But you do need to rest. Okay?"

Kennedy gazed up at Maureen, panic in her eyes.

"I won't budge from your side," her great-aunt responded to the unasked question. "In fact, why don't you and I visit the bathroom first, so you can wash your face with a cool cloth? Then, Ryan can carry you straight to the couch and we'll all be with you. Maybe a little later, you'll feel up to a glass of milk and a PB&J sandwich."

Kennedy shook her head. "I can't eat," she whispered. "But I do need the bathroom." Ever so slowly, she unfolded, releasing her death-grip on Maureen.

She looked pleadingly at Ryan, her face anguished and her eyes swollen from crying. "You don't have to carry me. But…are you staying?"

Ryan's insides twisted. "For as long as you need me."

She glanced around the room.

"We'll all be here," Garret assured her.

"You couldn't kick us out," Fiona added.

"Okay, then." Kennedy let Maureen lead her to the first floor bathroom.

***

"She's totally broken," Ryan said once they were out of earshot.

"You're not much better," Nolan said, studying his brother. He and the whole family knew how tight Ryan and Shane had been. "We're all here for you, too."

"And for each other," Colin added. He raked a hand through his salt-and-pepper hair. "There's a wake and a funeral to plan. I don't want the whole burden to fall on your mother."

"I'll help Mom," Fiona said. "And I'm sure the FBI will have some input, too."

"Garret and I know a few of Shane's friends," Nolan told them. "We can get a list together. What about Caitlin's friends? How do you want to handle them? She's Shane's wife. We have to give her the respect she deserves. I know both her parents are gone, and she has no other family, but there must be someone we should contact."

Fiona frowned and shook her head. "I'm not sure we should go that route, at least not yet. We don't know where Caitlin is or even if she's alive. The FBI might prefer we keep things quiet. I'm just speculating, but let's see what they say before we open that door."

"I agree," Colin said. "We'll take our cues from law enforcement. Somehow we'll find the right way to honor Shane."

Ryan swallowed hard. "No matter how this plays out, poor Kennedy has to face the gruesome finality. A wake. A funeral. No mother standing beside her. How much more can she take?"

No one replied.

In fact, the whole family stopped talking altogether as they heard Maureen and Kennedy's voices emerging from the now-open bathroom doorway.

"Let's go to the living room." Fiona was already heading for the door. "That way we'll be waiting for her. These plans can wait for tomorrow."

***

Ryan stayed for hours, as did his siblings. At Ryan's urging, Claire had joined them, meeting Kennedy and speaking to her in that gentle way Claire had. That had distracted Kennedy for a while, partly because she was curious about Ryan's girlfriend, and mostly because Claire was Claire. Not only did she temporarily stop Kennedy's tears, she even got her to eat half a sandwich and drink a glass of milk.

But, eventually, the novelty wore off and the nightmare slammed back to the forefront of Kennedy's mind.

She pushed away her plate and dissolved back into tears, this time pressing her face into Ryan's shoulder and drenching his shirt with her tears. "Daddy's dead, Ryan," she whimpered. "Oh my God, Daddy's dead." She raised her face to his. "And where's Mommy? Where did she go? Did that horrible killer take her?"

Ryan hugged her tightly. "We don't have facts yet, sunshine. But we will. I promise you that. I'll make sure of it."

And he meant it. He *was* going to solve the whole puzzle—not only if Caitlin was alive and where she was, but who had killed Shane.

He'd bring this to FI, get them to take this on as their number one priority case.

No matter how good the FBI was, Forensic Instincts was better.

***

The smell of the sea air wafted through the slightly-open window of the motel room. It went unnoticed by the room's sole occupant, who was busy opening their MacBook. The occupant started a terminal session, and proceeded to log in from one computer to another, the connection zigzagging halfway around the world to hide their tracks. When they arrived at the final destination, they opened the log file showing GPS tracking coordinates. There had been no changes in a couple of hours. The target had remained exactly where she was suspected to be.

The viewer logged out of all the remote computers and closed the lid of the Macbook.

4

Ryan's apartment
Park Slope, New York
Saturday, 5:30 am

Ryan stirred, rolling onto his back on the bed, and folding his arms beneath his head as the first pale rays of dawn peeked through his windows.

He hadn't slept a wink. How could he when all he could see was Shane's lifeless body, all he could hear were Kennedy's wrenching sobs?

He'd stayed put at his parents' house until Kennedy's body gave in and she passed out from sheer exhaustion. Then, he'd carried her up to Fiona's old room and tucked her into bed.

He sat beside her for a long time, just staring off into space.

Sometime later, his mother had come in. "It's time for you and Claire to go home," she'd instructed him. "I just shooed your brothers and sister out of the house. You're dealing with your own pain and shock. And, knowing you, you're ready to take on this investigation by yourself, with the help of your team. You need to recoup for that.

Dad and I are here. We'll stay at Kennedy's bedside all night. You'll come back tomorrow. Now go."

Ryan had been too spent to argue. Acting on his mother's orders, he and Claire had gone back to his place, where he'd collapsed on the bed out of total emotional exhaustion. Claire had waited long enough to send a Slack message to the entire FI team, providing them with all the information she'd been privy to, and arranging for a seven AM meeting in their first floor conference room. Customarily, the meeting would be held in their main conference room on the second floor, but everyone wanted to spare Casey the effort of walking the long, curvy flight of stairs.

That done, Claire had lay down beside Ryan, linking her fingers with his, silently being there to offer her strength and her support.

The rest of the night had passed in silence.

Moments ago, Ryan had vaguely heard Claire leave the room. She returned shortly thereafter, perching at the edge of the bed and handing Ryan a cup of coffee and two ibuprofen tablets.

"Hey," she said softly. "These will help your headache."

Ryan gave her a grateful look, pushing himself up until his back was propped against the headboard, and then popping the tablets into his mouth and washing them down with a swallow of coffee. "Thank you," he said, regarding Claire through red-rimmed eyes.

Claire lay her hand against his jaw. "No thanks necessary."

He turned his lips into her palm. "I barely heard you leave the room."

"I know. I was hoping you were resting."

"Yeah, well, that's not happening," he replied, his tone hollow. A deep sigh. "I'm guessing you Slacked the team. What did you tell them?"

"That we'd be meeting at the brownstone at seven am," Claire said. "I got responses from everyone. They'll all be there—including Casey."

Ryan nodded, taking another gulp of coffee. "What time is it now?"

"Five-forty. Do you want a PowerBar?"

"I don't think I can swallow it."

"Try," Claire responded. "You need to be at full strength—for Kennedy, and for Shane."

Ryan squeezed his eyes shut. "I know."

Claire rose. "I'll even eat one, along with my herbal tea, suffer though I will." She attempted the light humor, even though she knew Ryan wouldn't respond in kind. She was still accessing her inner strength and insights in order to best help Ryan cope. It wasn't going to be an easy process.

Ryan opened his eyes and turned to meet her gaze. "I don't even recognize myself. You know me. I can handle anything. Fix anything. But this time—I'm frozen, flailing, with no firm footing and no working strategy."

Claire ran her fingers lightly through his hair. "That will change. Once you're at work, with the team's support and your brilliant mind, you'll develop a plan and a strategy. Please…cut yourself some slack. This is a crisis that not even a superhero like you can surmount overnight."

She turned to go get the PowerBars and tea.

"Claire?" Ryan's voice stopped her, and she looked back at him in question.

"I love you," he said simply.

Her expression grew tender. "I know. I love you, too. And we'll get through this."

***

Offices of Forensic Instincts
1st Floor, Small Conference Room
Tribeca, Manhattan, New York
Saturday, 6:55 a.m.

The entire team was already settled in tub chairs, their work stations in front of them, when Ryan and Claire arrived. Between what Marc had briefly told them about the crime scene, and the details Claire had laid out in her Slack message, everyone was up to speed—at least on the basics.

Casey rose from her tub chair at the head of the room and walked over to Ryan, giving him a caring hug. "I'm so very sorry," she said quietly. "Your work family is here for you. And once you fill in all the blanks, we're going to solve this case."

"Thank you," Ryan replied, touched as the whole team stood, reaching out to him, and reiterating Casey's words. "That means a lot to me."

Yoda's voice resounded through the room. "My sympathies, as well, Ryan. I'm on standby for whenever you need me."

Ryan's lips curved a bit as he absorbed one of the very humanlike traits he'd added to Yoda's underlying AI model during retraining. "I appreciate that, Yoda."

He and Claire walked over to the JURA station, where Ryan poured himself a cup of coffee and got Claire her herbal tea. They then both joined the group, taking their respective seats.

Casey turned on her iPad, interlaced her fingers, and addressed the team.

"Before we begin, let me tell you the additional information Hutch passed along to me a half hour ago. As you know, he's personally heading up this investigation. He's already hand-picked the Violent Crimes squad supervisor he wants and assigned him the case. Ditto on the case agent, and the co-case agent. Not to mention all the others who'll comprise the team. A task force with agents from different squads will be organized. An Official Press Release will be issued about Shane's murder, Caitlin's disappearance, and the barebones facts about the ongoing investigation. There'll be an official media briefing on TV. Also, there'll be a press release added to the New York field office's website."

Casey concluded, "They'll be asking for leads pertaining to Shane's murder. They'll also obviously be seeking the public's help with regard to Caitlin's whereabouts. That's as much as Hutch can disclose, no matter how much he cares."

Marc nodded. "His hands are tied. We get it. Which is our weakest link. We don't know what cases Shane was working now, or what he worked during his past eight years in the Bureau. And the FBI sure isn't giving us access to any of that."

Casey continued, her tone softening, as she looked directly at Ryan. "All that's true. So we have to lean in with our strengths. The obvious one is the familial connection—you. I realize how painful this is, but we need as many personal details as you can provide, in order to be most effective." She paused, uttering her next words gently. "You and your cousin were very close, I assume?"

A muscle worked in Ryan's jaw. "Very."

Casey's fingers were poised over her keypad, as the rest of the team followed suit. "Tell us everything you can about him. Personal as well as professional. That will give us our first leg up on law enforcement."

Ryan took a swallow of coffee, then began. "My mother and Shane's mother were sisters. Shane was an only child, and both his parents are gone now. He is…was…a few years older than me. Even so, we'd been tight since we were kids, probably because we were both into gadgets and, later, into every conceivable sport. But Shane walked the straight and narrow, whereas I was the rebel. From the time he was in his teens, he was dead-set on being a cop. He blasted his way through his BS in Criminal Justice Administration, joined the NYPD, and earned his way up to detective. Then, eight years ago, he was accepted into the FBI, Violent Crimes, New York field office, where he stayed."

"What about Caitlin?" Casey asked, typing rapidly into her iPad. "When did she and Shane meet? Marry?"

A reminiscent look crossed Ryan's face. "They were high school sweethearts. That's why Shane and I stopped hanging out as much. He and Caitlin were pretty much inseparable. They got married a few years after I dropped out of MIT. Kennedy came along a short time later. I'm not really a kid person; that's never been my thing. But Kennedy and I just connected, even when she was a toddler clinging to my leg. We've had a special bond since then, even though I don't get to see her a lot. Months will pass where we're all too busy to get together, and yet things with Kennedy stay the same. She kind of adheres to me like a peppermint stick."

Ryan broke off, hiding his emotions by taking another swallow of coffee.

Casey steeled herself, knowing that her next question was going to push Ryan over the edge. She wished she didn't have to ask it. But she did.

"So Shane and Caitlin's marriage was solid—right up to the end? No affairs, problems, or issues that you know about?"

Ryan's mug clattered to the table, and his head shot up. "Are you suggesting that *Caitlin* killed Shane?"

"No, I'm not," Casey answered quietly. "But it's a thread the FBI is going to explore. The spouse is always at the top of the suspect list, and therefore, the first one questioned. In this case, that's impossible. Caitlin is missing. The Bureau will focus on that fact and pursue her with all their resources. So we have to do it first." Casey leaned forward, touching Ryan's sleeve. "I hate doing this to you. But you knew your cousin and his wife a hell of a lot better than the FBI did. We need to use that knowledge to our advantage. The sooner we get Caitlin off the suspect list, the better."

There was a long moment of silence, during which time Ryan dragged both hands through his hair. "This sucks," he said at last.

"I know," Casey agreed. "And I'm sorry."

He drew a swift breath. "Okay, here's the answer to your question. Shane and Caitlin were as tight as any couple I know. As I said, they were high school sweethearts. They've loved each other forever. The only things I've ever heard them argue about are who's a better driver and how to get Kennedy to go to bed at a decent hour. There was only caring and respect between them. And they both adored Kennedy. For her sake alone, Caitlin would never do this. Not to mention, she had no motive, nothing to gain. Let the Bureau explore this angle all they want. I'm sure they'll question me and my family—which I'd better prepare them for. Still, the answer won't change. This is a dead end." Ryan gulped down his cup of coffee, his hand shaking.

Without a word, Claire rose and refilled his mug. She squeezed his shoulder as she handed it to him. "Do you need a minute?" she asked.

"No. I need to move away from this subject."

"Done," Casey said. "Let's shift gears."

"Wait." Marc wished he could give Ryan time to compose himself. But that wasn't in the cards—not yet. "Before we bring this subject to a close, I need to add that I took a few quick photos of the crime scene. They're stored in the cloud. But I saw what I thought was an odd pattern. A pool of blood gathered beneath Shane, and a separate jagged line of blood on the floor several feet away. My gut tells me they belonged to two different people. The first was obviously Shane's. But the second—was it Caitlin's or the killer's? If it was Caitlin's, that's going to give the FBI more reason to consider a marital dispute as the cause of death."

Marc held up his palm as Ryan opened his mouth to blast him. "I'm not giving credence to the idea. I'm just stating facts. More importantly, since we're dismissing the idea that Caitlin would harm Shane, we have to probe the possibility that whoever killed Shane, injured either themselves or Caitlin in the process."

"Agreed," Casey concurred.

Marc cleared his throat. "I want to get my hands on the Bureau's lab report. I need proof that I'm right about the two separate bloodstains, not only that they're from different people, but who, besides Shane, did they belong to. I want the whole report, including blood types. It'll give us necessary information to figure out what actually happened, whether or not Caitlin is injured, and, if not, any analysis there is on the killer based on their blood type."

"Hutch will never cooperate," Casey stated flatly.

"I'm not asking Hutch. I'm asking Aidan."

A long moment of silence ensued.

Casey spoke up first. "Aidan? That's a rarity. You almost never involve him unless we're backed against the wall, with literally no other choice. You really are determined to get answers on this."

"Yeah. I am. I think they'll tell us a lot."

Aidan Devereaux was Marc's older brother, the head of the Zermatt Group—a covert team of military, corporate and spy agency operatives who took on emergent crises before they appeared on law enforcement's radar. His worldwide connections, both aboveboard and not-so-aboveboard, were beyond extensive. Zermatt and FI had joined forces on several overlapping cases. But asking Aidan a favor like this was not something Marc did lightly.

"Is Aidan home in New York?" Casey asked.

Marc shrugged. "Don't know. And it really doesn't matter. He can handle this from anywhere in the world. He'll have the contacts to pull this off, and fast."

"Then go for it. Just don't let Hutch catch wind of it."

"This is Aidan we're talking about," Marc replied. "No one catches wind of anything he's in charge of. Let's finish up our meeting. Then I'll call him."

"Okay," Casey responded, glancing at her iPad screen. "I want to backtrack long enough to ask what area Shane worked when he was an NYPD detective."

"Homicide," was Ryan's reply. "Every type from intricately planned professional hits to domestic disputes to killers for hire. That's another reason we have a lot of ground to cover. I'm sure Shane made more than a few enemies in his NYPD capacity, as well as his years at the FBI Violent Crimes."

Marc nodded. "That's definitely going to widen the suspect pool. However, in this case, it'll give us the parameters we need to get our answers. We'll have much better luck getting inside the NYPD than we will making inroads with the Bureau."

Patrick spoke up next. "Can we get back to the subject of Caitlin?" he asked, glancing at Casey.

"Of course," she said.

"I'll start with an obvious question. Ryan, I'm sure you've continued to try to reach her?"

"Repeatedly," Ryan replied. "But to no avail. Her iPhone is not in service. I'll have to find other avenues to pursue."

Patrick took that in, typing into his iPad. "I take it she doesn't work in law enforcement?"

Ryan shook his head. "She's an intelligence analyst with Scott Security, which is a nice-sized corporation in midtown. Her problem-solving skills rival mine—a compliment I don't often give. Anyway, she joined their company about five years ago. That's where I'll start my poking around. This morning will be my one shot, since the FBI and/or the details of their press release will reach Caitlin's associates in no time. So I'll call her office two hours from now, as soon as they open, to try to get a handle on which of her colleagues she's closest to, and to see if any of them has seen or heard from her."

"Unfortunately for us, it's Saturday," Casey reminded him. "There probably aren't a lot of people in the office. So you might be SOL. If you do reach someone who's tight with Caitlin, get their name to me ASAP. I want to take over from there. Not only am I the behaviorist of the team, I'm not personally involved the way you are. I'll follow-up right away—the moment I get your text—take a personal approach, rather than the professional one the FBI is bound to use once they're involved. It's a long shot, but maybe I'll learn something."

Ryan nodded. "If anyone can, it's you. No worries. You'll get my text pronto."

Marc was thinking and frowning, veering in a different direction. "Ryan, is there any way you can access a police report from yesterday's crime scene?"

Ryan flipped open his iPad, grateful to be doing something that helped him feel like his normal self. "Not a problem. The locals were on the scene before the Bureau. Which means they'll have a lean file they created before the FBI's ERT tossed them out. In a few days, I'll get into the NYPD's database, once the investigation expands to include them."

He began typing, making quick work of hacking into the New Rochelle Police Department's database. For now, this was his only shot. No way he'd try hacking the FBI's system. It was a virtual impossibility—and he'd lose his license and his freedom in the process.

Having located the local case file, he clicked into it, searching for details. Then, he tamped down on his personal feelings and began supplying the team with information.

"Okay, the local cops did a pretty decent cursory job. They found evidence of gunshot residue. Marc and I saw the casings that were beside Shane, so that makes sense. There was no blood cast on the walls—only that pool of blood Marc and I found on the floor near Shane's body, and the adjacent jagged bloody line." Ryan swallowed hard, and then continued. "There were smudged fingerprints on the doorknobs and the body—presumably the killer's. All doors and windows were checked, and indicated no evidence of forced entry. But the outside garage door was up and the inside door unlocked."

At that, Ryan looked up. "Pretty much everyone leaves their inside garage door unlocked. But I know that Shane and Caitlin always lower the outside door whether at home or away. I'm sure they had remotes in their cars to raise them."

"Which means anyone could have broken into the car and pressed that button," Marc muttered. "Did the cops check out the car?"

Ryan scanned the report. "Yeah. Long enough to find that there were indiscernible fingerprints and scratch marks on the driver's side keyhole. The car alarm was silenced. Your line of thinking is right, Marc. That's the way the killer got in."

"And it takes some level of skill to disarm a car alarm these days," Patrick noted. "So we're dealing with at least a minimally sophisticated subject—though not a rocket scientist. If he were *that*, he would have wiped his prints or worn gloves."

Casey nodded. "I agree. What about security footage? A Ring security camera would be a dead end if the killer entered the house through the garage. But was any activity caught on camera?"

"Nothing in the report about that," Ryan replied. "I'm sure that's when ERT arrived and the FBI took over. But my guess is that the killer avoided all cameras." He looked up. "As Marc and I saw firsthand, there were no signs of a struggle, and the house wasn't ransacked. This was quick and dirty. My cousin had no warning and no chance to defend himself."

"I'm sure the weapon is in a nearby dumpster somewhere," Marc said. "The Bureau will recover it. But, unless it has a history, it's of no use to us."

"Do you think the killer was already there when Shane got home?" Emma asked.

Marc shook his head. “No. Shane was an agent with Violent Crimes. He’d see the raised garage door and his antennae would go up. And he sure as hell wouldn’t stop to go to the bathroom before searching his house—unarmed, as we recall.” A quick glance at Ryan. “So that’s it?”

Ryan shrugged. “Yeah. Other than what we saw firsthand. Shane’s iPhone was smashed to bits—it was lying right beside him. But there are a lot of unanswered questions.”

“Damn straight,” Marc replied vehemently. “Starting with the car. Ryan, you told me that Caitlin always parked in the driveway and Shane on the street, right?”

“Yes.” Ryan’s wheels were turning. “Assuming the killer didn’t know that, and he saw only one car parked outside the house, how did he know it was Shane’s and not Caitlin’s? He’d want to be sure it was Shane who was home. So how did he figure that out?”

“Maybe he already knew,” Casey said quietly. “I’m assuming Shane wasn’t often home in the middle of the afternoon, right?” She waited for and got Ryan’s nod. “So why was he there yesterday? Could there be a reason the killer was somehow aware of? We’d better figure that out. And, further, one car—presumably Shane’s—meant no Caitlin. The killer’s target was alone, or so he thought.”

“But we know the car arrangements the Walshes had, so that’s not how it went down.” Marc furthered Casey’s logic. “For whatever reason we have yet to figure out, the killer thought it was Shane’s car he was breaking into. We know better. We know that Caitlin was working home that day. Which means we know that she was already inside the house.”

Casey paused. “Which brings us to the question we all have—was Caitlin killed, kidnapped, or is she on the run? Just as the idea of her being a suspect is out, I think the idea of her being killed is also out. If she walked onto the murder scene, the killer would have shot her dead on the spot. Could they have taken her with them and killed her later? It's possible, but weak. So the question is, was she kidnapped or did she run? And, if she ran, was she injured when she did?"

"Why would a killer kidnap her?" Emma wondered aloud. "She and Shane aren't rich, are they?"

Again, Ryan shook his head. "Not even close. And Caitlin's family is all gone, so there's no other fountain of wealth for a kidnapper to go to for ransom money."

Casey pursed her lips, looking adamant about whatever she was about to say. "I don't see this as a kidnapping. As you said, with Shane dead, there was no one to blackmail. No, my instincts tell me that Caitlin bolted. And we must find her, since she obviously has firsthand knowledge of the homicide. If she was home, which the presence of her car and the nature of her job suggest she was, then she saw something—if not the murder itself, then perhaps the killer coming or going. If Marc is right about her blood being on the scene, she could have been inadvertently grazed by a bullet, and then taken off. The only piece that doesn't fit is her leaving Kennedy behind."

"I agree." Claire set down her cup of tea, her gaze inwardly focused. "There has to have been a powerful reason for such a loving mother to vanish and leave her child behind. Caitlin didn't take her car. She didn't contact law enforcement, even though Shane worked for the FBI. She didn't contact us, although I'm sure she knows who Ryan works for and knows how successfully we'd handle this. That tells me she was in a panic. Maybe she knew the killer was right behind her, and she feared for Kennedy's safety if she took her on the run. Doing that would put Kennedy in the same danger as Caitlin herself was in."

Ryan turned to Claire. "Is that speculation or something you're sensing?"

"I'm not sure. Maybe both," she replied, her shoulders lifting in an uncertain shrug. "Remember, I sat with Kennedy for a while last night. Broken images are flitting about in my mind. But if Caitlin did see the killer and—more importantly—if she were aware that they'd seen her, she'd never rush to Kennedy's school and, as a result, lead the murderer there." A sudden spark of intuition lit Claire's eyes. "Caitlin would ensure Kennedy's safety by making sure she left her daughter in the best of hands before she tossed her cell phone and took off."

Ryan heard the conviction in Claire's tone, and jumped on it. "That last comment was more than just supposition. It was sensory awareness. Going with that, Caitlin is on the run, and the 'best of hands' would be my mom. No question." A pause, as he thought back. "My mom didn't recognize the cell number the text came from, and the number wasn't in service when she called back. To me, that screams a burner."

Marc nodded. "And she assumed it was Shane who used that burner, since his name was typed at the bottom of the text." A scowl. "A weak theory, at best. Clearly, Shane's assailant caught him off-guard. There was no time for him to react. So when would he have time to contact Ryan's mom? Plus, when would he have time to access a burner?"

"He wouldn't," Ryan stated flatly. "Which tells me that Caitlin sent that text. She witnessed the murder, escaped from the killer, and then sent the text herself to make sure Kennedy stayed safe." He sat up straighter, his expression filled with sudden realization. "Shane kept a couple of guns locked in his office desk. He was a just-in-case guy, so I know he also hid a few burners and some cash. I don't know the hiding places, but I'm sure Caitlin did. She must have grabbed the stuff, knowing she'd need it."

"Yes," Claire agreed—a statement not a conjecture. "That's just what happened. Shane was already gone. Caitlin took over from there."

"Making her the existing threat," Patrick followed through. "The killer knows she's very much alive and fleeing. I'm sure the burner phone she used to text Ryan's mother has long since been tossed, especially since Caitlin has others. She's a smart woman."

"Which makes finding her central to this investigation," Casey concluded. "She's alive. She has knowledge she's terrified to share, a possible injury, and a killer hot on her heels." A pensive pause. "We might get lucky. I can't imagine that Caitlin won't want to check on Kennedy again. Maybe she'll send periodic texts to Ryan's mother. Ryan, alert your mom to that. We have to be prepared to jump on it."

"Done." Ryan was clearly ready to move. "I'll have a long talk with her and my dad. They'll be prepped and ready. I'll also use my devices to log into Shane's iCloud and restore everything that was on his cell phone—particularly his calendar, so I can see what he had on tap for yesterday that the killer could have found out about."

"Good." Casey nodded. "Meanwhile, we're going to have to divide and conquer. Figure out who killed Shane, and locate Caitlin and bring her home. The latter would obviously help with the former, but we can't put all our eggs in that one basket. We need to investigate both simultaneously."

She glanced around the room. "Marc, call Aidan. Let us know when you hear back from him. In the interim, you and Patrick use all your FBI connections—retired as well as active—to gain information on Shane's investigations, as well as any potential enemies he might have made, these past eight years. I wish I could ask Hutch, but, as I said, there's no way he'd tell me anything. Nor, in good conscience, would I request that he did."

"Don't hold your breath on the active agents," Marc warned. "They'll be as tight-lipped as Hutch. The retirees aren't a much better option. They'd normally be more forthcoming, but not given it's FI they'd be talking to. Our best bet will probably be the former agents, those who changed careers and who don't have fierce loyalties to the Bureau."

"Then go that route, see what you can find out. We'll have to accept the fact that, in this particular investigation, the FBI is going to be our weakest source of leads. That means subverting them and focusing on everything and everyone else."

Ryan's mind was now in high-gear. "I'll hack into the NYPD's archived files. I'll get into every one of them where Shane was the detective or officer of record, or those in which he was even peripherally involved. I'll go back to the first year he joined the police force, and move forward from there, focusing closely on the last few years of his NYPD employment—his years as a detective. Yoda can cross-reference all Shane's cases against parolees or those who've completed their time, and then winnow some of them down."

"Good." Casey nodded. "Would you be okay with Claire and me talking with your family? Not until after the wake and the funeral, of course, and not until you give us the go-ahead. We don't want to intrude on your family's grief. I realize how traumatized they must be, and I'm sorry if I sound insensitive. But the fact is, they're the people who are and were personally closest to the Walshes. The FBI knows that. They'll be calling to set up meetings with every family member. We want to stay one step ahead of them. Fiona is the easiest for us to meet with. She's our friend, and arranging a meeting would be a piece of cake. What about your brothers? I know less than nothing about them other than the fact that they run a law firm. Would they be willing to talk to us?"

Ryan had steepled his fingers in front of him. "Definitely. Start with Fee. Then move on to Garret and Nolan. I'll give you their contact information. It makes the most sense to talk to them at their law firm in White Plains. That way, you can meet with both of them at the same time."

"Agreed. Can we do the same with your dad?" Casey asked, still typing. "Meet him at work? I know he teaches at the Bronx School of Science. Would he meet us there?"

"For sure."

Casey looked up. "I'm purposely avoiding conducting any discussions at your parents' house. I don't want Kennedy to be aware of any of this. It would be heart-wrenching for her."

"Yes. It would," Ryan said, following Casey's reasoning through to its natural conclusion.

Marc and Patrick exchanged glances.

"Unfortunately, that's not the way it's going to happen," Marc said. "The SA running the show is going to want to talk to Kennedy, to ask her about her parents' state of mind over the past few weeks. She's old enough to have absorbed any tension in the house, as well as to have overheard conversations. Out of respect for what she's going through, the BU will wait until after the funeral. But then, they're going to be calling your mother to set up a meeting with Kennedy. I suggest FI beats them to the punch."

“Dammit.” Ryan slammed his fist on the table. “Kennedy is at the end of her rope. How much more can they ask of her?”

Casey looked grim. “I didn’t think of that. But Marc is right. It sucks, Ryan, and I’m so sorry. But if the agents are going to question Kennedy, I want us to do it first.” A quick glance at Claire. “You and I?” she asked quietly.

Claire nodded. “Yes. Kennedy will open up more readily to women than she would to men. Plus, she and I have already met. I think we shared a nice connection. I’ll be a familiar face.”

Ryan forced himself to calm down, and turned his head to face Claire. “Kennedy really took to you. I’m way too close to her to handle this objectively. You and Casey do it. But wait until she’s calmed down after the wake and the funeral, which will be over in three days. She’s going to be a basket case.”

“The agents will give her a day or two after that to recover, as well,” Patrick said. “They’re not going to just barge in. They’ll call Ryan’s mother and see when the best time is. Casey, you and Claire just get there ahead of them.”

“We will,” Claire replied.

Ryan’s frown had returned. “That brings us to another complication. My mom is the best source of information where it comes to our family. Not only will you want to talk to her, SA Barkley will. Not when they talk to Kennedy. Alone. They won’t want Kennedy there and neither will I. So how do we handle that? The rest of my family lives elsewhere, and they’ll interview my dad at work. But how do we get Kennedy out of the house when she clings to my mom like a security blanket?”

“You could relieve her for a while,” Claire suggested to Ryan. “I saw the way Kennedy was with you. It’s sheer adoration. Is there somewhere special that the two of you go when you both visit at the same time?"

Another hint of a smile touched Ryan's lips. "That would be The Old Ice Cream Shop. The place is several blocks from my parents' house. Kennedy loves their peppermint stick ice cream with a deluge of rainbow sprinkles. I could easily keep her entertained there for at least an hour."

"Perfect," Casey said. "That's more than enough time for the FBI to do their own information-gathering. And Ryan, I know how devastating this is for you. I give you my word that throughout this process, we'll take our cues from you. You tell us everyone's limitations. We'll follow your lead. Just as long as we keep ahead of the FBI."

"Agreed, and thank you," Ryan answered gratefully. "I'll give you everyone's direct contact information now so you're ready when they are."

"What about me?" Emma demanded. "What will I be doing?"

"You're our social media pro," Casey replied. "Go through any accounts either Shane or Caitlin have. Shane was FBI, so he might not have any presence at all. Or he could have personal accounts using a different form of his name—talk to Ryan about possibilities for that after this meeting breaks up. Caitlin is another story. She's a layperson. She must have active accounts somewhere, even though she won't use her actual name. Find those accounts. I'm sure they'll be limited, given who she's married to. Still, do your best. Delve deep—photos, posts, friends—you know the drill. That can be started now. Later, when we start interviewing outside the family, I'll be calling on your chameleon skills." There was one more thing Casey wanted Emma to check out, but now was not the time to bring it up.

A grin. "You got it, boss."

Claire turned to Ryan, her expression gentle. “Do you have anything of Shane’s that I can physically hold? That always eases my way.”

Ryan didn’t avert her gaze. “I know. I’ve already run this through my mind. So, yes. I’ve got a zip-up hoodie of his that I borrowed ages ago and never remembered to return. And I’ve got some NYPD paraphernalia that he gave me when he joined the force. Is that enough for starters?”

“It is. I’ll give them right back to you after I’ve gotten all the sensory connections from them that I’m able to.”

Casey leaned back in her chair. “I think we’re good to go. We have plenty to keep us busy this weekend and the beginning of next week. After that, we’ll move on to talk to Kennedy and to the rest of Ryan’s family.”

5

The McKay Residence
Woodlawn, Bronx, New York
Saturday, March 11, 11:30 a.m.

Ryan pulled up to his parents' house, secured the convertible top of his prized new classic sports car—a rally red nineteen-sixty-seven Corvette 427—and cut the engine. He'd purposely driven to work and now to Woodlawn. Too restless to deal with hours of mass transit, he'd chosen to shorten his commute and ease his tension by zooming up to the Bronx, top down, so he could feel the wind in his hair and think.

He'd done a chunk of research probing Shane's NYPD archived cases, flagging all those that smacked of possible retaliation by the guilty party or parties. He'd then gratefully turned the project over to Yoda for analysis. At nine o'clock on the dot, he'd made his call to Scott Security, in an attempt to quickly locate one or more of Caitlin's colleagues. He did little to no damage, since, as Casey had suspected, only a skeletal staff was in. Plus, it was hard to ask questions without supplying information. So, when he finally reached someone in Caitlin's department, Lauren Robbins, he kept it simple, saying that he was Caitlin's cousin and that he and one of her good friends were trying hard to reach her, and had hoped they'd find her at work. Thankfully, Lauren had yet to see the FBI's press release on Shane's murder and on Caitlin being a person of interest. Nor had the Bureau yet contacted her.

Nevertheless, she was very reserved and more than a little reticent about having a personal discussion with him. He knew in his gut that she'd be more likely to talk to another woman—especially one as savvy as Casey. So he'd cut the conversation short, thanked her for her time, and hung up.

He'd then immediately passed her name along to Casey, who'd follow up in a heartbeat and play the part of Caitlin's close friend, admitting she was worried about Caitlin since she'd been very anxious the past week or two. That would be enough. Lauren would doubtless open up to Casey—almost everyone did. One name might grow to more. And Casey would work her behavioral magic to find out anything and everything about Caitlin's current state of mind.

As for Ryan—enough was enough.

He had to get out of there—not only his lair, but the whole brownstone. His concentration had totally deteriorated, and his mind kept going to Kennedy, wondering how she was holding up. Even though he'd made an early morning check-in call to his mom, he felt compelled to be there in person.

Now, he folded his arms over the steering wheel and took some deep breaths, readying himself to go inside and be strong.

As prepared as he could ever be, he headed up the walkway.

His mother greeted him at the door.

"You look so tired," she said, studying Ryan's face. "Did you get any sleep at all?"

"Not a wink," he replied. "How about you? You look pretty wiped out, yourself."

"I suppose I do," his mother replied, massaging her temples.

Concern knit Ryan's brows. He knew that his mother would push herself beyond her limits when it came to family. "Mom, you've got to take care of yourself. I'll watch Kennedy for a while. You take a nap."

"Your dad offered the same. We'll see."

Ryan didn't push, not yet. "When I called earlier this morning, you told me that Kennedy was out cold."

Maureen sighed. "She had a rough night. She was up every couple of hours when the memories resurfaced. Once they did, she'd get hysterical, sobbing that her daddy was dead and calling for her mommy. It broke my heart. Dad took over for me several times. But whenever Kennedy woke up, she wanted only me."

Ryan felt a knife twist in his gut as he, once again, thought about the nightmare Kennedy was living through. "That's no surprise," he murmured. "You're the emotional nucleus of the family."

"As it should be."

Ryan didn't dispute that fact. "So she conked out earlier this morning?"

His mother nodded. "Around nine-thirty. Right before you called. It's the first real sleep she's gotten, the poor baby."

Ryan glanced at the stairs. "She's still asleep?"

"Yes. And I'm glad. It gives me a chance to talk to you alone." Maureen led Ryan into the living room, where he sat on the sofa, brows drawn.

"Has something else happened? Or is there any news?"

Maureen lowered herself into an arm chair. "Nothing like that. I just wanted to fill you in on my call with Dr. Abel this morning."

"Did she speak with Kennedy?"

Maureen shook her head. "Kennedy was asleep. I told Dr. Abel that I'd make sure Kennedy knew she could call her whenever she needed to. In the interim, Dr. Abel passed along recommendations for dealing with Kennedy's grief." A frown. "There's an FBI employee assistance program that I'm able to access. I absorbed as much about it as I could. It offer specific kinds of counseling—I think it's online. But I'm still a little unsure."

Ryan jumped right on that. "I'll talk to Marc and Patrick at the office. They're both former FBI. One of them will explain anything you need. Hands on, if necessary, coming here and talking you through the process. We'll introduce him to Kennedy as my friend from work. They're both great with kids, so no worries there. No need to even mention law enforcement."

"Good." Maureen looked utterly relieved. "Thank them in advance for me. There's only so much of Dr. Abel's time that I feel comfortable taking up."

"What else did she suggest?" Ryan asked.

"She thinks we should encourage Kennedy to keep a journal of her thoughts. It will give her an emotional outlet. Also, possible grief counseling, either by a priest or another viable counselor. Kennedy can also access an FBI chat room, if posting there would give her some relief." Maureen sighed. "Dr. Abel is being tremendously supportive, not only of Kennedy, but of me. I'm moving blindly through this process, so I need as much professional guidance as I can get."

Ryan reached over and squeezed his mom's hand. "You're a miracle worker. You're doing great."

Maureen's brows were drawn, and she didn't respond to the compliment. "Given the circumstances—especially any outstanding danger as well as Kennedy's emotional state—I'm going to follow the FBI's suggestion. We'll have a small wake tomorrow and an equally small funeral the day after. Just the immediate family, plus any of Shane's law enforcement colleagues who choose to honor him. Aside from the agents posted outside our house, a few more of them will be at both events, for security purposes. Originally, Fiona and I were planning on a larger scale, given how many people loved Shane. But the FBI felt something more contained would be safer and easier on Kennedy."

Ryan nodded. "Her mother is missing, and we can't ignore the fact that Kennedy could be another of the killer's targets. I agree with the Bureau."

"As do I."

"Listen, Mom, the team and I met this morning and did a fair amount of brainstorming."

Maureen's brows rose, hope flickering in her eyes. "Anything you can share with me?"

"A few major things. We all agreed that it's likely Caitlin will want to check up on Kennedy, probably on a steady basis. She'll find a way, and it will be through you. So you and Dad have to be aware of that fact and, should those kind of instances occur, you have to report every detail to me the minute they happen. Not law enforcement. Me. Okay?"

Maureen studied Ryan's face. "You believe Caitlin is alive."

"Yes." There was no hesitation on Ryan's part. "We do. Alive, scared, and on the run. I can't get into details, other than to tell you that we've concluded it was Caitlin, not Shane, who texted you. Shane was already dead by then. All this information is for you and you alone."

"And the FBI—do they know this, as well?"

"Not from us, they don't. Although I'm quite sure they'll think of it on their own. But as far as FI, this is pure conjecture and we therefore have nothing we need to share with law enforcement."

A hint of a smile. "Walking that fine line again, I see."

"Yup. And before Agent Barkley calls to come over and interview you—which he will the day after the funeral—I'll coach you so that you can field his questions. I'll get Kennedy out of the house when you speak to him. I can review all aspects of that plan with you later. For now, just remember that no matter what, if Caitlin makes contact with you, the first person you go to is me."

Maureen nodded. "All right. I'll fill your dad in. We'll follow your instructions—and be on the alert." She paused, focusing on the rest of what Ryan had said. "Agent Barkley will want to talk to all of us, won't he?"

"Yes," Ryan replied, holding his mom's gaze. "Including Kennedy."

Maureen's hand flew to her mouth. "But she can't—"

"Unfortunately, the Bureau thinks she can. She's old enough to have picked up on tensions, conversations, arguments, and whatever else she heard at home. They're going to ask her questions about that. Just know that we'll talk to her first, bolster her in any way we can." He paused, feeling ill at what he was about to say and bracing himself for his mother's stunned fury. "There's more."

"I'm listening." Maureen was starting to bristle.

"It's about Caitlin. And it's going to set you off big-time. It sure as hell did me."

"And what is that?"

Ryan went for straightforward and frank. "The FBI is going to question each of us about the inner workings of Shane and Caitlin's marriage. You've watched enough detective shows on TV. The wife is always first on the list of suspects."

Angry color suffused Maureen's face. "Are you telling me that the FBI believes Caitlin killed Shane?"

"I'm telling you they have to pursue that possibility. We'll set them straight. But this is procedural, not personal. We have to answer their questions. We can't blow up, the way you just did and I did back at the office. Whatever they ask you and Dad, answer candidly. I'll do the same. We all know how special Shane and Caitlin's marriage was, and how devoted they were to each other and to Kennedy. It's up to us to nip that theory in the bud so the agents can get out there and pursue the right ones."

Another stoic nod. "All right. I'll tell your father, as well as Fiona, Nolan, and Garret, so everyone is prepared for questioning. Including Kennedy. But I won't tell her until after her father is laid to rest and the trauma of that day is behind her."

"I agree." Ryan felt ticked off and utterly spent. "Just remember, FI is one step ahead of the Bureau where it comes to this. We know Caitlin's innocent. So we're moving on to more valid theories."

Maureen's fury banked. "I know. It's okay. We'll handle the FBI."

Ryan sighed, grateful to have gotten past that. Now he had a different question to ask. "Mom, please think. Do you know the names of any of Caitlin's friends? Personal or professional? Maybe one of them can help us figure out where she is."

Thoughtfully, Maureen tapped her chin. "I feel as if I do. Let me think. Give my middle-aged memory a chance to warm up."

On the heels of Maureen's words, Kennedy descended the stairs, calling out to her great-aunt, as she did. "Aunt Maureen?" Her voice was filled with pain and fear.

"I'm right here, lovey." Maureen walked over to the foot of the stairs, extending her arms to her great-niece, who stepped right into her embrace, burying her face in Maureen's shoulder. Her hair was tousled, the nightgown Maureen had slipped her into during the night was rumpled, and her face was drenched with tears.

Reflexively, Kennedy reached for her pendant, holding it as if it were a lifeline. "Did the FBI find mommy?"

Maureen rocked her in her arms. "Not yet, sweetie. But soon. Besides, not only is the FBI working on this, so is Ryan's company, Forensic Instincts. Sometimes I think they're better than anyone at solving puzzles like this one."

Ryan felt a lump in his throat, and he walked right up behind his mom.

"Hey, sunshine," he said, gently stroking Kennedy's hair.

Kennedy lifted her head and stared at him. "Ryan?"

"In the flesh."

"Did you sleep here last night?"

"Almost." He wiped the tears from her cheeks with his thumbs. "I left really late and just got back here now. I thought you and I could have lunch together." Seeing the panic on Kennedy's face, he clarified. "Not at a restaurant. Right here. I make a wicked stack of waffles, remember? And you're always the best helper. Should we give it a go?"

Kennedy swallowed, then gave him a shaky smile. "Okay. But Ryan, do you promise that your company is looking for mommy and for the horrible person who…?" Her voice broke off.

"You bet we are. We started at the crack of dawn. I took a short break just to come here and spend some time with you. Then I'm driving right back to the office and picking up where I left off." He cupped Kennedy's face between his hands. "Trust me, sunshine. I'll take care of everything."

"I know you will."

Kennedy's absolute faith in him humbled Ryan, doubling his determination to get the bastard who killed Shane and to bring Caitlin home, alive and well.

He eased Kennedy out of his mother's grasp, and seized her hands in his. "Tell you what. Let's let Aunt Maureen lie down for a while. You and I will whip up the waffles, with more than enough for her. While she's sleeping, we'll cook and eat. Then we'll wake her up to enjoy her own portion. And I'll head back to the office. Is that okay?"

With the maturity beyond her years that had always been hers, Kennedy studied her great-aunt's face. "You're very, very tired, Aunt Maureen. Get some rest. I'll be fine with Ryan."

Hesitation shot across Maureen's face. "But if you need—"

"Then I'll handle it," Ryan interrupted in a quiet voice. "Kennedy and I are a team. We'll be great together. And you need the energy to take over once I leave."

For one last second, Maureen hung back.

"Good night, Mom," Ryan said. "Dream of waffles."

Maureen's smile was soft. "Okay, I will."

6

Offices of Forensic Instincts
Main Conference Room, 2nd floor
Saturday, March 11, 2:10 pm

Casey finished typing up the last of her notes on Lauren Robbins—the woman Ryan had called in to report was a close work colleague of Caitlin's. His instincts had been dead-on. Lauren was a quiet and cautious woman—one who thankfully, the FBI had not yet contacted. So Casey had tried to extract as much relevant information as possible from her. She'd told her that she was worried about Caitlin, who hadn't been herself for the past few weeks, and then asked Lauren if she'd noticed anything different about her behavior.

Lauren had hesitated, then asked, "You said that you and Caitlin are very close?"

"Yes," Casey replied. "We have been for years, since high school. Which is why I'm so worried about her."

Lauren blew out a breath. "Actually, so am I. Caitlin is usually an upbeat, happy person. The last few Wednesdays when she came into the office, she seemed very preoccupied and jumpy. When I asked if she was okay, she barely heard me. I had to repeat myself twice. I was starting to worry that something was wrong, either at home or with her health."

"That really upsets me," Casey said, pressing the charade. "Did she say anything specific?"

"Not really," Lauren replied. "Only that she's feeling fine. She's a very private person, and we've never exchanged confidences. But I knew her well enough to notice the sudden change in her behavior."

Casey made an on-the-spot decision. This was going nowhere fast. And even if she wormed some names out of Lauren, there was no way to rationalize asking for personal email addresses or phone numbers. That would raise too many red flags. And calling on Monday was out. By that time, the whole office would know that Caitlin's husband had been killed and that Caitlin was a person of interest.

It was a definite dead end.

"Thank you for your time, Lauren," Casey said. "I'm even more determined to get Caitlin to talk to me. I'll let you know if I learn anything important."

***

Casey glanced up from her iPad when Ryan walked into the first floor conference room, looking taut as a bowstring.

Casey sat back in her chair and studied his expression. "How's Kennedy? And your mom? Any news? And did she handle all you had to tell her without breaking down?"

He sucked in his breath. "Kennedy is still a mess. I could barely get her to eat. My mom's reserves are depleting; she's with Kennedy every breathing moment. And, other than a bolstering call from the FBI's victim specialist, things are status quo. I passed along the information I had to. It didn't go over well. But my mom will do what she has to. She always does. How about at your end? Did you reach Lauren Robbins?"

"Yup." Casey went on to fill him in.

Ryan poured himself a cup of coffee and sat down on one of the room's tub chairs, his lips thinned into a grim line. "Caitlin is as calm as they come. I've never seen her on edge. And now she's so much so that her coworker noticed? Something major had to have happened. Given how tight she and Shane were—I'm going to go out on a limb and say that Shane was involved in something dangerous, something risky, and that he shared some or all of what that was with Caitlin."

Casey nodded. "That makes complete sense. Unfortunately, Lauren is now a dead end, since Caitlin didn't confide in her. My gut tells me that, if Caitlin opened up to anyone, it would be one of her closest friends, someone outside the office. I'm counting on your mom to remember at least one name."

"Knowing my mom, she'll wrack her brain until she does. And, yeah, when that happens, it's definitely a stronger angle to pursue." Ryan took a gulp of coffee. "Caitlin would never betray Shane, nor compromise his position with the Bureau. But even if she hinted at something, it'll be enough for us to run with." He rubbed the back of his neck. "I hate waiting. But we can't press my mom now. The funeral is on Monday and we have to give her time to recover and, most important, to soothe Kennedy, who'll be a wreck."

"Of course. I'd planned on giving her a call on Wednesday."

"Uh-uh. Tuesday will be enough time. Despite her grief, my mom wants this case solved yesterday. So set up a visit for either Tuesday afternoon or Wednesday morning, first with her and then with Kennedy. For the first part, it'll be no problem to get Kennedy settled with a movie, far away from your conversation. After that..." A pained shrug. "Who knows how Kennedy will react?"

"Claire and I will be as gentle and reassuring as possible. I promise."

"I know you will. And it'll be way easier for her to talk to you than it will be when she has to talk to the FBI."

"We'll prep her for that, as well," Casey said.

Ryan's mind vaulted to another subject, one that was less urgent, but which had been bothering him on the drive back.

"Look, Case, *I* want this case solved yesterday. But I'm realistic enough to know that's not possible. We've got a ton of ground to cover, all of us." He frowned. "With that as a given, there are other plans to be made for Kennedy. Even though my mom is making her the number one priority, I still feel responsible for her. Maybe that sounds crazy. It's hard to explain."

"You don't have to. I understand."

"It's not just the connection Kennedy and I share. It's my role in the family," Ryan continued. "I've always been the grounded one, the one my mom counts on to be logical and pragmatic, rather than emotional. Well, that's what I'm trying to do with Kennedy, regardless of my own pain. I've got to strive for as much normalcy for her as possible. Today we made waffles together. Tomorrow and Monday, I'll be by her side. But eventually, we've got another area to address. School."

Casey's brows knit. "She's at home, living through a major crisis, and under FBI protection. Returning to school isn't an option."

"Yes, I know." Ryan took another swallow of coffee. "Even with the FBI agents posted there, she's terrified of leaving my parents' house. When she thought I meant to take her out to eat, she started freaking out. I'd never suggest her physically attending school. But she loves it, and catching up with homework would be a great distraction for her. Maybe not this coming week. But, after that, I want to arrange for her school work to be sent home, maybe once a week, and then returned when it's complete. At that time, I want the next week's assignments sent home. I'm sure her teacher and her principal would cooperate, under the circumstances. It would just be until the crimes are solved and Kennedy is safe. If it turns out that I'm the one to ferry things back and forth, I'll more than compensate for the time I'm away from the office. Like I said, I'm on these cases twenty-four-seven."

Casey tapped her fingernails on the table. "I wasn't worried. And actually, your idea makes a world of sense. The only thing is, I'm guessing your mom is the one who has to initiate the process, since she's acting as Kennedy's guardian. After that, I'm unaware of the procedure. I'll give Angela a quick call to research the legal formalities."

Ryan looked surprised. "You already brought Angela up to speed? I thought she wasn't starting until Monday."

"She's not. But I want her to hit the ground running. So I detailed what she'd be walking into. Now I'll be able to call on her expertise right away."

"That was smart. It also takes a load off my shoulders. I'll be able to explain the procedure to my mom, so she can follow protocol and make it happen." Ryan paused, abruptly glancing around the room. "I saw Emma at the computers, digging around for social media profiles. Where's Claire?"

"In her yoga room with the things you gave her of Shane's," Casey reported, swiveling in her chair and wincing as she spoke. "As soon as she comes down, we'll talk to her."

"Uh-uh." Ryan gave an adamant shake of his head. "*I'll* talk to her. You'll go home and rest. You look beat, and you're obviously in pain. You did too much and for too long. Hutch is going to have my head."

"I won't tell if you won't."

"I won't have to tell. He knows you. I'm sure he'll be sending over a car service to take you home. You've been here since seven. Count on being escorted out of the brownstone soon. So let's wrap up. You can continue working via phone or Zoom."

"But there's still so much to do—"

"And we'll do it, in steps." Ryan raised his head. "Hey Yoda," he called out. "Anything I should know about?"

"Yes, Ryan. I red-flagged all applicable cases I found together with the NYPD members who worked those cases with your cousin. Some of the criminals involved are still incarcerated and some are on parole. Many of the pertinent detectives have retired. Many others are still at NYPD homicide. And still others have moved on to work in different police departments in other locations in the country. How would you like me to proceed from here?"

A scowl. "The current detectives are not going to be amenable to providing us with information. Even Marc and Patrick will be limited, since, other than task forces, they weren't working in tandem with the cops. They're handling the retired FBI-agent questioning, and I'm sure they can eke out a conversation or two with retired cops. But the rest…that's going to be tough. Start with the retired detectives first. Make a list. I'll go through it with Marc and Patrick."

"I'll begin immediately," Yoda responded.

"Thanks." Ryan frowned in thought, then abruptly his head shot up. "What about having John Nickels spearhead this part of the show?"

he asked Casey. "I know he's Patrick's main guy for our security team, but he also served with NYPD homicide for twenty-five years, before he retired and Patrick snatched him up for FI. He's got a hell of a lot more viable contacts than any of our other team members. And those contacts will be much more open and willing to talk to John than to talk to the rest of us. We can share Yoda's list with him, as well."

Casey considered that possibility, and nodded. "Another good idea. Even though we've never used John in that capacity, his record stands on its own. I want to run the idea by Patrick, see where his head is on the concept."

"Where is he?"

"He and Marc are having lunch with a retired special agent Shane worked with at the New York field office. They hadn't contacted any retired cops yet. They were going for the few FBI contacts they could muster up. As for the NYPD, your idea of using John in that capacity is great. It'll yield far better results." Casey glanced at her watch. "Marc and Patrick should be back within the hour." She winced again. "I'll wait until they get here."

"No you won't," Ryan countered, leaning over to shut her laptop and her iPad, and shove them into her case. He rarely took such an authoritative role with Casey; he knew she'd shoot him down in the blink of an eye. But when it came to her health, he was willing to take the risk. "Sorry for the disrespect, boss, but you're going home. You'll recap and set up a plan with Patrick and Marc via a Zoom meeting. I'll talk to Claire right here. You and I will give each other verbal reports. We've certainly done it before, especially when you were in the hospital. So call either Hutch or a car service—now."

Casey had no chance to ream Ryan out. As if on cue, the doorbell sounded.

"Casey's car service has arrived," Yoda announced. "The driver is waiting to escort her home."

Ryan's lips twitched, and Casey rolled her eyes.

"I rest my case," he said, going around to help Casey to her feet. "She's on her way," he called out to Yoda.

"Very good. I'll let the driver know," Yoda responded. "Oh, and Hutch sent a message along with the driver. He said to tell Casey that he expects her to be in bed and resting in forty minutes. He'll be calling her to verify that his orders are being followed."

Casey sighed, steadying herself on her feet. "Okay, Yoda. I won't even finish my coffee. I'm just getting my devices and related case notes."

"There were no instructions prohibiting that."

"Glad to hear it," she replied. "Also, no verification from my husband will be needed. I'll call him once I'm all tucked in and reassure him that I've followed his orders to a tee."

"That conversation is out of my jurisdiction," Yoda replied.

Ryan bit back laughter. "I'll carry Casey's stuff to the door," he told Yoda.

"Good. Hutch will be pleased."

Casey wasn't laughing as she turned to Ryan. "I'll call Angela, as well as Marc and Patrick, while you talk to Claire." A frustrated shake of her head. "I wish I could stay. I feel as if I'm deserting you."

"You're not," Ryan assured her. "The next part of my work has to be done solo, anyway. I'll be here pretty much round-the-clock, other than tomorrow afternoon and Monday morning, when I'll be at the wake and funeral with my family. This afternoon, I'm working on recovering all the data on Shane's cell phone. First up, is checking out his calendar for yesterday. Maybe he had something scheduled that'll clue us in to how his… killer knew he'd be home." Even now, Ryan tripped over the word "killer" as it pertained to his cousin.

Casey lightly touched his arm. "Keep me posted. I'm only a text away."

7

Casey and Hutch's apartment
Battery Park City
Manhattan, New York
Saturday, March 11, 3:40 pm

Casey had just settled herself on the bed with an afghan thrown over her, a cup of tea on the nightstand beside her, and Hero stretched out on the rug beside her, when the phone rang.

"Good afternoon, Supervisory Special Agent Hutchinson," she greeted her husband. "I was just about to check in. I'm positioned as ordered."

Hutch didn't laugh. "You spent almost eight hours at the office," he said in a steely voice. "That's at least four hours too many. If you get off that bed, I'm calling your surgeon."

A soft smile touched Casey's lips. "Don't bother. I'm more intimidated by you than I am by him."

"Somehow I doubt that."

Casey heard beyond the drill sergeant tone to the worry beneath it. "I'm really fine, Hutch," she said in a gentle voice. "Promise."

Hutch blew out a relieved breath. "Okay. I'll take your word for it, until I can confirm it myself. I'm inundated here. But I'm going to try to get out at a reasonable hour. I'll bring home dinner."

"Inundated? Anything you can tell me?" Casey asked like a hopeful puppy awaiting a treat. "Maybe something that's not classified?"

Hutch chuckled. "No, my beautiful wife. But nice try. Now put your head down and sleep."

"Okay," Casey reluctantly agreed. "Even though I'm not tired."

Hutch's lips curved as he heard her yawn. "That's fine. I'll stay on the line while you settle in to rest."

He waited three minutes. "Case?"

No answer. As he could have predicted, his exhausted wife was out cold.

Smiling, he disconnected the call and sent out the necessary group text.

***

Ryan's lair
Offices of Forensic Instincts
Tribeca, Manhattan, New York
4:10 pm

Ryan was peering at his computer, working with Yoda to restore Shane's cell phone data, when Claire knocked lightly at the door.

"Am I interrupting?" she asked, poking her head inside. "Because if it's not a convenient breaking point for you, I'll come back later."

Ryan raised his head and swiveled his chair around to face her.

"No problem," he said. "Restoring data off a cell phone that's shattered and in FBI custody is slow, tedious work. I could use a diversion." For a brief second, a hint of the old Ryan emerged, and a corner of his mouth lifted, his brows arching in hopeful anticipation. "Is this a booty call?"

Claire smiled. "Sorry to dash your hopes, but this is work-related." She held up two evidence bags containing the personal items of Shane's that Ryan had given her. Seeing the pained expression that crossed his face, Claire softened the discussion that lay ahead. "Although I have felt neglected. Maybe a raincheck for tonight, when we're both here working until God knows when?"

With a hard swallow, Ryan nodded. "My pleasure. Yours, too." That was about all the lighthearted conversation he could muster up. "Did you pick up on any sensory connections from holding Shane's stuff?"

Crossing over, Claire perched on the wobble stool that Ryan had engineered for his restless moments.

"Not the NYPD-related items," she responded. "But the hoodie—yes." She set aside the NYPD evidence bag, opened the other, and took out the zip-up hoodie. She held it gently, running her finger along the jagged edges of the zipper. Her eyes slid shut, and when she spoke, she was unmistakably repeating an awareness she'd accessed and was now recounting. "Shane's had this since he was just out of college. Caitlin gave it to him because he always forgot his regular jacket. He was more of a sweats' guy. So this jacket-like hoodie was a no-brainer. She wound up buying him several, which is why he was okay with lending this one to you."

Ryan nodded, stifling a choked-up sound.

Claire's brow furrowed, as she sought an answer she didn't quite have. "I see the unrelated past so clearly. But the more immediate past? The present? All I perceive is an aura of danger. It doesn't just surround Shane. It surrounds Caitlin, too. Before. After. Impending death is still out there. I can't reach its source. I'm trying..." Claire's fingers tightened around the hoodie. "But it hasn't come yet." Her eyes opened, and her gaze was torn with sadness and grief. "I've got to reach it. I must." A pause. "I'm so sorry it's taking this long."

Ryan rose, walked over and tugged Claire to her feet and into the circle of his arms. "Don't be," he murmured. "You're doing everything you can, stretching yourself as far as you can go." He could feel moisture burning behind his eyes. "I realize you're going above and beyond. Please know how much it means to me—how much you mean to me." He pressed his lips into the crown of her head.

Nodding, Claire wrapped her arms around his waist. "I know. You mean the same to me. I wish I could take away your pain. But, Ryan, we will resolve this, bring peace to Shane's memory, find Caitlin, and help heal Kennedy."

"Wishful thinking?" Ryan asked.

"Maybe. But my every instinct is telling me I'm right." She eased back. "You go back to what you were doing. I'm ordering a couple of sandwiches for us. We haven't eaten since our five-thirty AM PowerBars."

Despite the sober feeling permeating the room, a corner of Ryan's mouth lifted. "Those PowerBars don't count, at least not for you. You barely choked yours down without heaving. And my appetite wasn't exactly great. So a sandwich sounds good about now. Nothing with alfalfa sprouts in it though, not for me."

"I'll try to restrain myself." Claire was, not only a vegetarian, but a health food nut. Ryan, the carnivore, always teased her about it. She usually shot back a playful barb. Not this time.

Grateful that she'd infused Ryan with a bit of laughter, she went over, retrieved the hoodie, and zipped it back in its storage bag. She'd reexamine it after a brief lunch break.

"I'll slide your sandwich under the door," she called over her shoulder. "Hard at work or not, you'd better eat it. Or you can forget the midnight booty call."

That didn't please Ryan at all. "Every morsel will be gone in record time," he assured her. "Do I get extra points for that?"

Claire smiled from the doorway. "Most definitely."

***

Offices of Forensic Instincts
Marc's office, 3rd floor
Tribeca, Manhattan, New York
4:30 pm

Marc leaned back in his office chair, not even waiting for Patrick to get settled in the chair on the opposite side of the desk before opening the frustrating conversation.

"All today proved to us is that, in order to accomplish what's necessary, we need Ryan to hack the Bureau's database and get us a comprehensive list of present, former, and retired agents," he stated flatly. "We both know that's not happening. Which results in meetings like we just had with SA Groban—unproductive and a waste of time."

Patrick sighed, rubbing the back of his neck. "The only worthwhile bit of information that he passed along to us was one name—SA Tricia Adams—a just-retired agent who worked the same VC squad as Shane did during his freshman year at the Bureau. And even she, unfortunately, moved out west after retiring. We'll contact her and set up a Zoom meeting, but I'm not too optimistic about finding out anything pertinent from her either."

Marc scowled. "Plus, Shane was young and only with the Bureau for eight years. There are going to be a slim number of either retired or former agents who worked closely with him. Which narrows the possibilities even more."

"I'm as disgusted as you, but equally unsurprised," Patrick replied, seeing how pissed off Marc was, and trying to be the voice of reason. "I can't blame any of the agents, retired or current, for not wanting to spill their guts. We might have once been Bureau, but now we're not. Worse, we operate by our own set of rules—rules they don't respect. They'll never trust us."

"I know." Marc took his irritation down a notch, speaking in his customary pragmatic fashion. "As for the current agents, they have an additional reason to shut the door in our faces. Hutch must have put the fear of God in them where it comes to us. And I don't blame him, either. He's just doing his job. Casey is his wife and FI is her family. He knows our methods only too well."

"Which leaves us where?"

Marc folded his hands behind his head. "With one approach left to tweak. When we talk to SA Adams, we have to shift our line of questioning. Rather than asking about former squad members and specific cases, we have to ask about BU employees who Shane was tight with—not just agents he worked with, but agents in other squads or field offices, and support staff, as well."

"You're going for a personal connection," Patrick said.

"Yes. I want to reach out to anyone Shane might have expressed his concerns to. It's our only hope of gathering pertinent information. It might be a long shot—but it's the only one we've got."

With that, Marc opened his iPad. "I'll email Tricia Adams now. It's only one-thirty on the west coast, so hopefully she'll answer sometime today. While we wait to set up the Zoom meeting, you and I will strategize."

***

Casey and Hutch's apartment
Battery Park City
Manhattan, New York
6:30 pm

Hutch walked into the apartment, quietly shut the door, and crossed over to the kitchen. He put the bag of Chinese food on the kitchen island, then turned and headed into the bedroom. He smiled when he saw Casey curled up on the bed, still sound asleep. Her cell phone had dropped onto the pillow beside her.

Hero leaped up, tail wagging, and came over to welcome Hutch home.

"Hey, boy," Hutch said quietly, squatting down and scratching behind the bloodhound's ears. "Thanks for keeping an eye on our girl." Rising, he crossed over to the bed, sank down beside Casey, and bent to give her a tender kiss.

Casey's eyelashes fluttered, then lifted.

"Hi," she said with a small smile. "I guess I nodded off."

Hutch steeled himself for the explosion. "You didn't just nod off, sweetheart . . . You've been asleep for almost three hours."

Sure enough, Casey bolted into a sitting position. "*What*?" she demanded. "*Three hours*?" As if to confirm, she picked up her cell phone and looked at the time. "Dammit!" Shoving waves of hair off her face, she glanced frantically around, as if she didn't know which thing to do first. "Patrick...Claire...Angela—*shit*!" She squirmed to get up, determined to get to the living room, grab her iPad, and initiate a group Zoom meeting.

"Hey, easy." Hutch pulled her against him, ignoring her furious expression, and pressing her head to his shoulder. "You'll make it all happen." He kissed the crown of her head, easing her struggles to free herself. "I know you're ripping pissed at me, but you were wiped. You needed your rest."

Casey stared up at him accusingly. "I was fine until you pulled the whole caveman thing on me."

A grin tugged at Hutch's lips. "Really? Did I also hypnotize you into falling asleep?"

Casey frowned, realizing how irrational she was being. "I was supposed to talk to members of my team hours ago. They must be worried and angry."

"They're neither. I texted them all, and told them you'd conked out. They're waiting patiently for you to get back to them. And, no, I didn't ask what they were doing or why. No sabotaging your investigation—you have my word."

Easing herself to standing, Casey shot him a sideways look. "You're enjoying this, aren't you?"

"Your reaction? Yes. Your pushing yourself too hard? No."

Casey grimaced. "You made your point. Now I have to get to my iPad and get to work."

"Fine. One condition. Group text your team and let them know you'll be initiating a Zoom meeting in fifteen minutes. Then, come to the kitchen and eat. No shoveling while you work. Please, Case. For me."

Between Hutch's plea and how worried he looked, Casey relented. "Fifteen minutes. Then I get our office to myself—for as many hours as I need it."

"Within reason," Hutch clarified. He didn't wait for an answer. "Go ahead and send your text. I'll put out the food."

8

Casey and Hutch's apartment
Battery Park City
Manhattan, New York

Six-forty-seven on the dot, Casey shut the door to the second bedroom—the one that she and Hutch shared as their home offices—armed with her iPad and her notes. The newly married couple had effectively split the spacious room in two, with his and hers matching workstations, each with a swivel office chair, side table, and bookshelves, all in a classy, modern teak. Rather than using up the office's space with a guest bed, they'd instead put in a printer, copy machine, and coffee-maker, opting for a couch in the living room that opened up into a queen-sized bed, and a more expansive, hi-tech Jura station in the kitchen.

All in all, it was a perfect layout for their needs.

That being said, the office furnishings were the last thing on Casey's mind as she headed straight to her desk and settled herself behind it.

She'd already planned her agenda.

The topics would be: What Patrick and Marc had learned at their lunch. Patrick's opinion on having John Nickels heading up the NYPD facet of the investigation. Claire's feedback on any sensory connections she'd made with Shane's possessions. Ryan's progress on restoring Shane's phone and, if completed, what data he'd pulled off of it. Emma's social media findings on both Shane and, more likely, Caitlin. And last, Angela's legal take on the proper procedure to follow in order to ferry Kennedy's homework to and from school, plus, knowing Angela, anything else she'd already thought through and researched regarding the case.

After that, Casey was open and willing to listen to anything and everything from the team that she hadn't already covered, and to brainstorm the next ideas to pursue.

A minute after Casey initiated the Zoom meeting, six invitees joined the session and the whole team's faces appeared on her screen. All of them, save Angela, were still at the office.

"Hi all," Casey said, taut and ready to roll. "I want to begin by apologizing. I left you all in the lurch."

Ryan spoke without thinking, as was his usual MO. "Come on, boss. Cut yourself some slack. You were on the verge of collapse when I finally got you into that Escalade Hutch hired to drive you home. And you didn't go willingly. The last thing we need is an incapacitated president—again."

You could have heard a pin drop on that Zoom meeting.

The irked tone. The take-charge attitude. The reference—yet again—to a time when Casey couldn't be in command and control. For the second time that day, Ryan had way overstepped, and the results wouldn't be pretty. FI might be a family, but Casey was its undisputed leader.

Her eyes flashed as she leveled her gaze on him, opening her mouth to put him in his place.

Claire interceded. "Casey, not all of us expresses it artfully, but we're all worried about you. We're asking a lot—way more than your surgeon would agree to. Sometimes you have to give in to your body's needs in order to stay healthy."

The anger in Casey's eyes banked, and her lips twitched. "Ah, Claire, the consummate diplomat. Ryan might not know it, but you just saved his ass."

"Yeah, I kind of do know it," Ryan said sheepishly. "Sorry, boss. I was out of line. I'm still not holding it together too well."

"I realize that. So apology accepted."

"We're all on edge," Marc put in. "The important thing is that, while you were catching up on some much-needed rest, we were carrying out our assignments. I'm sure we've all got a lot to bring you and each other up to speed on."

Casey nodded. "And we will. But before we get started, welcome to your first official FI full-team Zoom meeting, Angela. Thanks for giving up your weekend."

The former defense attorney waved away the thanks. Even on a Saturday evening at home, wearing little-to-no makeup and a sweater and jeans, she looked über-professional and, as always, strikingly attractive. "No problem," she assured Casey. "I wasn't surprised by your call. After consulting with you on your last case, I was prepared for the way you ran things here. Twenty-four-seven. And with an electrifying energy. That's one of the reasons I was eager to join your team—*our* team," she clarified. She cleared her throat. "Ryan, I'm very sorry about your cousin."

"Thanks," Ryan replied. "You're a great add to the team. I already have a question to run by you after we've caught Casey and each other up."

"I'll be all ears."

"Okay, let's get down to business," Casey responded. "Marc, I'll start with you and Patrick. How are things on the FBI front? Oh, and did you reach Aidan?"

"I did and he's on it. I'll let you know when I get results."

"Fair enough. Go on."

Marc went on to fill Casey—and the whole team—in on his and Patrick's lackluster meeting with SA Grogan, and Marc's follow-up email to SA Adams. "I cc'd James Harkins on the email, as well. That's probably a long shot, since he's currently at the New York field office, a high-level specialist in the office of public affairs. But it's worth the risk. I've met him several times. He's got a good handle on inside work relationships. Maybe he'll have some insight into Shane's inner circle—insight he's willing to share with me as long as it doesn't tread on Hutch's toes."

"Excellent. Have you heard back from SA Adams yet?" Casey asked.

Patrick nodded. "She agreed to a midday Zoom meeting our time on Monday. Grogan definitely prepared her for us. Her email was stiff as a board and sounded about as enthusiastic as I do when I'm about to have a cavity filled. I think she only agreed to talk to us because of the way Marc phrased the email. As you just heard, he made it personal, not investigative."

"Smart," Casey acknowledged. "And James Harkins?"

"I got an Out of Office message," Marc replied. "Maybe he took a long weekend, which would explain it. But there was no indication that he was away for any length of time. So, with a modicum of luck, he'll get back to me. Hopefully on Monday."

"Hopefully at all." Casey blew out a frustrated breath. "You guys have an even tougher path to follow than I anticipated." A pause. "What about the NYPD? Any contact there?"

"Not yet," Patrick replied. "We're brainstorming to try to come up with the best in we can. It's going to be another tough nut to crack, our only advantage being that Ryan can access their database."

"Maybe not our only advantage," Casey modified. "Ryan came up with another way in. John Nickels. John spent over twenty-five years with the NYPD. He must have a substantial number of friends and contacts. What do you think about letting him head up that effort?"

The whole team looked enthused, and Patrick nodded his head vigorously. "Great idea, Ryan. John is more than capable of handling this. He can join our next meeting, or I can just develop a game plan with him alone. Whichever you want, Casey."

She contemplated that for a moment. "You talk to him first, bandy ideas about. Once you have a prospective game plan, we'll have a team meeting so we can put things in motion stat. You've got tonight and tomorrow to connect with John and come up with an approach. We'll reconvene as a group on this Monday—with John included."

No one was surprised by Casey's fast-track approach. And not just because this case was so personal. FI operated on supersonic speed all the time. It was part of their winning formula.

"Ryan, you next," Casey said interlacing her fingers on the desk. "Were you able to resurrect Shane's cell phone data?"

Ryan gave a tight nod. "It took most of the day, but yeah. I went straight for his Friday calendar entries. He'd taken a half-day at work. His annual physical was scheduled for one-thirty PM. He kept the appointment; I called his doctor's office to make sure. The appointment wrapped up at around two-fifteen. The doctor's office is in Ardsley, which is about twenty minutes from New Rochelle, but it wouldn't be worth it to go back to the city. He'd get there in time to leave."

"So he went home—straight home," Casey noted. "Otherwise the timing of the murder would be off."

"Right." Marc looked thoughtful. "No stopping to do errands or pick up dinner. Which is what busy professionals—who also happened to be family-minded—usually do when they get a rare few hours off. He didn't even give Caitlin a break by going to pick up Kennedy. From Ryan's description, that doesn't sound like Shane."

"No," Ryan said. "It doesn't. So what are you getting at?"

Marc pursed his lips. "I'm operating on pure speculation. But let's see it through. Kennedy was still at school. Caitlin was working at home. Maybe Shane had a serious situation to discuss with her, something dark that would affect them both, or even them all. Whatever that something was, it would be a good chance for them to talk in private."

"Yes," Emma agreed at once. "You don't get much couple time when you have a nine-year-old, not even at night when you *think* the child is asleep." She grinned when she saw the surprised looks gazing at her. "I babysat a lot," she explained. "I needed the cash. I know the drill."

Ryan wasn't smiling. "My guess is that the assailant was targeting Shane, so he was probably following him. I doubt he had access to

Shane's personal calendar. So, unless we're dealing with a professional killer—which none of us believes we are—he used traditional methods to keep an eye on my cousin."

Claire was frowning. "That's not right. Correction: it's partly right. But mostly wrong."

"Can you please unscramble that statement?" Ryan pressed her.

"I can think of one reason why it's wrong," Patrick interrupted. "Parking. We're talking about Federal Plaza and lower Manhattan. It's a zoo. There are barely enough spaces for the employees and no way to see who parked where. Not to mention, there's no niche for a tail to hang out in for a full work day in order to follow someone from that building."

Ryan's mind kicked back in, and he looked grim. "Claire's right for another reason. If the bastard was tailing Shane anywhere he'd know his car. In which case, he would have seen him arrive at home and park on the street, and another car—presumably Caitlin's—parked in the driveway. Meaning he'd realize that Shane wasn't alone in the house. That punches a hole in the entire theory."

"Both those explanations make sense, and explain my ambivalence." Claire was pensive, and she looked totally puzzled. "Still… I can't dismiss the concept that Shane was being watched. It's just that something is out of whack—something we're missing. I'm just not sure what."

"Shit." Ryan dragged both hands through his hair. "Nothing fits."

Claire shook her head. "Something does. It's just out of reach. Like everything else I'm grasping for."

That made Casey turn her gaze to Claire. "Does that mean you hit a brick wall when you held Shane's possessions?"

"So far, I'm just getting flashes and an overriding sense of danger." Claire filled Casey in on her frustrating sensory awareness. "I'm not even close to being done. I need more tools to get my answers." She turned her gaze to Marc. "Is the Walshes' house still sealed off?"

Marc wiggled his hand from side to side. "Not in the way you mean, no. ERT has done its job. So has the coroner. But I don't know if Hutch already has agents canvassing the area, talking to neighbors to get leads on Caitlin's whereabouts, not to mention pressing for information on whether anyone spotted or heard anything out of the ordinary at the time Shane was killed. Why? What do you need?"

"Physical items that Shane and Caitlin shared," Claire replied. "A remote control. Matching coffee mugs—I somehow sense that they shared their first cup of the morning together each day. His and hers towels. Whatever you can readily get your hands on. This crime involved them both. I need their combined energy. It might help fill in the blanks and unblock me."

"That's reason enough. I'll take a ride to New Rochelle right after lunch and borrow whatever I can from the Walshes' house. I'll make sure I'm not seen."

"I guess that's one of the pluses of being a former Navy SEAL," Emma muttered. "You learn to be invisible."

"You bet," Marc responded.

"Thank you, Marc," Claire said, visibly relieved.

Casey nodded. "That's a good idea." She angled her head toward Emma. "Emma, did you learn anything from the Walshes' social media accounts? Because I talked to only one of Caitlin's friends today—a work friend. I need more. I'm hoping you can come up with personal friends, hopefully long-time ones, whose names or faces Ryan's mom might recognize."

"No worries there," Emma assured her. "Caitlin likes posting photos on Instagram. That's primarily where she goes, other than an occasional tweet on X. Her captions tag social media handles, but don't use real names. I'm still figuring out which handle belongs to whom. Then, I'm digging into each of their backgrounds and cross-referencing their other friends."

She sighed, speaking before she could think. "I ran those dating sites, too, Casey. No sign of either Shane or Caitlin participating in..." She clapped a hand over her mouth.

Ryan bristled. "I thought we dropped the whole cheating idea. No way. Not ever. Subject closed."

Casey quickly jumped in. "This one's on me, Ryan. I asked Emma to dig into all possible dating sites. No matter how certain you were and how much we agreed with you, I had to cover every base. The Bureau will. And, if you calm down and think objectively, you'll realize I'm right."

There was a long taut silence.

"Yeah, okay," Ryan said at last. "It only served to prove my point."

"Yes, it did." Casey turned back to Emma. "Back to social media. What else?"

Emma wet her lips and continued, after shooting an apologetic look at Ryan. "Unfortunately, looking for platforms of Shane's was a dead end. No social media presence at all, not under his own name or any other."

"That doesn't surprise me," Ryan said.

"It didn't surprise me either," Emma replied. "I just made sure to cover all my bases. That done, I switched entirely over to Caitlin. Other than Instagram photos, she doesn't post too often, maybe every other week. No LinkedIn account either. Nothing business. Nothing personal. That's not stopping me. I can shoot you over some names and profiles now, including the backgrounds I've put together, or I can keep going and send it all to you at once, after I'm done."

"Separate what you've completed versus what you're still working on," Casey instructed. "Forward the completed list on to me now. Finish the incomplete list between now and when the funeral is over. Then, I can review everything, first alone, and then with Ryan's mom on Tuesday or Wednesday. That's the most efficient way of handling things without holding up the process."

"Okay, I'll get back on it right after this Zoom meeting is over," Emma replied.

"What about other platforms, like Facebook?" Patrick asked.

Emma wrinkled up her nose. "Only old people still use Facebook. Caitlin has a barebones page there, but that's not where she posts." She gave Patrick an apologetic look. "No offense."

His lips curved. "None taken."

"Incorrect, Emma," Yoda piped up. "While Instagram and, secondarily TikTok, rank high in popularity on the social media platforms for Millennials, who span the ages of twenty-eight to forty-three years old—an age span that would include Caitlin—Facebook still holds its own. It is used at least once a week by eighty-seven percent of Millennials. So it would be foolish for you to discount that platform while doing your research."

That took the wind out of Emma's sails, and she let out a sigh of defeat. "You win, Yoda. Fortunately, I've included Facebook in all my analyses." She turned to Patrick. "And I withdraw my inaccurate statement."

Casey stifled a smile. "Let's move off the social media aspect of our investigation," she said, simultaneously glancing from one face to the other. "Anything else?" She paused to look at Ryan. "Go ahead and run your question about Kennedy's schoolwork by Angela."

Ryan did exactly that.

Angela listened intently. "I'm going to answer off the cuff, but I'll follow up with hardcore research. Fact: Your mother is acting as Kennedy's guardian, unofficial though it may be. Have her make the initial call to the principal and set up a meeting between her, Kennedy's principal, and her school counselor. Maybe include her teacher; I'm not certain—yet. When they meet, your mother should reveal only the facts released by the FBI: Kennedy's father was killed and her mother is missing. As a result, Kennedy is living with her and her husband. Let the group of them work this out and decide how things should be handled. My guess is, they'll agree to allow a designated person from the family to transport Kennedy's assignments to and from the school. The school will want her to stay current on her homework, and her counselor will want to help her focus on anything other than the loss of her father and the whereabouts of her mother. Give me a few hours to verify or embellish on what I've said. In any case, it's a good idea."

"Thanks for the advice," Ryan replied. "I'll wait for you to give me the go-ahead. It's not urgent since I won't be bringing this up to my mom until after the wake and funeral. I know she'll be happy to do anything in her power to ease things for Kennedy."

"Speaking of which," Angela added. "I've done some research into the idea of your mother acting as standby guardian for Kennedy, at least until Caitlin's fate has been resolved. It's a complicated process that takes months to complete. Forms have to be submitted to Family Court and you need a judge to approve them. My advice? Continue to deal with the Office of Child and Family Services and avoid the legal path. OCFS is aware that your mother is Kennedy's next of kin, and that she has a large, supportive family she's close to. So they'll be willing to keep the current arrangement in place as long as they can."

Ryan gave her a grateful look. "I appreciate your handling that—even before I thought of asking."

"No thanks necessary. Besides, that was the easy part. I'm sure that keeping FI out of jail will be a lot harder."

With a hint of a smile, Casey brought the meeting to a close. "We all know what we have to do. I'll hold Monday's meeting at the office, with John included. Ryan, you and Claire, of course, are excused."

Ryan shook his head. "I want to be there, to stay current with you guys. As it turns out, the funeral isn't until two PM. If we have our meeting in the early morning, Claire and I can get to my parents' house, no problem, with time to spare for being with Kennedy before we leave for church." He frowned, looking at Marc. "Unfortunately, I'll miss hearing what you gain from your Zoom meeting with that retired FBI agent—plus a whole lot of other things that'll happen the rest of Monday. And Claire won't be at the office to hold the personal items you bring back from Shane and Caitlin's house."

"We'll fix all that on Tuesday," Marc replied. "You and Claire do what you have to."

Casey nodded. "Sunday is a lost day anyway, since most of the world isn't working. We'll hold our meeting on Monday at seven AM, so you and Claire can attend. Whatever minimal updates we have, we'll bring to the table. And John will be there. He'll have had more than enough time to coordinate with Patrick and to adjust his schedule so he can join us." A compassionate look crossed her face. "But Ryan, as for the rest of Monday—we'll bring you up to speed whenever you're ready. I don't want to hear from either you or Claire until sometime on Tuesday. You're officially off. Be with your family. They need you. Kennedy needs you. And you need to honor Shane."

Ryan's eyes grew misty. "Yes, I do. But I also need to find his killer."

"And you will. We all will."

9

Ryan's apartment
Park Slope, Brooklyn, New York
Sunday, 10:35 pm

Claire lay quietly in Ryan's bed, her head pillowed on his chest, his arms wrapped tightly around her.

The sense of peace that pervaded them was a godsend.

The wake had been hell—for Ryan, for his family, and, most of all, for Kennedy. Her tears had been interminable, her pain something no child should have to endure.

The funeral parlor had been quiet, with only family, fellow FBI agents, former NYPD detectives, and a couple of Hutch's Special Agents overseeing the event to make sure that no dangers presented themselves. The aura of death, exacerbated by the violence that had preceded it, hung like a heavy cloud over the room, extinguishing any nostalgic stories or cherished memories that usually accompanied such a meaningful occasion.

Claire had tempered the darkness to the best of her ability. She'd weaved her way among the members of Ryan's family, conveying as much of her positive energy as possible. But overall, she stayed with Ryan, her fingers linked with his as she offered him her closeness, her strength, and her support. She'd felt his pain as her own, even as she watched him manage to stay strong, especially for Kennedy, who alternately wept against Ryan's shoulder and buried her face in his mom's loving arms.

The whole event had been heartbreaking, including the family gathering at the McKay house afterwards.

Ryan had held it together until, several hours later, when he and Claire finally left his parents' house. He was unsettled about leaving, since he was worried that Kennedy might need him. But Maureen felt otherwise. She'd given Ryan and Claire a firm wave of her hand, her expression clearly stating that they needed time alone for Claire to comfort Ryan while he gave in to his own grief. By that time, Kennedy was curled against Maureen's side, half-asleep, and there was nothing more that could be done tonight. Tomorrow at the funeral, Ryan and Claire's strength would, once again, be called upon, and they required some recoup time.

The drive home had been silent, Claire letting Ryan stay inside his own head, grappling with his memories and his feelings. Once inside his apartment, she shut the door and turned to him. "Do you need to be alone?"

Ryan gave an adamant shake of his head, his tough veneer cracking. He reached out and drew Claire against him. "Come to bed with me," he said, his voice trembling as he spoke. "I need you. I need us."

"You have both," Claire replied softly.

Their lovemaking was intense and urgent, a deep manifestation of their love and a reaffirmation of life. Even after their passion was spent, Ryan held Claire to him, unwilling to release her and to, once again, be inundated with the pain of loss.

Claire tipped up her chin, her gaze meeting his. "I love you," she whispered. "You're not alone."

"I know." Ryan's eyes shut, as he let the balm of Claire's love ease his emotional torture. "I also know that, since this nightmare began, I've been asking way too much of you."

"No you haven't. Not even a little." She kissed his shoulder. "Besides, I just got a reprieve. This more than made up for that booty call we never managed to have last night."

A hint of a smile curved Ryan's lips. "It was just a start. We have the rest of the night for encores." He pressed his lips into her hair, all humor having vanished. "I don't want to think. Not until tomorrow. For tonight, I just want to make love to you."

Claire looped her arms around his neck. "That sounds ideal."

***

Asia
Location: unknown
Time: unknown

The room was dark, except for the glow of several large displays.

Inside, the operative shoved aside his half-empty can of Red Bull and leaned over the keyboard. He'd received his orders. Penetrate the FBI database and exfiltrate the necessary information.

Swiveling around, he glanced over at the refrigerator humming in the corner. He rose, checked the contents behind its dirty glass door. It was well-stocked with shelf upon shelf of liquid human fuel.

Given the intense security he needed to penetrate, it would be at least a three-can night.

He shut his eyes and began the journey into hell.

***

Offices of Forensic Instincts
Tribeca, Manhattan, New York
First floor conference room
Monday, 7:00 am

The team—John Nickels included—had already helped themselves to coffee, and were gathered around the room in tub chairs, iPads open and ready.

"Welcome, John," Casey began, a twinkle in her eye. "Given the role you customarily play with the team, I feel safer already."

John didn't smile. "That's kind of you, considering I fell down on the job when you needed me most," he replied. "I'm *so* sorry, Casey. I never saw that bullet coming."

"Neither did Hutch and he was right beside me," Casey responded without missing a beat. "You're the best there is, John. It all happened too fast for anyone to stop. And I'm just fine. So toss the guilt."

"Consider it tossed." John's rigid posture eased. "As for running the NYPD aspect of this investigation, I'm looking forward to the challenge. And I can still be FI's lead security guard, as needed."

The whole team knew that was true. John was always Patrick's go-to person when security of any kind was needed. Not only was he as professional and conscientious as they come, his track record was superb. Plus, he looked the part. At well over six feet tall, John had the body of a linebacker, and an icy stare that could freeze a criminal in their tracks. As for the NYPD, he'd served in the homicide department for two-and-a-half decades before retiring. During his successful career, he'd also worked a few joint task forces with Patrick. So when the time came for John to say good-bye to his old life, Patrick had cleared it with Casey and snatched John up for Forensic Instincts.

There'd never been any regrets—not from either side. John fit right into the group, and they called on him time and again, sometimes to protect clients, sometimes to protect team members themselves. He was smart, he was shrewd, and he knew when and how to fly by the seat of his pants.

Now, Casey leaned forward, interlacing her fingers on the workstation in front of her and addressing Patrick. "What did you and John work out?"

Patrick was ready with his reply. "First of all, other than emergencies, I've relieved John of his security responsibilities and substituted strong replacements in his stead until this case is solved. Much as I know he can handle both, I want his efforts focused on the NYPD aspect of this investigation."

"I totally agree," Casey responded.

"John and I amassed a long list of his current and retired allies in a multitude of precincts, and not only homicide cops," Patrick continued. "He'll start reaching out to them today. I was stunned by the number of people he knows, and how many of those people he'd feel comfortable approaching about Shane."

Ryan jumped in at this point, turning to face John. "That's great. I already hacked into the NYPD's database, and Yoda and I compiled a list of Shane's cases, as well as the cops who worked with him and the criminals who were involved. Tomorrow, you and I can start cross-referencing them with your contacts. Anything else you need as we move along, just tell me. I'll get back into the NYPD system and dig up answers. Sporadically. So I don't raise suspicions."

John nodded. "We'll accomplish what we need to. Count on it. And Ryan, it goes without saying how sorry I am about Shane."

"I know. Thanks."

Casey cleared her throat. "We've all got a lot to do today, since yesterday was a bust other than Emma working on the list of Caitlin's friends." Casey's gaze shifted to Emma. "Judging from what I've seen so far, you're doing a great job. I'm looking forward to getting the complete list. And I'm proud of you."

Emma beamed. "Thanks."

"I'll analyze the entirety of what you put in the cloud as soon as it's there. Then, I'll take it all to Maureen McKay, the instant she's up to seeing me. Given her nuclear role in the McKay household, I have a strong feeling she'll contribute a lot to pinpointing what's necessary."

With that, Casey paused, her lips thinning into an annoyed line. "Just so you all know, I'll be here today only until after Marc has his Zoom meeting with SA Adams. Hopefully, by then he'll also have heard back from James Harkins. I doubt he'll have collected what Claire needs at the Walshes' house—it'll be too early. I'm going home to rest before two o'clock, per my husband's *request*. I reminded him that I'd relaxed and worked in a recliner under an afghan most of yesterday, but that didn't seem to help. So I'll take a late-afternoon nap, eat dinner, and be available by Zoom this evening. Let's make it seven-thirty."

Marc's lips twitched at the irked note in Casey's voice. "Got it. Seven-thirty it is. We'll fill you in on anything you miss."

A tight nod. "I'll be back in the office at the crack of dawn tomorrow. In addition, we're moving back to the main conference room next week. That's where we have our team meetings, not to mention that it's also my office. Things need to get back to normal. I can manage one flight of stairs."

Marc didn't argue. "Just make sure to run it by your surgeon." His lips twitched again. "And your sentry."

Casey shot him a look. "I will. And I'm not amused."

"I'll also be in first thing tomorrow," Claire announced. "I want to connect with whatever Marc brings me from Shane and Caitlin's house as soon as possible."

"And I'll be with Claire," Ryan said. "It'll be time for me to get back to work. Casey, I'll pull my mom aside tonight and make sure she's okay with your calling her tomorrow and setting up meetings—first with her and then with Kennedy. We'll still be mourning in our hearts. But we've got to move forward with this investigation."

Casey studied his face. "Are you sure it's not too soon?"

"Positive."

"Then I'd appreciate it. Claire, when I go to the McKay house, I want you with me," Casey continued. "Given your gift of claircognizance, it would be the right decision under any circumstances, but especially under these. You spent time with Kennedy. You were at the house when the FBI broke the horrible news to her, and again at the wake and now the funeral. Given who and what you are, I'm sure she already feels comfortable with you. You can ease the way through our talk."

Claire nodded. "Of course. I'll also be with you when you interview the rest of the family. We can work those meetings around the all-important ones with Ryan's mom and with Kennedy."

"All my siblings and my dad will be on board," Ryan assured them. "You can call them tomorrow, as well, and get things rolling."

"That's ideal," Casey responded. "Thank you, Ryan." She glanced from one team member to another. "So we're all set?"

Nods across the board, although Ryan looked upset and torn.

"You'll be back at full steam tomorrow," Casey said gently. "Today you're needed elsewhere—the same elsewhere you need and want to be. Go. Our thoughts and prayers are with you and your family."

***

Podgorica, Montenegro
6:05 PM CET

Owen Willard slammed the empty whiskey glass down on the table in disgust. His two guys, who were surveilling the house from that nearby apartment over the store, had turned up shit. Just hour upon hour of boring conversation. And the video was worse. Just the family marching in and out. Mostly, that stupid overbearing hen clucking around the kid.

He swore under his breath, leaned back in his chair, and massaged his temples. The drink hadn't done anything to ease his migraine or his stress. He might have killed the FBI guy, but that didn't end the problem. His boss was all over his ass about the threat the fucking agent had left behind, and leaning on him to finish the job. Easier said than done, especially since he couldn't handle the situation firsthand. But a return trip was not in the cards. Thanks to his fuck-up, he'd be stuck in this bullshit country for the rest of his life, the only good thing being that he couldn't be extradited, tried, convicted, and sent to a supermax prison.

That wouldn't keep him safe from his boss. He had to do something to get the wife to resurface—and fast. Increased pressure might up the incentive. He'd kick-start that right now.

Maybe that would ruffle the feathers of that old hen and make things happen.

***

East 236th Street
Woodlawn, Bronx, New York
12:15 pm

Ryan and Clare had left Manhattan early and were about to turn onto the McKays' street. The entire family was meeting at the house before the funeral. Being together to share in the somber mood of the day and the personal agonizing everyone was going through was as important as being at the church. This way, they could travel there, car by car, in a line and as a unit, as tight as any family in crisis could be, lending strength to each other and standing as one to endure the ordeal of saying good-bye to Shane.

As they neared the house, Claire reached over and took Ryan's hand. "I'll be wherever my instincts tell me to go," she said softly. "But mostly I'll be by your side. I'll know when you need me."

Ryan squeezed her fingers. "What would I do without you?"

"Don't waste your time on that one. I'm not going anywhere."

Ryan had just opened his mouth to reply, when his cell phone rang. He glanced at the caller ID, then, brows drawn in puzzlement, pressed answer. "Hi, Mom. You okay?"

"No." Maureen's voice was trembling. "Where are you?"

"Driving down your street."

"Thank God. I need you here. Now. I just got a text message. I don't know from whom. But it's thrown me. Please just get here."

Ryan accelerated. "Give us two minutes."

***

Claire and Ryan were out of the car almost before it came to a stop.

Maureen was standing on the outside step, her expression grim, her cell phone clasped in her hand.

She walked across the lawn to meet them. "I don't want anyone else to know about this," she began. "Not yet. Especially Kennedy. She's falling to pieces as it is." With that, Maureen handed her phone to Ryan, the text she'd received open and ready.

Wordlessly, he scanned the message, which was comprised of two cryptic sentences:

I'm watching Kennedy. Are you?

"Shit," Ryan muttered, his jaw clenched. "A pointed threat about Kennedy's safety, sent, no doubt, via a burner. Either Kennedy herself is a bigger threat to the killer than we thought, or they're using texts like this to draw Caitlin out. Or both." He turned off the phone and pocketed it. "I'll need to take this back to the office with me, Mom. Use your home phone for both incoming and outgoing calls. I'll reroute your cell calls to that number here, as well. I want things to seem like business as usual."

"But it won't be," Maureen said, her forehead creased with worry. "You'll be trying to trace the text and do whatever else you need to do. The problem is that there will be FBI agents stationed at the church. Don't we have to share this with them first?"

Ryan shook his head. "Not today. Today is about saying good-bye to Shane. No one will expect us to address the investigation, or even to check our phones. Give me tonight. I'll get what we need. Then first thing tomorrow, you can share the text, and your phone, with the Bureau. Tell them you just checked your cell and found the message."

Claire was looking unsettled. "Hutch would be furious."

"He won't find out. I'll work all night. My mom can have her phone back by dawn."

Claire was still visibly uneasy. "Okay."

Ryan turned to her and frowned. "You think Hutch will somehow figure it out?"

"No." Claire massaged her temples. "But something isn't right. Something about the text message. And about the danger that exists."

Maureen blanched. "Is Kennedy at immediate risk?"

Claire took her hands away from her forehead, confusion and anxiety clouding her expression. "I don't think so. At least not from the text."

"Or the person who sent it?" Ryan demanded.

At that, Claire nodded.

"So the sender isn't the killer," Ryan surmised, brow furrowed. "They could be a hired hand, some flunky. But the killer is out there, threatening, not only Caitlin, but Kennedy, as well."

"Yes." Claire was looking more and more confused. "I...maybe I'll hold the cell phone on our drive home tonight—if that's okay with you?" she asked Maureen.

"Of course," Maureen replied. "I'm grateful for any help you can offer."

Claire placed a hand on Maureen's arm. "Ryan will figure this out. You'll see."

Maureen fought back tears. “I know.”

From the corner of his eye, Ryan saw his father and Nolan hovering at the open doorway, looking puzzled.

“Let’s go inside,” he urged his mother. “I don’t want you to have to answer questions as to what was going on out here. We’ll just say you came out to hear if we had any updates. Then we’ll drop the subject and turn our attention to Kennedy and the day ahead.”

10

The Offices of Forensic Instincts
Tribeca, Manhattan, New York
Marc's office, 3rd floor
12:20 pm

Marc ended the bullshit meeting with SA Tricia Adams, and sat scowling at the blank computer screen.

Other than praising Shane as a fine human being and an even finer agent, Adams had dodged Marc's carefully-worded questions. She'd claimed that she couldn't recall specific BU employees with whom Shane had had a tight relationship, nor could she recall any stand-out cases their squad had been working on seven to eight years ago.

Effectively, she'd told Marc nothing.

Special Agent Groban had obviously prepped her, just as Marc and Patrick had predicated. Even though Marc had taken a very low key approach, she'd played an effective game of dodge ball. So had James Harkins, who'd answered Marc's email by saying that, given he'd been out of the office for several days, he was backed-up with work and couldn't schedule a Zoom meeting.

In short, Marc had hit the ultimate immoveable brick wall, making the whole FBI aspect of this investigation a dead end.

It wasn't hard to figure out why—or rather, who.

Marc left his office and walked down to the first floor conference room, where Casey was reviewing some of Emma's social media results.

"Bad time?" Marc asked, hovering on the threshold.

Casey sighed, ran a hand through her hair, and waved Marc in. "No. I'm trying to figure out who each of these handles belongs to, and coming up empty. I doubt I'll get anywhere until I have more details from Emma, and ask the right questions of Ryan's mom. I could definitely use a diversion." Her brows rose in question. "Anything from Tricia Adams?"

Marc walked across the room, grabbed a mug of coffee, and sat down. "Nope. Not from her or from James Harkins, who emailed me back just to blow me off. Let's cut to the chase. We're not getting anything out of these BU employees or special agents—not the active, former, or retired ones. This time it's Hutch who's running the show. And he did an A+ job of shutting everyone down."

"He's too damned good at what he does," Casey muttered. "And he knows only too well how my mind works—and how our team operates. As a result, on this investigation he and I are like two cats, facing off with our backs arched. I guess the honeymoon phase is over."

Marc chuckled. "Not a chance. The honeymoon phase is a given with you guys. The problem is that, even though you're ideally suited, you're also too damned much alike. Both intense leaders who, in this case, are butting heads. With you and Hutch, that's called marriage. It's just the first time you've been truly pitted against each other."

"Why doesn't that make me feel all warm and fuzzy inside?" Casey's question was rhetorical, asked in a sarcastic tone. "What you're telling me is that, no matter what approach FI takes, pursuing Shane's FBI connections will yield a big, fat goose egg."

"Yup. That's what I'm telling you."

"How encouraging." Casey shook her head in frustration. "And, as I said, the social media end of things is still way up in the air. I've got nothing tangible."

"Emma will give you more by tonight," Marc reminded her. "And you'll get to run all those names by Ryan's mother tomorrow."

"I hope I get the chance to do that before the media and the public at large read about Shane's death, and Caitlin's disappearance, and make the connection between the Walshes and the McKays. When that happens and word gets out that Kennedy is staying with her great-aunt and great-uncle, which we know it will, all hell will break loose in Woodlawn. Ryan's parents' house will be swarmed with nosy media mongers and curious folks from the neighborhood who have yet to be interviewed by the FBI. Plus, the agents assigned to the Walshes' place will be ready and eager to question the McKays, the press will descend...Dammit." Casey gave a hard shift in her chair, the motion causing her to wince and moan softly with pain.

She waved away Marc's instinctive motion to help, fighting the pain—and losing. "I'm okay." Even as she spoke, she sagged back in discomfort and fatigue. "Dammit. It's not the time for me to slow down. Why can't I just be back to myself already?"

"You will be—soon." Marc took the bull by the horns, going straight for the diehard reality Casey refused to discuss or to allow herself to fully recall. "Case, we're not talking about recovering from the flu," he stated bluntly in a way that only he was allowed. "You were shot. You lost so much blood that you nearly died. Your spleen was removed. You spent days in the ICU. That was only three months ago. Cut yourself some slack. Try to have some patience. And look at how far you've come rather than at how far you still have to go."

Eyes lowered, Casey gave a terse nod. "Message received. I'll try. But I got nothing accomplished today and I have to leave in an hour and a half just to lie down and recoup my strength. This whole situation is driving me crazy."

Marc downed the rest of his coffee and set down the mug, simultaneously rising to his feet. "I tell you what. I'm at a standstill. You're at a standstill. I'll take that ride to Shane and Caitlin's house a little early, before that swarm of media mongers show up. As it is, I'll have plenty of canvassing agents to avoid."

He paused, pursed his lips. "I'll park a few blocks away and walk. That area of New Rochelle has lots of trees between houses. I'll weave my way through them and enter via the back door. Ryan gave me his keys, so it's no problem. I'll get what Claire needs and send you a text and photos before the car service comes to collect you. You can review it all as you ride home. You won't be violating Hutch's wishes. And you'll be all ready for a preliminary discussion of this topic during our evening Zoom meeting, before Claire's even seen the stuff. Plus, just my *doing* something will get our juices flowing—yours and mine. And who knows? It might just yield some results."

Abruptly, Casey perked up. "Why don't you take some time to discreetly chat with some of the Walshes' neighbors yourself? People are psychologically more inclined to help family or friends than they are cops. Maybe you'll find someone who saw or heard something they'd forgotten." She waved away what she knew was about to be Marc's protest. "Yes, I'm sure Hutch had a team do that already. But, again, they're law enforcement. You're a close friend of Shane's cousin. Tell them how devastated Ryan is. Go for their heartstrings. That might make them remember something. I wish Ryan could do this himself, but he's in no shape to do so. It's up to you. And, yeah, Hutch won't be happy. But what you're doing is absolutely legal."

A corner of Marc's mouth lifted. "This is a first for me. I'm not usually the heartstrings type."

"But you are the covert type. You won't be spotted. Plus, I've seen the sensitive side of you. You'll pull it off." Casey held up a palm. "And before you stress it yet again, I realize Hutch will be über pissed. I'll deal with that later—after we have the information we need."

"Brave girl," Marc said drily. "But you've got a valid point. Let's see what I can do."

A glint of hope lit Casey's eyes. "Go for it."

***

15 Marigold Terrace
New Rochelle, New York
1:35 pm

Marc slipped in the back door of Shane and Caitlin's house, then crept to the front window, standing to a side and peering into the street.

Several FBI agents doing their jobs, subtly traveling from door to door to interview people. A bunch of curious neighbors milling around and watching them. The end result? No one was focused on Shane and Caitlin's empty house. Excellent. Now Marc just had to continue to evade them.

Just to be safe, he waited a few minutes before he began his search—and when he did, it was slowly, cautiously, squatting down as he moved from room to room.

Claire's suggestions had been good ones. On the kitchen drain board were two mugs, one that read "Shane" and one that read "Caitlin". Right beside them were two teaspoons. It was a good guess that the combined items were used for their last shared early morning cup-of-coffee ritual.

Marc opened the backpack he'd slid over his shoulder and put both mugs and spoons inside.

From there, he glanced into the living room and shook his head. Warm and cozy, but not intimate enough for what he needed.

He turned, easing his way up the flight of stairs and to the master bedroom. His gaze darted about. There was a coaster on each nightstand, each of which had a coffee ring on it. Obviously, the spots where the couple placed their mugs. Marc grabbed those, too, as well as the remote control that was between the two pillows on the bed.

Lastly, he went into the master bath, hunting down the final items Claire had mentioned. Sure enough, there was a pair of hand towels on the hooks beside the sink, monogramed with Shane and Caitlin's initials.

Marc stuffed those in the backpack, as well. He even stepped into the stall shower and took the bottles of shampoo and conditioner—personal items that both Shane and Caitlin had held in their hands.

He'd just left the room and was inching his way toward the stairs, when a sudden thought occurred to him. It might be useful. It might not. But it was worth the try.

He pivoted and crept down to Kennedy's room. There was no mistaking it, he thought with a hint of a smile. It was light pink and filled with stuffed animals, together with a kid's desk and a clothing bureau, all in a bright lacquered white. In contrast, there was a slew of gymnastics equipment clustered in one corner and three taekwondo medals on the far wall. Definitely a well-rounded kid.

Marc's gaze swept the room, settling on a school project that Kennedy was in the midst of working on. It was a half-completed historic building, comprised of Legos, that, when finished, would be the Eiffel Tower. It was complex and finely detailed—a project that would require a parent's help. Whichever parent had provided that help would have had to handle the blocks, as would Kennedy.

Taking it would be a great idea—and a tough execution.

There was a solution for every problem.

Instead of picking up the whole structure and risking its demise, Marc plucked a short column of Legos off the top—the area where Kennedy and her mom or dad had most likely been currently constructing. He put those in his backpack and slung it over his shoulder.

He waited until he was back in his car before texting a message and all the photos to Casey.

Then, he went off to dodge the agents and question the neighbors.

***

Casey and Hutch's apartment
Battery Park City
Manhattan, New York
4:50 pm

At the sound of Hero's bark, Casey squirmed in the bed and opened her eyes. After reviewing all the photos Marc had sent her, in addition to reading the tidbits of information he'd gathered on his neighborhood tour—all of which he'd share with the team later—she'd tossed and turned for an hour before drifting off for a nap. Now, judging from the sounds emanating from the front door, Hero was greeting Hutch, who'd just arrived home.

She sat up amid the rumpled covers, running her fingers through her hair and pushing it away from her face. A moment later, Hutch walked in, looking weary and preoccupied. Clearly, he'd had a rough day, yet he was home early. His gaze swept over Casey, assessing her and making sure she was okay.

"Hey, did I wake you?" he asked, sitting on the edge of the bed and leaning forward to kiss her.

Casey's earlier irritation ebbed as she saw just how exhausted her husband was. Between his responsibilities at the Bureau and his insistence on taking care of her, these past three months had taken their toll on him.

She kissed him back and smiled. "Technically, Hero woke me when he realized his favorite wrestling partner was home. But it's fine. Nap time is over."

Hutch frowned, tracing the dark circles under her eyes with his forefinger. "It shouldn't be. You're still wiped out. You spend way too many hours at your office. And you don't get enough rest. I'm worried about you."

Casey kissed him again, this time tenderly. "I know you are. And I love you for it. I've kept all my PT appointments, and I have a follow-up with my surgeon next week. But, Hutch, please understand. I can't just lie here in between health checks. Especially with a major investigation going on. I'm losing my mind."

"I do understand. That doesn't stop me from worrying."

"Or from taking charge of my life," Casey noted dryly, holding his gaze. "Marc is right. You're acting like my sentry."

A corner of Hutch's mouth lifted in amusement. "Your sentry? Maybe so. But it doesn't work well enough. What you really need is a full-time security guard and a full-time medical professional assigned to you. Unfortunately, there'd be no applicants. You're way too difficult to manage. You're impossible."

"You're pretty impossible yourself. A knight overseeing his fortress—and strengthening it to the max."

Hutch didn't pretend to misunderstand. "If I am, then it's only because you and your team are impeding a Federal investigation—or trying to."

"And you're shutting us down."

"That's kind of my job."

"And getting past you is mine."

Rather than angry, Hutch looked amused. "Go for it."

Casey lightly punched his shoulder. "Have I told you how arrogant you are?"

"Frequently." He caught her fist and brought it to his lips. "Have I told you how sexy you are when you battle me?"

"Once or twice." Seeing the darkening look in Hutch's eyes, she scooted over on the bed. "Let's call a short truce. You want me to stay put? Give me an incentive to."

Hutch was already unbuttoning his shirt. "With pleasure. My libido is what brought me home early."

Casey laughed and tugged off her t-shirt. "Then let's take care of that now."

***

The McKay house
East 236th Street
Woodlawn, Bronx, New York
6:35 pm

The funeral mass had been held at Basilica of Saint Patrick's Old Cathedral in Manhattan, the beautiful church where Ryan's family were long-time parishioners. The ceremony had been solemn, painful, and Ryan had somehow managed to give the eulogy without breaking down. He'd relished the time for reflection, done in reverent silence, where he could think about Shane, the years of memories they'd made together, and the gaping hole his death had left behind. There were readings, prayers, and songs, all of which had been soothing and inflaming at the same time. Quiet sobs, glistening tears, and—worst of all—Kennedy's frozen silence as she clung to her great-aunt, had twisted a knife in Ryan's gut.

The burial site was closer to the McKay's home, a grassy plot that held the few members of their small family. Seeing the coffin lowered into the ground had been almost surreal, with Kennedy gripping Ryan's fingers so tightly that her knuckles turned white, and Claire on his other side, gently holding his arm. Then came a handful of condolences, after which the attendees disbanded and the procession of McKay cars traveled back to Maureen and Colin's house.

Hours later, seated on the living room sofa, Ryan glanced around, noting that the last few guests had trickled out of the house. It was just the immediate family now, with everyone clustered in this one room, sipping a cup of coffee or tea and talking quietly about the day. Maureen hadn't yet sat down, and was moving around to make sure her children and her husband were all holding up.

Every few minutes, she turned to gaze at Kennedy, who'd been curled up against Ryan's side, and had nodded off minutes ago, her face streaked with tears, her fingers tightly clutching her pendant. Ryan had eased her head onto his lap so she could sleep more comfortably. Claire, who'd been talking with Fiona, had made her way to the sofa moments ago, settled herself on Ryan's opposite side, and begun stroking Kennedy's hair with a gentle hand.

"She's wiped," Ryan murmured, pain etched on his face. "I really don't think she can hold up much longer."

"We'll make sure she does," Claire replied. "We'll also help her move on to the new challenges she has to face."

"Other than praying for her mother to come home and mourning the death of her father?"

"Yes." Claire nodded. "Her loss and her worry will remain. But the wake and the funeral are behind her. It's time to deal with the grief she's holding inside. I researched the appropriate child psychologists, spoke to a few, and selected the right one for Kennedy. I'll share the information with your mom when she's ready."

Ryan looked surprised. "I didn't know you were doing that."

Claire sighed. "Ryan, you're grieving much more deeply than even you realize. You're also shouldering your family's grief. In short, you have the weight of the world on your shoulders. This was something I could do, and do well. I have contacts in this field. There was no need to burden you. You play an enormous part in two investigations. Until they're both solved, you can't make peace with Shane's death."

Briefly, Ryan shut his eyes, reaching for her Claire's hand and squeezing it. "You're amazing."

"So are you." Claire slid to the edge of the sofa. "Stay with Kennedy. She needs your presence. Your mom and I communicate well. I'll talk to her about Casey and me interviewing, first her, and then Kennedy, tomorrow. We'll get here early—before Kennedy's awake, so we can talk to your mom alone, and I can also return her cell phone to share with the FBI. We'll bring the completed list of Caitlin's social media friends that Emma compiled. As for your siblings, I've already touched base with each of them. Your dad, too. I set up times for Casey and me to meet with them individually. That eliminates the need for Casey to make a slew of phone calls, and expedites our strategy."

Ryan gave her another surprised look. "Pretty damned organized, Claire-voyant. And here I thought I was the grounded one in our relationship."

"Most times you are. But, once in a while, it's okay for our roles to reverse." Compassion softened Claire's gaze. "This time, I get to be the rock and you get to be scattered and out of sorts. It's a good balance. That's why you and I share what we do. Give in gracefully, tough guy."

A corner of Ryan's mouth lifted. "I'll try. But when these cases are solved, all bets are off."

11

Casey and Hutch's apartment
Battery Park City
Manhattan, New York
7:05 pm

Casey and Hutch were sitting at the kitchen nook, munching on their pizza and drinking one glass of wine each—Casey's stipulation, since she was about to get on a meeting with her team. Hutch had agreed since he'd brought home a ton of work, too.

"I get the office for an hour," Casey said, sipping at her wine. "After that, I'll work in the living room armchair and the office is yours. Deal?"

"Deal." Hutch helped himself to another slice of pizza, speaking in an offhanded tone. "And while you're on the call, mention to your team that contacting retired FBI agents is going to be a no-go. Former agents, too. All your creative attempts are going to strike out. So save yourselves the time and aggravation. It'll all end the same way it did with SA Grogan and SA Adams. Oh, and James Harkins, too—current FBI members are the biggest no-no of all."

Casey put down her glass. “Have you wiretapped our office?” she asked, her tone laced with sarcasm.

“I don’t need to. I know how you think and how your team operates.” Hutch took another bite of pizza, chewed, and swallowed. “And by the way, I know we made light of it, but I meant what I said about impeding a federal investigation. That’s a crime I can’t ignore—not even for you. So stop. Now.”

By this time Casey was bristling, partly because she hated taking orders, but mostly because she knew her husband was right.

“I get your point,” she replied in a tight voice. “And, just to reassure you—and to take you down a notch—we’d already reached that conclusion on our own.”

“Good.” Hutch leaned forward, folding his hands in front of him, a grim expression on his face. “And one more thing. I expect to be kept in the loop about everything FI uncovers—regardless of the source. No exceptions. No games. I mean it, Casey.”

Casey blew out an angry breath. “Or what? You’ll shut down FI?”

“That’s not what I want, and you know it. So just cooperate and all will be well.”

Casey took a hard bite of her slice of pizza. “I hear you.”

“I know you do.” Hutch didn’t avert his gaze. “I’m concerned about whether you’ll *listen* to me.”

“I’ll do my best.”

Hutch’s eyes twinkled. “At least you’re being honest with me. If you’d out-and-out agreed, I’d know you were lying.” He reached across the table, interlaced his fingers with hers. “I don’t mean to be a hard-ass, Case. I’ll give you as much leeway as I’m able. But it’s a short leash. I have no choice.”

Casey's anger dissipated. "I know. I respect that. But please respect me and my team. We have a job to do. Not to mention that Shane was Ryan's cousin. That's as personal as it gets. We'll stick as close to the straight and narrow as we can, and share our findings with you—soon after we get them. And our poking into the bureau is over. Is that enough?"

"I'll try to make it enough."

"Have I told you what a great guy and an even better husband you are?" Casey asked, squeezing his fingers.

Hutch's gaze turned tender. "On occasion, yes. Lucky for you, you happen to be my soft spot."

***

Casey and Hutch's home office
7:30 pm

The FI team, sans Ryan and Claire, but plus John, signed onto the Zoom meeting promptly.

"Hi guys," Casey began. "It's good to connect up."

"How do you feel?" Marc asked, not revealing to the rest of the team just how bad Casey had been earlier. "Did you get rest and eat dinner?"

"Both," she replied. "And thanks for the photos. I assume you shared them with the rest of the team."

Marc nodded. "All except Claire and Ryan. Today was a day to respect their privacy. And they'll see the actual items first thing in the morning."

"That was the right thing to do." Casey leaned forward with great interest. "I'm sure you also told the team you were canvassing the Walshes' neighborhood. Did you elaborate on what you learned?"

"Nope. Not without you there." Focused on his laptop screen, he pulled up his notes and then screen-shared them with the team. "I'll store these notes in the cloud right after we talk. Here's the scoop: The whole group of residents in the Marigold Terrace area were incredibly sympathetic and understanding about my questioning them even though the FBI had already done so. They expressed their condolences and tried hard to recall anything suspicious. The majority of them couldn't recount any more than they already had. Two of them provided some input. As luck would have it, neither were home when the FBI made its rounds."

"Excellent." Casey was reading Marc's meticulous notes closely as he spoke.

"Let's start with Norma Holbrook. A middle-aged homemaker. Lives at 25 Marigold Terrace, half a block away from the Walshes. Spends a lot of time in her front garden, pruning her hydrangea to perfection." Marc's lips twitched.

"So she has a bird's eye view of everything that goes on," Emma said.

Marc nodded. "Yup. Especially Shane. She was very impressed with the fact that he was FBI. So she noticed him—a lot. She told me she'd seen him come home twice this past week in the middle of the day, which was highly unusual for him. In addition, on both occasions he was on edge when he got out of the car, glancing up and down the block before walking into his house. Each time, he stayed about an hour, then hurried off."

"He was making sure he hadn't been followed," Patrick surmised aloud. "Plus, it sure sounds as if whatever he was investigating, he wanted it done in private—outside the walls of the field office." A long, drawn-out pause. "Do you think he was investigating something on his own? And, if so, what?"

"That's a good question," Casey said with a nod. "And if he was, was it a private matter or did he mistrust someone at the Bureau?" Her brows drew together. "What about Caitlin? Was she at home? Or didn't this Mrs. Holbrook notice?"

"Oh, she noticed," Marc assured him. "And, yes, Caitlin's car was parked in the driveway—and Shane's on the street—on both occasions."

"Wow." Emma's eyes were wide. "This is starting to sound like a spy thriller."

"Don't jump the gun," Casey warned her. "This is all supposition." She glanced at the notes Marc had shared on their screens. "What about the second person you talked to—George Rainley?"

"Rainley is a retired widower, who lives at 35 Durling Street—a block away from Marigold Terrace. He walks his dog three times a day, passing the Walshes' house each time. One day last week around lunchtime, he noticed Caitlin sitting on her front doorstep, drinking her coffee and quietly weeping. He stopped and asked her if he could help, but she politely refused, thanking him for his offer and then going back into her house."

"More inexplicable drama," Casey said.

Marc nodded. "I could have continued interviewing neighbors, maybe covering another block or two. But I didn't want to push my luck. There was still a limited FBI presence in the area. I had no desire to tempt fate. So I jumped into my car and headed back to the office."

"Nice work," Casey commended. "We can always pursue this further once the Bureau directs their investigation elsewhere."

"Yeah, we can...*carefully*," Marc amended. "For all we know, the agents acquired enough vital information to go back. Let's cool our heels for a while, Case."

She gave him a reluctant nod. "You're right...unfortunately." With that, she turned her attention to Patrick and John. "Anything worthwhile to report in your neck of the woods?"

John wiggled his hand in a so-so gesture. "Nothing momentous—*yet*. But I did reconnect with several of my former colleagues, who are going to do some internal digging around for me. Plus, I've got dozens of feelers out, some of whom I hope to hear back from tonight. It's a solid start."

Once again, Casey nodded. "Yes it is. Several can snowball into many. We knew this was going to take time. And, as you just heard, patience is *not* my virtue. But keep going as quickly and effectively as you can."

"Will do."

"Speaking of Marc's concerns, we've been ordered off making contact of any kind with BU-related personnel, past and present, and of doing anything else that could be regarded as impeding a federal investigation."

Marc's bit back a grin. "Tell Hutch he's made his point."

"I did," Casey answered flatly. "We'll do the best we can."

"Yeah. Right." Patrick scowled. He was the strings to the team's kite, yanking hard whenever the team was stepping way too far over the line. "I'll keep us on track."

"And I'll keep us out of jail," Angela added with a hint of a grin.

"Sounds great," Casey responded. "Let's hope it doesn't come down to that."

With that, she turned to Emma. "Where do things stand on Caitlin's social media platforms? Have you completed the list of her personal friends?"

"I was as thorough as possible," Emma told her. "I uploaded everything to the cloud, so it's all set for you to review." She hesitated for a moment, then went on. "I don't know if this falls under Yoda's jurisdiction, but maybe, if it comes down to it, he could sort through some of this, even categorize it? It's pretty complicated and time-consuming for us mortals."

"Good thought," Casey replied. "Well, Yoda?" she called out. "How are you at analyzing social media data?"

"I'm exceptional at analyzing any data you ask me to, Casey," Yoda stated. "Ryan has trained me to be extraordinary in all areas."

Casey rolled her eyes. "Why did I even ask?" She angled her head toward Emma, shot her a proud look. "It's a great idea. I'll start with what you've given me and take it to Maureen McKay. Hopefully, she'll meet with Claire and me tomorrow. After that, we'll run the situation by Ryan, and then turn the project over to Yoda."

"Just a heads' up," Emma added. "I don't know if it means anything, but one of Caitlin's friends showed up on Instagram a lot more often than the others; sometimes mentioned in posts, but mostly referenced in a fair number of photos—more than any of Caitlin's other friends. None of the photos was actually of the two of them, so we can't identify her with a visual. Lots of pictures of the places they visited together, along with a significant number showing great-looking dinners and desserts they made. Oh, and one was of a mouthwatering-looking brunch that I would have died to take part in. But no matter how hard I tried, I couldn't come up with the friend's name, only her handle."

"What is it?" Casey asked.

"@mimosagirl121. I'm not sure if it has significance. But one thing's for sure. She's going out of her way not to disclose her real name anywhere. I cross-referenced with Caitlin's Facebook friends and posts. Even tried to find that gorgeous brunch photo. Nothing. So you might want to show everything I compiled to Mrs. McKay and ask if she knows anything about her."

Casey typed in a note for herself. "I will."

***

Offices of Forensic Instincts
Ryan's Lair
Tribeca, Manhattan, New York
11:05 pm

Ryan settled himself behind his computer. He and Claire had stopped for a cup of coffee and herbal tea on their way back from the Bronx, to bandy about the filaments of sensory perception that Claire had picked up off Maureen's cell phone. Most of them were too vague to give credence to. But the strongest one was the absence of malice, the sense of harmlessness that emanated from the initiator of the text. An unwilling ally? A detached hire?

Something didn't fit.

The remainder of the drive to FI's offices was quiet and pensive. As soon as they got there, Claire reluctantly turned the phone over to Ryan. She'd then switched gears, locating the items Marc had left for her, and taken them right upstairs to her yoga room, eager to see what energy she could pick up from them.

At the same time, Ryan had headed directly downstairs to his lair, his mom's cell phone in hand.

Now he readied himself for a long and intricate process.

"Hey, Yoda," he said. "We're on duty tonight. No rest for the weary."

"I don't rest, Ryan," Yoda replied. "I'm always processing data, and I also survey the brownstone when everyone is away."

"I meant me," Ryan responded, rolling his eyes. "Unlike you, I require sleep. But I won't be getting any tonight. And I'll need you on standby."

"Consider it done. I'll await your instructions."

"Good. We're tracing a text, sent to my mom from a burner. That's all we've got."

With that, Ryan logged into his Phonneo account and got busy.

Forehead furrowed in concentration, he went about finding the right API call that would enable him to determine the carrier used to send the cryptic text to his mom's cell phone. He shifted in his chair, impatient and annoyed at the shitty documentation and examples Phonneo provided.

Finally. He found something he could use. Following the proper syntax, Ryan entered the cURL command in his terminal window. Instant success.

The carrier was National Mobile Telephone, or NMT as it was known colloquially.

Next up was the trickier part of the process, but one that Ryan had grown proficient at leveraging, having honed his craft over many years of investigations. He started a series of sequential logins, bouncing between various servers all across the globe, all of which was necessary to cover his tracks and avoid detection by NMT's security systems and law enforcement should his efforts ultimately be discovered.

He was in.

Ryan moved quickly, finding the billing logs where all U.S. terminated cell phone calls were stored. He smiled at how little had changed since the last time he needed to access NMT's logs. These systems were huge, incredibly expensive, and making even the slightest of changes took careful planning and even more rigorous testing beforehand. IT execs hated messing with these software beasts as mistakes meant lost revenue. And lost revenue meant goodbye exec who'd effed it up.

His first query asked the system how many texts and or phone calls were made from the originating burner phone. The billing system told him it had only been used once—just to send that single text message. Ryan reflected on that for a moment. The person sending the text had gone through a lot of trouble to send only one message.

He shifted gears to look at how that particular cell phone interacted with NMT's network—what towers had been contacted for coverage. Once he knew the tower IDs, he could work backwards and determine their physical location and then, based on a little math and triangulation, perhaps even figure out the location from where the text message had been sent. A few minutes later he had the relevant cell tower logs.

Authentication request initiated. Authentication request approved. Authentication token issued. IP Address issued. Text message received from IP address x.x.x.x. Text message sent. Text message delivered to recipient's carrier. Authentication token expired.

Only a handful of towers had reported any interaction with that cell phone number. And then nothing. This told Ryan that the phone was no longer in use.

It didn't take a scholar to figure out what had taken place. The sender had taken out the cell phone battery until they'd chosen a secluded spot. Then, they reattached the battery and turned on the cell. The phone booted up, and then they sent the text to his mom, waiting for delivery confirmation. Once received, they turned off the phone, removed the battery and took off.

"Yoda," Ryan commanded, "analyze NMT's cell tower log. Triangulate between the tower data and their physical locations and tell me approximately where the cell phone was used to send the text message."

"Yes, Ryan," Yoda replied. "Triangulating right now..." The AI system immediately began the process of narrowing down the geographic origin of the text message.

"We're looking for a large open space Yoda, one that has very few cameras," Ryan instructed. "The sender would want privacy and seclusion to send the text and shield their identity from curious onlookers."

"I've narrowed my search to a half-mile radius." Yoda paused. "My analysis indicates that the most likely place based on the calculated probabilities is Franklin Park. It is a 485-acre park that remains Boston's largest open space. It has acres of woods, miles of trails, and a renowned cross-country running course. With a constant flow of people both into and out of the park, it appears to be an ideal spot for someone who wishes to remain inconspicuous."

"Makes sense." Satisfied as he was with Yoda's response, Ryan remained frustrated. True, they now had limited information about where the text was sent from. But they were also left with an impossible task—locating a potential source of video surveillance near the park to ferret out just what the sender might have looked like. Without knowing anything at all about the sender, this avenue was pointless.

Whoever they were, they were long gone. The question was, were they still in Boston?

Possibly. Maybe even probably. There were no guarantees.

But Boston was a congested city of over four million people, easy to get lost in. So it was a good place to start.

***

Offices of Forensic Instincts
Claire's Yoga Room, Third Floor
Tribeca, Manhattan, New York
Tuesday, March 14, 12:15 a.m.

Claire sat in lotus position on her yoga mat, the door tightly shut, the room lit only by two dim candles.

Spread out in front of her were the items Marc had brought back from the Walshes' house. She'd already handled the his and hers coffee mugs and spoons, and gotten only the same flashes of a shared morning ritual, along with the aura of a warm and loving partnership. The same applied to the twin coasters.

The personalized towels were more telling.

Claire's eyes closed as she held each one, her hands sinking into the soft terry, her fingers tracing the letters of their names.

Shane's towel emanated a gamut of emotions, ranging from love and commitment to duty and responsibility. Claire's brows knit as she picked up on the worry and the protectiveness Shane had been feeling the last time he'd used his towel. Not self-protectiveness. Protectiveness for his family. They were in danger. Grave danger. And it was up to him to eliminate it.

Caitlin's towel screamed worry and fear. Unlike Shane's structured emotions, Caitlin's were abstract and all over the place. Intense. Fearful. Spreading out from her and Shane to Kennedy. What would happen to their daughter? How could Caitlin keep her out of the equation and safe—especially when Kennedy wasn't with her, when she couldn't keep an eye on her every move?

The bottle of shampoo both Caitlin and Shane had used was white-hot with terror and an equal amount of determination.

But whose—Shane's or Caitlin's? And what was it based on?

With a premonition of dread, Claire set aside the bathroom items and reached for the LEGO blocks Marc had taken.

Surges of darkness jolted through her the instant her fingers touched the blocks. At the same time, a clear vision popped into her head. Caitlin. Kennedy. Sprawled on the carpet, assembling pieces. Building the tower together. Caitlin putting up a brave front. Kennedy concentrating on her project, unaware of her mother's anguish.

The danger was imminent. And Caitlin had done what she could to protect her family. But mostly Kennedy. She'd protect her with her life, never take her eyes off her.

Never take her eyes off her.

The phrase slammed through Claire's brain with the force of a tidal wave.

I'm watching Kennedy. Are you?

Claire bolted to her feet and raced down the stairs to Ryan's lair.

12

Offices of Forensic Instincts
Ryan's Lair
Tribeca, Manhattan, New York
Tuesday, March 14, 1:35 a.m.

Claire didn't even bother to knock. She just burst inside.

"Hey." Surprised, Ryan looked up from his gym rat corner, where he sat, bare-chested, lifting weights with frustrated purpose. Seeing the expression on Claire's face, he set down the weights, stood up, and grabbed a towel to wipe his face and neck. "You sensed something."

"Yes." Claire didn't even sit down. "Where's your mom's cell phone? I need to hold it."

Wordlessly, Ryan walked over and handed it to her.

Claire clasped it tightly, closing her eyes, and letting the energy flow through her. "Yes," she whispered as images shot through her mind.

"Yes what?"

Claire's eyes opened, and rather than looking dazed and faraway, there was utter certainty reflected in them.

"The person who sent that text—it was Caitlin."

A moment of dead silence.

Then Ryan reacted.

"*Caitlin*?" His jaw dropped. "Are you sure?"

"Very. She's alive. Running. And terrified that someone will hunt her down *and* go after Kennedy to find out what she knows."

At that, Ryan went very still. "Kennedy knows something? What?"

"I'm not sure." Claire set down the phone, her hand shaking with the aftermath of her vision. "I'm sorry, Ryan. I'm not zeroing in on that part—not yet. I just know that this is the reason I kept feeling as if someone without malice had sent the text to your mom. It wasn't the killer, or even someone who worked for the killer. It was Caitlin."

"Damn." Ryan dragged his hands through his hair. "I don't believe this."

"I got a clear image of her sending it," Claire continued. "I saw a lot of greenery and open space around her. As if she'd texted from a public garden or a park."

"The latter," Ryan replied. "The text originated in Boston. In Franklin Park."

Claire nodded. "That makes sense."

"Yeah." Ryan blew out a breath. "What also makes sense is that she feels compelled to reiterate that she wants my mom to do what she herself can't—watch over Kennedy. Is Shane's killer hovering nearby? Is that what Caitlin is implying?"

Claire's shoulders lifted in a shrug. "I don't know that either. All I'm sure of is that we have to keep Kennedy safe—and trace Caitlin. Did you and Yoda get any more specific information from the text? Because Boston is a big city."

"Nope." Ryan began pacing, his mind working through the problems they faced. "Plus, even if I'd narrowed down our search a little, rushing up to Boston would wave a red flag in Hutch's face. He'd be all over us for an explanation. As things stand, we can just give the cell phone back to my mom, have her show the text message to the FBI, and keep the rest of our newfound knowledge under wraps."

He paused, pulling out his own cell phone. "I'm Slacking the whole team. I don't care what time it is. We have way too much to discuss to wait til seven o'clock. Besides, you and Casey have to get to my parents' house by eight at the latest. Otherwise, you run the risk of Kennedy waking up before you've had the chance to talk to my mom alone. Not to mention, you've got to get my mom's cell phone back in her possession ASAP. *And* you've got to interview my mom and Kennedy before the FBI does."

Claire nodded. "Maureen is expecting us to arrive early. That won't be a surprise. But I agree with you—we need to have a team meeting right away. There's too much information that's not yet shared. We need everyone on board. We also need Patrick to put extra security on Kennedy." She gestured at Ryan's phone. "Go ahead. We'll see how many of us are awake enough to respond."

***

Casey and Hutch's Apartment
Battery Park City, Manhattan, New York
Tuesday, March 14, 2:05 a.m.

Casey was in the living room, curled up on the couch with a flashlight, reviewing Emma's list so she could be ready to discuss the names with Maureen sometime tomorrow. She had an afghan thrown over her and a novel at the ready—in the event that Hutch awakened and came out to check on her. Working in the bedroom was out. The slightest flicker of light and Hutch would be up and grilling her about what she was working on in the middle of the night and why. Nope. Times like these called for craftiness and utter seclusion.

Her cell phone vibrated.

She glanced down at it, seeing the arrival of the Slack message. Without pause, she opened and read it. Her brows drew together and her adrenaline started pumping. She knew Ryan's tone. And whatever this was about, it was urgent.

She doubled Ryan's efforts by also Slacking the team, adding her voice to his and initiating an immediate invitation for a Zoom meeting.

Come as you are, she typed. *PJs welcome.*

***

Offices of Forensic Instincts
Ryan's Lair
Tribeca, Manhattan, New York
Tuesday, March 14, 2:13 a.m.

Ryan read Casey's message and chuckled. "Our president is on board," he told Claire. "She's summoning the troops." He headed to the chair in front of his computer, pulling over a second chair as he did. "C'mon," he invited Claire, patting the seat. "Let's jump on the call."

She did so at once, and an instant later, Casey's face came into view. "Let's give the others a chance," she said. She shot Ryan a worried look. "You okay?"

He nodded. "More or less. Most important, I'm back in the saddle."

"So I see. You're at the office in the middle of the night. Why?"

As Casey spoke, Marc and Patrick joined the session. Both of them looked tousled, tired, and with a five-o'clock shadow, but completely alert.

"What's up?" Marc demanded.

Before Casey could reply, Emma joined the chat. "I'm here," she said. "But I'm not wearing a shred of makeup. So don't judge."

"We'll do our best," Casey replied dryly.

"I'm not so brave." Angela's voice entered the conversation. She'd turned on her audio, but not her video. "You'll have to visualize me. Just know I'm here."

This time, Casey's lips twitched. "Gotcha. No problem."

As she spoke, John's face appeared. "Present and accounted for," he said.

"Great." Ryan looked both pleased and relieved. "The whole team is here. Thanks. I know an emergency Zoom meeting is the last thing you want to be having at this hour. But it can't be helped. Our whole timetable has been pushed up." He paused to inhale. "Claire and I have a lot to talk about. I'm sure all of you do, too. But Claire and I are going first."

Waiting only long enough to receive Casey's go-ahead nod, Ryan plunged in. He went for the most crucial information first: the text his mother had received, quickly followed by his cell phone data accumulation, and Claire's epiphany that Caitlin had sent that text.

"Caitlin?" Emma managed. "That changes everything."

"It does indeed," Casey concurred. "Although we probably shouldn't be as shocked as we are. We determined that Caitlin sent the initial text to Maureen, asking her to take care of Kennedy. Why wouldn't she send this one, as well?"

Marc rubbed a palm over his jaw. "Because of the way it's worded. It's meant to sound like a threat from the killer, probably to throw off the FBI and the killers if the text were to be intercepted. Whereas, in fact, it's a plea for help. Caitlin is a smart woman. She's frightened for herself, but she's frantic for Kennedy. This suggests that she has reason to feel that way. It's up to us to figure out how Kennedy fits into the mix."

"I'll put extra security on her as soon as we wrap up this meeting," Patrick said. "I don't like the implications here."

"Agreed." Ryan's lips were drawn into a grim line. "Also, Casey, you and Claire have a meeting set up with my mom at eight this morning, before Kennedy wakes up. Once the poor kid is awake, you'll interview her next. Claire made the arrangements with my mom, so she'll ease Kennedy's way. She'll make sure Kennedy knows it's just Claire and another friend from FI who'll be chatting with her. That'll calm her down. We've got to get ahead of the FBI. They'll be setting up interviews with her and with my mom by later today."

"I agree," Casey replied. "I assume you kept your mother's text message private?"

"The FBI knows nothing about it," Ryan said. "They'll find out this morning—after Claire returns the phone to my mom. At which point, my mom will show it to the agents and let them take it from there."

"The line she's giving the FBI is that she was too overwrought about the funeral to check her messages until this morning," Emma surmised aloud.

"Exactly."

Claire spoke next. "Casey, speaking of jumping the gun, you and I have appointments to talk to all the McKays today. I'll give you the times and places." She waited for Casey's thumbs-up. "And Marc, thank you for all the items you brought me from Shane's house. I wouldn't have sensed any of the things I did without them."

"Glad it helped. Oh, and by the way, I also canvassed Shane and Caitlin's neighborhood, dodging federal agents as I did. I had a few interesting conversations. I shared them with the rest of the team earlier. Ryan, you and Claire go check out the cloud. I posted my notes there."

"Anything significant?" Claire asked.

"Just appetite whetters—things to keep on the back burner in case we need to revisit them."

Ryan leaned forward with interest. "Did any of the agents spot you?"

"Fortunately not." Marc frowned, remembering what he needed to warn them about. "Without getting into unnecessary detail, Hutch has blocked all our efforts to speak with Bureau staff, past and present. He also informed Casey that he's taking a hard line with us. That closes the door on our information-gathering from the Bureau. So how do we pursue Caitlin's probable hideaway in the Boston area?"

"My question exactly," Ryan said, visibly frustrated. "We've got to put our heads together and get creative."

"Not *too* creative," Angela interjected. "We're already withholding information. With Hutch laying out rigid parameters, any move we make that hints at obstruction of justice will result in having Forensic Instincts shut down and land our asses in jail."

"Agreed," Casey said. "So from this point on, we primarily stick to John's efforts with the NYPD and any covert snatches of information we can figure out on our own to finding Shane's killer. Most of our efforts have to be channeled into locating Caitlin, and finding and eliminating any threats to Kennedy that exist. Ultimately, all these things are tied together. And my gut tells me that if we accomplish the latter, it will lead to the former."

"I'm totally on board with that," Ryan said. His brows drew together. "I've got to come up with some way to figure out a more precise location in the Boston area for Caitlin without tipping off the FBI in the process. Maybe Yoda and I can come up with something—fast."

"I think you're the best one of us to tackle that," Casey replied. "None of us has your strategic skills where it comes to technology."

"Yeah," Ryan said. "I know." His gaze shifted to John. "Let's get to the NYPD aspect of things. Any new developments to report?"

"Actually, I made decent headway tonight," John replied. "A lot of return calls. At this point I'll need Yoda's help in bringing order to chaos."

"Consider it done. I'll give you access to it right after this Zoom meeting is over."

"No need, Ryan," Yoda chimed in from the lair. "I'll make it available to John right now. You continue your strategizing."

John stifled a grin. Yoda's participation and omniscience were still new to him. "Thanks, Yoda. I'm sure that'll enhance my scope. As things stand, I talked to a few of Shane's most recent former colleagues. They offered up whatever they could remember: names of some released felons who Shane helped put away, and names of still-incarcerated ones, just in case they have contacts on the outside doing their dirty work for them. Yoda's list will verify and expand on that."

"On a more personal note," John continued. "I also have meetings scheduled with the detectives who attended Shane's funeral. Hopefully, they'll be able to provide additional information, since they were tight with him. And, lastly, I'm waiting for the rest of my own contacts, who are researching and paring down cases for me. I'll interview as many of them as I can—hopefully, all of them. The combination of everything I just outlined should cover all our bases at the NYPD and, with a modicum of luck, lead us where we need to go."

"*If* that's where we need to go," Casey clarified.

"Right."

Ryan shot John a grateful look. "Thanks so much. What you're doing is huge."

John's lips thinned into a grim line. "Thank me if it leads us to our killer."

***

Marc and Madeleine's Duplex
Upper East Side
Manhattan, New York
Tuesday, March 14, 4:35 a.m.

Marc had barely dozed off when his private line buzzed, with the caller ID blocked.

Beside him in bed, Maddy stirred. "You're a busy man tonight," she murmured, shifting position to get more comfortable.

Marc frowned, glancing quickly at his pregnant wife. "You okay?"

She smiled. "We both are. The baby and me. Go answer your phone." She squeezed his hand, then settled in.

Reassured, Marc snatched up his cell. “Devereaux.”

“Morning, frogman,” Aidan greeted him. “Time for breakfast.”

“No problem, leatherneck,” Marc quipped back. “I never went to sleep. Busy work night.”

The frogman-leatherneck jibes went back to their military days, when Marc was a Navy SEAL and Aidan was a Marine captain. It was a comfortable ritual, one that had never changed.

“Well, it’s about to get busier,” Aidan replied. “I’ve got the serology and DNA results you need. Verbal overview now, more detailed fact sheet via the necessary channels in Yoda’s memory banks by midmorning.”

“I’m listening.”

“Two different blood types. Pool of blood gathered underneath Shane was AB positive. Jagged stream of blood alongside it was A negative. The former belonged to Shane. The latter belonged to Caitlin. All designated blood markers consistent with that conclusion.”

“That’s all I needed,” Marc said, pleased that his instincts had been right. “How much did this set you back?”

“Not a penny,” Aidan returned dryly. “Some terrorist group has less money to destroy the world. So it’s a win-win. Still, I did get you the information. Therefore, you do owe me. I’ll just have to come up with the right payback.”

A corner of Marc’s mouth lifted. “I can hardly wait.”

“Enjoy your day, frogman.”

“You, too, leatherneck. And thanks.”

13

The McKay Residence
East 236th Street
Woodlawn, Bronx, New York
Tuesday, March 14, 7:03 a.m.

The sun was barely poking its head up and there was a drizzle of frost on the ground when Claire and Casey arrived at the McKay house.

Maureen greeted them at the front door, and Claire immediately introduced Casey.

"Ms. Woods, thank you for coming," Maureen said, showing them in. "I appreciate everything you and your company are doing to help us."

Casey waved away the thanks, extending her hand and clasping Maureen's. "Please, it's Casey. And before we even begin, I want to extend my condolences to you in person. I know you're suffering deeply. I apologize that, at the last minute, I moved this talk up to such an early hour, especially since the funeral was just yesterday. But I was concerned about waiting until eight. We have a lot of territory to cover, and I want to do so before Kennedy wakes up."

"I agree." Maureen took their coats and led them into the living room, gesturing for them to have a seat on the sofa. Once they were settled, she poured and handed each of them a cup of steaming tea. "Here. This will warm away the March chill."

"Thank you. This is perfect." Casey took an appreciative sip, as did Claire.

Maureen poured herself a cup, as well, then sat down in an adjacent armchair. "I appreciate your kind words. As for the earliness of the hour, I haven't been getting much sleep these past days anyway. I hope I'm able to help you before the FBI contacts me." She shot a brief glance toward the staircase. "And before Kennedy wakes up."

"We're hoping the same." Casey followed Maureen's gaze, a sympathetic look on her face. "How is she, especially after the funeral?"

A deep sigh. "Not good. She wept half the night. The idea that Shane is gone, much less murdered, is eating away at her. The funeral was a horrifying reminder that she'll never see her daddy again. As for Caitlin's disappearance—that she can't accept at all."

"The poor little girl," Casey murmured. "My heart breaks for her." For the time being, that was all she said.

Claire picked up from there, leaning forward and placing her hand over Maureen's. "We'll be as gentle as possible when we talk to Kennedy. We just want to figure out what, if anything, she either picked up or overheard between her parents that might make her a threat to the person who shot Shane."

"I want the same thing," Maureen replied, her lips drawn into a grim line. "After reading that text…" A hard shudder. "Kennedy must be kept safe."

The team had uniformly decided not to say a word to Maureen about their suspicions where it came to Caitlin. It was too unfair a burden to place on her. The less she knew, the less obstruction of justice she'd be guilty of. Also, she wouldn't have to agonize over what to tell not only the FBI, but Kennedy. For now, all the FI team's research and suspicions would remain with them.

"We assigned extra security for her," Casey said. "Trust me, no one will get past Patrick's team."

"Thank you." Maureen put down her teacup and shifted nervously in her chair. "Now ask me anything you want to know, and then please prepare me for the FBI."

Casey and Claire exchanged a quick look. Clearly, Maureen was unnerved about the Bureau's interview.

Claire took the lead on this one. "Talking to the FBI is an anxiety-producing experience for everyone who goes through it," she said. "Especially given the bigger-than-life images portrayed of them on TV. Honestly, they're just regular people, doing their jobs."

"Yes, but you're not regular people doing your jobs," Maureen stated in return. "And I don't want to hurt your investigation."

"You won't," Casey assured her, impressed by Ryan's mom's candor and insight. Nevertheless, years of behavioral experience had taught her that eliminating someone's fears and putting them at ease before they tackled a separate task would yield far better results over the long haul.

To that end, she said, "Why don't we start this discussion by prepping you for your FBI interview. Then, we'll ask our own questions."

"I'd very much appreciate that."

"Speaking of the FBI..." Claire reached into her purse and pulled out Maureen's cell phone. "Here. This needs to be back with you." She handed the device to Ryan's mom. "Once Casey and I leave, feel free to contact SA Barkley about the text. That will flow nicely into scheduling a time for his visit."

Maureen placed the phone on the end table beside her. "I will. And I'll tell him exactly what Ryan instructed—that this is the first I'm seeing of the text; that I haven't so much as glanced at my phone until now. The funeral consumed me and my day."

"Perfect," Casey said. "They can now run with the text message as they see fit."

"Because Ryan already did just that." It was a statement not a question. "I know my son. Did he get answers?"

"He has suspicions," Casey replied. "He's probing them."

"Understood." Clearly, Maureen realized Casey was hedging in her response, but she was smart enough not to press the issue.

"Back to the Bureau." Casey sat back in a relaxed stance and proceeded to clearly delineate what Maureen should expect: the points Barkley would touch on, where and in what ways he'd apply subtle pressure, and what his objective would be coming away from the meeting.

"Remember," she concluded. "He's not coming after you as the enemy. He doesn't assume you're lying. He might think you're holding back a few details because of Ryan's and FI's involvement. But mostly, he'll think it's possible you know something you don't realize you do. The same applies to Kennedy, when he talks to her. From what I understand, he's a good man and a good agent. He's not going to twist your words or act accusatory. He'll be frank, but kind. Don't be afraid to show how broken up you are, and how devastated your family is. And go with your instincts. Anything Ryan has advised you or anything your gut tells you should be kept between you and FI, refrain from mentioning it. Remember that silence is not the same thing as lying."

"Most of the time," Maureen qualified. "But in this case, that's true." She drew a sharp inward breath. "It's going to be hard for me to stay calm when Detective Barkley alludes to Caitlin as anything but a victim."

"I know. And it's natural to be indignant, even offended. Just don't lose your temper. Not only will that be counterproductive, it'll make you more likely to say something you'll wish you hadn't. State the truth. Caitlin and Shane had a strong, solid relationship. By all means, emphasize that—without sounding defensive." Casey leaned forward and squeezed Maureen's hand. "You're more than ready. You were ready before this talk. You're a very intelligent woman. Trust your instincts."

A nod of relief, followed by a new tension. "I will. But Kennedy… How will this affect her? How will she hold up under this kind of pressure?"

"The tenor of that interview will be entirely different," Claire spoke up. "Much softer and less probing. We'll prepare Kennedy. We'll tell her that Agent Barkley just wants to know if she recalls anything she might have forgotten. As Casey said, he's a kind man. He doesn't want to further traumatize a nine-year-old whose father was just killed and whose mother is missing. He's not expecting any great revelations from Kennedy. I'd be surprised if the interview lasted more than ten minutes."

Given Claire's explanation, Maureen's tension ebbed. "Hearing that, I think my little lovey will be okay. Especially if she hears all that from you." A quick glance at Casey. "I mean no offense, Casey. But Claire has a lovely rapport with Kennedy. I felt it from the start. Regardless of how short a time they've spent together, I know she trusts her."

“No offense taken.” Casey smiled. “Claire has a quality about her that draws everyone in, particularly a child. I think letting Claire take the lead with her is an excellent idea.” A pause, during which time Casey glanced at her Apple Watch. “Do you feel ready to go over a few things with us now?”

Maureen picked up her teacup. “Yes. Go ahead. I’ll help in any way I can.”

“Great.” Casey flipped open her iPad. “I’ll begin by filling you in on Ryan’s recap of his memories of the Walshes. See if there’s anything you want to add or change.” Concisely, she told Maureen everything Ryan had said.

Without interruption, Maureen nodded her agreement. “All accurate.”

“Good. Now it’s your turn. Talk to us about your memories, overall and then specific—no matter how insignificant they might seem. Did you see the Walshes often? And not only with Ryan there. Were you close with them?”

A hard swallow. “Yes. Ryan was like a brother to Shane, but I was like a second mother. My sister passed away many years ago, her husband even before that. At that time, Shane became Colin’s and mine. And when Shane married Caitlin, and Kennedy was born, our bond deepened. They were family, not extended family. We used to see them frequently when they were newlyweds and new parents. Then, just like with my own children, life took over, commitments happened, and our visits became more sporadic. But the love between us all never wavered, and when we did get together, it was as if no time had passed.”

“When was the last time you saw them?”

Tears filled Maureen’s eyes. “We were all scheduled to have a family dinner this past Sunday. The entire clan, including significant others. A rarity indeed. Obviously, that dinner never happened. Before that, the three of them dropped by maybe a month or two ago. And, before you ask, at that time, nothing seemed out of the ordinary. No stress or tension at all."

Casey typed into her iPad. "That suggests that whatever and whoever was threatening Shane didn't yet exist. Okay, next give me more specifics about Kennedy's role in Shane and Caitlin's relationship. I know how much they loved her, but how open were they about discussing things in her presence? Did they send her off to play when they needed to talk? Or did they customarily allow her in the room during their discussions?"

Maureen's brow furrowed. "That's not something I can be absolutely certain about. I know the three of them were a very tight unit, and that Kennedy spent a great deal of time with her parents. She has friends her own age, but she's a very mature nine-year-old. She's also an only child. So she hung out with her parents a lot. Would it shock me if she overheard her parents talking? No. With something this serious, they wouldn't just converse in front of her. But could she have picked up snatches of a private conversation between them, or been aware of their extreme anxiety? Yes. She's a very bright, curious child."

Claire nodded, her expression drawn with worry. "As we touched on, she might know something and not even be aware of it. I'm hoping I get some insight into that when Casey and I talk to her."

Casey leaned forward. "I'm assuming, given the kind of person Shane was and the line of work he was in, that he didn't discuss his professional life with you."

"You assume correctly."

"Okay, then I'm going to abandon that line of questioning and get to what you might know about Caitlin. Did you spend one-on-

one time with her? Did she discuss her friends, her work, anything about her life other than family?"

A sad smile touched Maureen's lips. "Caitlin's parents are both gone, too. And she has no other living relatives that I know of. So, yes, we spent time together. Infrequent, given how busy she is, but there was an occasional lunch, some chats on the phone, that kind of thing. She did mention work, on occasion, but, frankly, the kind of work she does, like Ryan's, is foreign to me. I'm not exactly a high-tech person, nor a scientific person like Ryan and my husband. I'm lucky I can check emails and pay bills online. My realm is family, people, and emotions."

Casey chuckled. "None of us measures up where it comes to Ryan's skills. So I wouldn't judge yourself using those standards. So let's move away from work. What about Caitlin's friends? Did you ever meet any of them? Or did she talk to you about them, mention someone by name?"

"Meet them, no. But hear about them…as I told Ryan, I have the niggling sensation the answer to that is yes. I've been racking my brain on the subject since Ryan brought it up. You're hoping to come up with someone Caitlin confided in?"

"Yes." Casey was tapping her iPad screen, studying it with a frown.

"But if that's true, if a friend of Caitlin's knew anything about the cause of her disappearance, wouldn't they have contacted the FBI?" Maureen asked.

Casey's shoulders lifted in a shrug. "Maybe. Maybe not. Often people don't immediately think of calling the authorities, especially if they're unsure about the significance of what they know. They feel uncertain, foolish, even reticent. However, the reciprocal doesn't apply. The Bureau will most emphatically contact everyone Caitlin knows. We've just got to beat them to it. And, given that we have a family connection, we're hoping you can help us do just that."

With that, Casey brought up Caitlin's Instagram page, and swiveled the screen around so it faced Maureen. "I'm going to show you some photos and posts that Caitlin put up on her key social media account—Instagram, where she has a strong social media presence. All the people here use what are called 'handles.' Think of them as nicknames for themselves. Like you might use '@lovingmom' as your handle, rather than Maureen McKay. There would be a page dedicated to you, and you would decide what about yourself you wanted displayed there: a photo of you, additional photos of your family, a bio of sorts, maybe your interests, that kind of thing. There would be links to your followers, who you would develop over time. In any case, Emma, the social media guru on our team, has dug deep into Caitlin's social media presence and sorted things out for you. Pages, handles, bios, lists of followers—the whole nine yards."

Maureen frowned. "You know, of course, that I understand very little of what you just said."

"That's okay." Casey gave her a rueful smile. "I just gave you an overview. I promise that Ryan will give you more details and a more thorough explanation. Even though social media isn't his thing, he more than gets it. But I don't want to waste any of the time you have with Claire and me. Ryan coming over and having long visits with you is a natural occurrence. Not so for us. So I want to move things along. To that end, let's start with the handles, see if any of them strikes a chord as belonging to friends Caitlin mentioned. That would be a huge plus."

Casey was just about to start by asking about @mimosagirl121 when they all heard footsteps approaching from upstairs, followed by Kennedy calling, "Aunt Maureen?" as she padded down.

Maureen shot Casey a worried look.

"Before we leave, I'll find a way to show you the most pressing handles and photos that are on my list," Casey said in a quiet voice, closing her iPad. "Hopefully, something will ring a bell. The rest I'll email you from the car. Review them as quickly as you can. Ryan will be here later. He'll finish up the process with you. Now go ahead to Kennedy. We'll wait here."

Maureen nodded and rose to her feet. "I'm right here, lovey," she called back, heading for the staircase. "We have some visitors, and I was just chatting with them."

As Kennedy came into view, Casey could see that she was wearing flowered PJs, fluffy slippers, and that she was reaching behind her neck to fasten a pendant. Her head came up and she gazed toward the living room with red-rimmed eyes—and a touch of apprehension. "Is it people from the FBI?"

"No, lovey, not the FBI. Friends of Uncle Ryan's. They came to talk to me, and to you."

The anxiety on Kennedy's face was supplanted by interest. "Which friends of Uncle Ryan's?"

"Come and I'll introduce you. One of them you already know." Maureen finished the task of fastening the pendant, giving Kennedy an approving smile. "Good girl. I'm glad you listened to me and took off your necklace last night. It's dangerous to sleep in it."

Kennedy nodded. "I know. Mommy tells me the same thing. It sits on my nightstand every night." A closer, more curious look into the living room, and a shy smile as she recognized Claire.

"Hi," she greeted her. "You're not just a friend. You're Uncle Ryan's girlfriend. You're very pretty, and I can tell from the way he looks at you that he likes you a lot." She screwed up her nose. "Maybe more than likes."

Claire was already on her feet and walking over, her lips curving at Kennedy's assessment. "Thank you for the lovely compliment. I'm so glad to see you again." She squeezed the girl's hands, held on to them for a few seconds, then released them and gestured toward the sofa. "I brought another friend—someone who really wants to meet you, as well. This is Casey Woods. Casey, this incredible little girl is Kennedy Walsh."

Casey rose and walked over to join the group, a genuine smile on her face. "Hi, Kennedy. I've heard a lot about you. You're a very brave girl, and everyone is so proud of you. Especially your uncle Ryan."

Kennedy's brows rose. "You know Uncle Ryan, too?"

"Mm-hmm. I work with him. So he's my friend and my colleague."

Kennedy's eyes grew wide. "You're part of that amazing company he works for?"

Claire answered for her boss. "Actually, Casey is president of Forensic Instincts. She's pretty awesome—a great leader and an even greater person. We all love her. I think you will, too."

Kennedy walked alongside them to the edge of the living room, then hesitated. "Can I come in? Or are you talking privately to Aunt Maureen?"

Casey waved Kennedy in. No behavioral analysis was needed here. Ryan was right. Kennedy was a bright, polite, and insightful girl—mature way beyond her years. "Of course, come in. We'd enjoy talking with you. Your uncle Ryan is not easy to impress, but he's totally impressed by you."

With a soft smile, Kennedy perched on the arm of the sofa. "He's biased," she replied. "But that's okay. I think he's wonderful, too."

Casey watched Kennedy fiddle with her pendant and went with that.

"What a lovely necklace," she said, leaning closer. "Delicate and beautiful."

A shadow of pain shot across Kennedy's face. "It was a present from my mommy." She met Casey's caring gaze. "Would you like to see it?"

"Very much, if that's okay." Casey waited until Kennedy leaned forward, offering her the silver heart-shaped pendant for inspection. "It's pretty and distinctive, just like you," Casey murmured, gently touching the intricate mesh trim and tracing the tiny diamonds that formed the letter *K* in its center. "And given that it's a gift from your parents, no wonder it means so much to you."

Kennedy nodded, tears glistening on her lashes. "Thank you."

Hastily, Maureen gestured for Casey and Claire to reseat themselves on the sofa, and for Kennedy to join them. "All of you relax. I baked Irish soda bread for everyone. I'll go get it while you ladies chat."

Kennedy watched her aunt head off to the kitchen. "If Aunt Maureen baked, that means she knew you were coming. I get the feeling this was planned." A panicky look crossed her face. "There's no bad news about Mommy, is there?"

Immediately, both women shook their heads.

"We're searching hard for her, sweetie," Claire said, patting the cushion between Casey and her, waiting until Kennedy had plunked down. "And we'll find her, bring her back to you. You'll see."

The panic dissipated, but the insightfulness did not.

"You want to ask me questions, don't you?" Kennedy asked, glancing from one of them to the other. "To see if I remember anything that could help? I know that Agent Barkley from the FBI plans to do that. Late last night, I heard Aunt Maureen and Uncle Colin talking."

Ideal, Casey thought. *Not only smart and intuitive, but a good eavesdropper.*

Casey didn't have to glance over at Claire to know she was thinking the same thing. But she fell silent, letting Claire take the lead.

"Yes, sweetie, we do have questions," Claire began. "And not only to prepare you for Agent Barkley. To help us figure out the reason all this happened." She squeezed Kennedy's hand. "You know your uncle Ryan. He likes to be first at everything, including getting answers."

"Your team is competing with the FBI for first place," Kennedy stated. "Just like when I'm in a taekwondo competition." She swallowed hard. "Only, in this case, it's to figure out who'd do such horrible things to my parents."Claire nodded, taking Kennedy's hand in hers. "You're incredibly smart and mature, Kennedy. So I know you get it. Casey and I are counting on your thinking back over the past few weeks, even months, and hopefully remembering something that would help us."

A frightened spark flickered in Kennedy's eyes. "Like what?"

Claire continued to hold Kennedy's hand, her expression taking on that all-too-familiar crystallized awareness. "You've been reliving Friday over and over—ever since Agent Barkley told you the heartbreaking news. I understand. I also understand you're forcing yourself not to think about the week or two before that. But now I need you to do just that, to try to recall anything you either felt or overheard at home. Did your mom and dad talk about anything that scared you? Did they seem scared themselves? Were you worried about them—or about anything that might happen to them?"

It was obvious that Claire's gently spoken questions had struck home.

Kennedy began to tremble. Tears welled up in her eyes and slid down her cheeks as she responded. "Lately, when they talked, it was in their room with the door shut," she said in a voice that was little more than a whisper. "They never did that before. Except for surprises, we didn't keep secrets. But this wasn't just a secret, it was something bad. Very bad. I just knew it."

She paused, sucked in her breath. "Then, a week ago, when I'd gone back to my room, I heard Daddy open the door and walk out into the hall. So I crept to the doorway and listened. Mommy was crying, saying how scared she was. Daddy told her he'd make everything right, that he wouldn't let anyone hurt our family. But I knew someone was trying to."

"Did he say who that someone was?" Claire asked. "Or where he knew him from?"

Kennedy shook her head.

"Okay." A soothing nod. "What else did your daddy say?"

"Nothing. He went downstairs to the kitchen and brought back two cups of coffee. I was crouched in my room, so he didn't see me. He just went back into their bedroom and shut the door again."

"But you tried to listen," Claire said.

A shaky nod. "I pressed my ear against the door and held my breath so I could hear. Mommy was crying and crying. Daddy was talking quietly to her. I heard him say something about digging for information and finding enough to take action. I don't know what kind of action, because their voices got very low, and all I could hear were Mommy's sobs. I didn't want them to find me there, because it would upset them more than they already were. So I went back to my room. But after that, they were different. Sad. Worried. Mommy hugged me a lot. Daddy spent more time on his computer."

Kennedy broke down, pulling her hand away and covering her face as sobs racked her body. "Now Daddy is dead. And I don't know where Mommy is. Who did this? Why? I should have listened harder."

Claire squatted down in front of Kennedy and gripped her shoulders. "Sweetie, none of this is your fault. Whoever did this is evil. The fault is theirs. You're a wonderful daughter and a wonderful person. I promise you, we'll figure this out."

"How can you be so sure?" Kennedy wept.

"I just am." Claire paused, glanced quickly at Casey, and—despite their original decision to avoid conveying any concrete hope—received her nod. "Kennedy, let me tell you something about myself, something I only talk about with my friends. I sometimes just know things. I have no idea how or why that happens, but flashes of awareness come to me, and I'm very sure they're true. After talking with you, holding your hand—this is one of those times."

Kennedy's head came up, and she stared at Claire through her tears. "Are you a psychic?"

Claire shook her head. "I'm what's called a claircognizant. Everything I just described to you—that's what a claircognizant is. I realize that no one can bring back your daddy. But the rest—my instincts tell me that everything will be okay." She could sense Maureen's presence in the doorway. "I'm asking you to believe me."

Kennedy didn't avert her gaze. "Mommy's alive, isn't she?"

"I believe she is, yes."

A long pause as Kennedy fought for control. "Then I believe it, too." New tears flowed. "How will you find her?"

"We're working on that round the clock. Especially your uncle Ryan. Have faith in him, in all of us. We won't let you down."

Kennedy flung her arms around Claire's neck. "Thank you. Thank you so much." She dried her eyes. "Do I have to tell Agent Barkley about this?"

"No," Casey intervened. "And not because you're lying. We'd never ask you to do that. The truth is, Agent Barkley would probably think it was just wishful thinking on your part. More importantly, we have no proof to share with him. Once we do, we'll tell him right away." She gestured for Maureen to join them. "For now, let's just sit together and have some of your aunt Maureen's soda bread. Be strong. As soon as we have answers, so will you."

14

Offices of Forensic Instincts
Ryan's Lair
Tribeca, Manhattan, New York
Tuesday, March 14, 5:35 p.m.

Claire rapped lightly on the partially open door.

Rather than typing furiously at his computer, Ryan was on his feet, pacing around impatiently. He stopped when he saw Claire peering around the corner.

"Come on in," he greeted her. "Did you just get back?"

She nodded. "First, I made sure Casey got home without collapsing. She was totally wiped. A very long day for her. Where is everybody?"

"They all headed home a few minutes ago. They're on high alert, should they be needed. Marc was really antsy about Maddy. Since she's on bed rest, her nurse has been working round-the-clock, and he's barely seen her since Friday. Adele called Patrick to announce that she was making him his first hot meal in days. Emma is going out to dinner with her roommates. And Angela is wrapping things up with the last few of her former clients."

"I'm glad," Claire replied. "We're all on overdrive. A little come-down time is necessary—except for you," she hastily amended. "Meanwhile, any news? Updates?"

"Yeah," Ryan said with a nod. "Aidan called Marc about the blood on the floor at Shane's house. Marc was right. Aidan confirmed that the blood belonged to two different people—Shane and Caitlin. Different blood types, specific DNA markers—the works. Caitlin must have gotten injured when Shane was killed. We have no idea how severe the wound is, although logic dictates it wasn't too bad, given how little blood there was. Still, Marc and Patrick were digging around all day, unsuccessfully, trying to come up with where Caitlin went to get treated—*if* she got treated at all."

"That makes sense." Claire was eyeing Ryan as he shifted from one foot to the other. "You're obviously waiting for Yoda to process something. Do you want me to come back later?"

"Nope." He drew her to him, gave her a deep, tender kiss. "Screw our office rules. That kiss was just what I needed." A corner of his mouth lifted. "Actually, I could use a whole lot more."

"That's going to have to wait," Claire returned with a smile. "You can barely stand still, much less indulge in our fantasies. Tell me what's bugging you."

A grimace. "I can't get a better handle on where in the Boston area Caitlin is, even though my gut tells me she's still there. Yoda and I have been at it for hours. No clear path to figuring it out."

"*Yet*," Claire stipulated. "You'll find answers."

"I sure hope so." Ryan plopped down on the wobble chair, rolling around in a clockwise circle to try to get rid of his excess energy.

"What about you? You've spent the entire day interviewing my family. Any of them think of something we haven't?"

"Overall? No. There were no surprises or contradictions. Everyone saw the Walshes the same way: as a warm and loving part of your family. None of your family members had seen them recently enough to pick up on tension or anxiety."

Ryan knew Claire too well. "*Overall*? Then something did strike you."

"Kennedy did." Claire's brows drew together in reflection. "She and I have a strong connection. When she sat down beside me, I could perceive much of her internal turmoil these past few weeks."

Ryan stopped moving around. "Go on."

Claire proceeded to fill him in on her conversation with Kennedy, as well as what she'd sensed when holding the young girl's hands.

"And she's been bottling all this anxiety up," Ryan said with a frown.

"Not only the anxiety. The awareness. She knew her parents were going through something—something that threatened their family unit. She just didn't hear enough to determine the who or the what." Claire's inner concentration deepened. "I'm going to have to combine all the knowledge I do have and use it while holding Shane's and Caitlin's personal items again. Maybe something will click."

She paused, studying Ryan's pained expression.

"Please don't be stubborn. You and Yoda take a break," she said quietly. "Head over to your parents' house for dinner. Emotionally, you need to see Kennedy. And practically, you need to talk to your mom, to complete Casey's explanation on Caitlin's social media handles. The two of them only spoke for ten minutes at the end of our visit. I chatted with Kennedy to keep her occupied. Casey told me that the @mimosagirl121 handle definitely struck a chord with your mom, as did the photo of the brunch table—complete with mimosas—that Caitlin posted on Instagram."

"What kind of chord?" Ryan demanded.

Claire shrugged. "She's not sure yet. She's racking her brain. Also, Casey emailed her a bunch more handles and corresponding data from the car, but there's information attached to all of them that has to be explained in person. You do it. Be there. Your dad can watch a movie or play a game with Kennedy while you talk to your mom. Then, you can tuck Kennedy in and head back to my place." A hint of a smile. "I'll wait up."

"Good to hear." Ryan grinned. "Yoda?" he called out. "Give it a rest. We'll pick it up in the morning."

"I think that's wise," Yoda responded. "Perhaps by then we'll get beyond our impasse."

Ryan shot a quick look at Claire. "You go home. You look pretty wiped out, too."

Claire hesitated. "I will—soon. But, while it's all fresh in my mind, I want to go up to my yoga room for a while and see if anything clicks." She turned and headed for the door. "Give Kennedy a kiss for me."

***

The McKay Residence
East 236th Street
Woodland, Bronx, New York
Tuesday, March 14, 9:30 p.m.

Ryan pulled up a chair beside Kennedy's bed and lowered himself into it, studying her pale face with concern. Dinner had been tense, with his mom serving the meal, and then sitting down at the table beside Kennedy, scrutinizing her as they ate. His dad had done his share of the scrutinizing, as well. For her part, Kennedy had been very quiet, as she had been since SA Barkley called. He'd thanked Maureen for turning her phone over to his people so promptly. Then, he'd set up appointments for the following afternoon to interview first Maureen, and then Kennedy.

None of that was unexpected. Still, that didn't make it any more palatable.

Ryan had managed to lighten the mood by telling Kennedy he planned to take her to the Old Ice Cream Shop while the FBI was with his mom for a "who can eat the most rainbow sprinkles on the hugest ice cream serving" contest. A sparkle had lit her way-too-serious eyes, and she'd given him a big smile.

"You're going to lose," she'd stated flatly. "So what's my prize?"

Ryan didn't miss a beat. "A return trip there so I can steal the championship from you."

Kennedy giggled. "And if you lose again?"

"Winner's choice. You'll pick the prize and I'll suffer."

Even Maureen's lips had twitched at that reply. "Don't sound so cavalier," she told Ryan. "Kennedy has yet to choose a destination that doesn't excite you as much as it does her."

Ryan grinned. "True. But I've got to seem humble."

"Humility is not your strong suit," his father pointed out, straight-faced, as his wife spooned out second portions of stew. Kennedy hadn't done much damage with her first portion.

"Touché, Dad," Ryan had replied. "You got me on that one."

The light banter had continued throughout the rest of the meal, after which they'd enjoyed dessert and the latest family-friendly movie streaming on Netflix.

Nonetheless, when it came to bedtime, Kennedy's tension and anxiety screamed to the forefront.

"I don't think I can sleep," she managed, her voice trembling. "When I try, all I do is cry or have nightmares."

Ryan had stood, exchanging a quick glance with his mom before addressing Kennedy. "How about if I help Aunt Maureen and Uncle Colin clean up while you change into your PJs, and then I hang out in your room for a little while until you feel sleepy?"

A flicker of hope. "Would you?"

"My pleasure." Ryan waved her toward the stairs and rolled up his sleeves, heading for the kitchen. "Be up in a minute."

Kennedy nodded, walking up the steps with a heavy tread.

Maureen watched her disappear from view. "Every day, my heart breaks for her all over again," she murmured to Ryan as she joined him at the sink, and Colin carried in the dishes.

"Mine, too." Ryan's hand paused on the faucet. "I'm sorry it's going to be a late night. I still have social media stuff to go over with you. But right now—"

"Right now, Kennedy needs you," Maureen finished for him. She patted her son's arm. "I'll be fine. I'll fill Dad in and put up my feet while you sit with Kennedy. You and I will talk afterward."

Ten minutes later, Ryan was sitting beside Kennedy, waiting while she undid the clasp on her pendant and placed it on the night table beside her. She then lay back, staring silently at the ceiling.

"It was a rough day, wasn't it, sunshine?" Ryan asked gently, tucking a strand of hair off her face. "Getting that phone call and having to prepare?"

"Talking to Claire was easy," she replied. "She's wonderful and the whole claircognizant thing is amazing. But thinking about the interview with Agent Barkley—it's really freaking me out." She turned her head toward Ryan, and there were tears glistening on her cheeks. "Claire says he's nice, that he won't upset me, at least any more than I already am. Do you think she's right?"

Ryan took Kennedy's small hand in his. "Claire is usually right, so yes, it'll be the way she says."

"She believes Mommy is alive. I think she's right about that, too."

A hard swallow. "I agree. But don't mention any of that to Agent Barkley."

"I won't," Kennedy replied, shaking her head. "Claire already told that to me and explained why. She's right. He'll think that's just wishful thinking on my part. Or he might think I know something I'm not saying." She smiled through her tears. "She and I both know that you're trying to beat the FBI. That's just who you are."

Ryan threw back his head and laughed. "So the two of you are gossiping about me, huh? Should I worry?"

"Uh-uh." Kennedy looked at him with wisdom and maturity beyond her years. "She gets that same expression on her face when she talks about you that you get when you talk about her. At first, I thought that was yucky. But now, I think it's kind of romantic."

"Do you?" Ryan's chest tightened at the tenderness of Kennedy's young heart. "I'll tell you a secret: So do I."

"I'm glad. She's really special. And not just because she's a claircognizant. She cares about people. She cares about you." Kennedy leaned forward conspiratorially. "Be good to her. She's what Mommy calls 'a keeper.'"

Ryan's lips twitched, and he ruffled Kennedy's hair. "Your mommy's right. And don't worry. I'm not dumb enough to let Claire go. So you can get used to having her around."

"Good." Kennedy settled back against the pillows. "Ryan—I know I keep asking you this, but you're going to find Mommy, right?"

"Right," Ryan confirmed. "Like you guys said, I plan to win this contest. So trust me. I'll bring your mommy home."

Kennedy's eyelids began to droop. "I'm glad I have you and Aunt Maureen to watch out for me—until Mommy's home. Then she'll take over, the way she always does."

With that, Kennedy was asleep.

Ryan sat quietly, thinking about Kennedy's words, and reflecting on the fact that Caitlin had implied much the same thing in her text message.

I'm watching Kennedy. Are you?

Ryan's gaze fell on the silver pendant, lying safely just as Kennedy had placed it.

I'm watching Kennedy...watching Kennedy...

Ryan's spine straightened. How? How was Caitlin watching Kennedy? Not figuratively, but *actually*.

She'd chosen those exact words, so they were no coincidence. And it was counterintuitive to believe she'd used them to throw FI off track, make them believe the text was coming from the killer. No. She was conveying a message to them, one she wanted to keep hidden from the killer's probing eyes.

With a flash of insight, Ryan realized how obtuse he'd been when the truth was staring him in the face.

"Idiot," he muttered under his breath. He picked up the heart-shaped pendant that Kennedy wore every waking minute, turning it over in his hands and carefully studying its intricate design. Two layers of delicate mesh, with the letter *K* in the center. The letter was made up of tiny pavé diamonds. The center diamond, where all the arms of the letter met, was larger than the others.

Almost as if it were a camera lens.

Ryan grabbed his cell phone, making sure that Kennedy was sound asleep before he texted his sister.

Fee—I need to FaceTime with you now. Can you free up and get to your workshop? Could be urgent. R

Not thirty seconds later came the responding text.

Ready and waiting. Call.

Ryan did just that, easing silently out of Kennedy's room, pendant in hand, and shutting the door partway. He leaned against the adjacent wall, squatted, and slid to the ground until he was in a sitting position, his back braced.

Then, he initiated the FaceTime.

A moment later, Fiona's face showed up on his iPhone screen.

"What's going on?" she demanded. "I was just about to call it a night."

"Shh," he whispered. "I'm in the hall right outside Kennedy's room. She finally fell asleep. I don't want to wake her." A pause as he considered the fact that the killer's henchman might be listening. Fine. Let them. The worst that could happen is that they'd realize he'd figured out Caitlin's communication device. He'd deal with that fact when it became necessary.

"Ryan?" Fiona pressed.

"Sorry. We'll keep our voices low, but loud enough so we can still hear each other. We've got ground to cover."

Fiona turned her palms up in question. "Am I supposed to understand what you're talking about?"

Ryan shook his head. "No. You're supposed to help me figure something out. Consider it a jewelry consult."

He held up the pendant, bringing it as close to the screen as possible. "Are you on your tablet or your laptop?"

"My laptop."

"Good. That'll give you the broadest visual. Sorry we can't do this in person, but obviously, I can't take the chance of disappearing for hours with Kennedy's precious possession, which, these days, is her only constant."

Fiona nodded, eyeing the necklace. "Can you make the image sharper somehow?"

"Yeah." Ryan applied one of his special filters to do just that. "Better?"

"A lot." Fiona's practiced eye studied the face of the pendant. "What do you need to know?"

"Anything you can tell me about how this was made. Also, if you see something unusual or different."

"For starters, the double layer of mesh is lovely and makes the face of the pendant decorative—but it's an odd choice. It looks less like silver than it does like two layers of woven metal sintered together."

"Sintered? Explain."

"You mean I can teach you something?" she teased.

"Fee, I'm not laughing. What does *sintered* mean?"

When she heard the taut note in Ryan's voice, all Fiona's amusement vanished. "Sintering is a process where metal mesh is laminated together in a high-temp furnace under mechanical pressure in an inert gas environment."

Ryan did a double-take. "How the hell did you know that? It sounds über technical *and* scientific, like it's coming from me rather than from you."

"I'm smart. Plus, I took lots of adjunct courses. One of them was in materials science." Fiona's brows drew together in puzzlement. "Ry, the sintering process that was used to make the front of the heart is not something that's normally used in jewelry-making. It's used in industrial metal fabrication."

Ryan's blood was thrumming through his veins. "Go on."

"You don't sound surprised."

"I'm not."

"Check the entire necklace," Fiona instructed. "Look for a 925 marking. That'll tell you if the pendant is made of genuine sterling silver."

Ryan searched closely. "Nope. Nothing. Again, not surprised."

Fiona made a frustrated sound. "I wish I were holding the piece so I could weigh it. Is it lighter than the pendants you've handled before?"

A grunt. "Pendants aren't exactly my thing. How would I know?"

"Okay, fine." Fiona sighed. "Does it feel hollow?"

Ryan placed the necklace in his palm and shifted it around. "No. But it doesn't feel like it's solid through and through."

"It's not sterling. I'd bet on that—and I'd win."

More certain than ever that he was on the right track, Ryan pressed on, watching his words carefully. Fee had no knowledge of Caitlin's text to their mom, nor to the fact that Caitlin was the one who'd sent it. And it was imperative that she not find out.

"Fee, what about the diamonds, especially the center one. Anything there out of whack?"

"I was just getting to that. The placement of the center diamond looks weird, and it looks more synthetic than real."

"You mean like cubic zirconium?"

"No. I mean like not jewelry at all. There's not even a setting holding the stone. From what I can make out, it looks to be attached from the inside out. Honestly? This isn't something a silversmith would create. It's something an engineer would create, with its decorative quality an afterthought."

"Or a diversion," Ryan muttered.

"What does that mean?"

It means that Caitlin is a lot smarter than even I realized, Ryan thought to himself.

Fee was clearly getting exasperated. "Are you planning on filling me in on what you're looking for?"

"Later." Ryan sidestepped the question. "I need to follow through on this by myself. In the meantime, not a word about anything we said or did tonight to anyone. Okay?"

"Of course not."

"Good. And Fee? Thanks."

He ended the call, waiting impatiently for his home screen to reappear. Once it did, he went straight for BUGGY, the highly sophisticated bug detecting scanner app that he'd created and installed on his cell phone.

He opened the app, waiting until it was ready, then held his phone up to the front of the pendant, moving it slowly around. The mesh had more than enough pores to allow sound to penetrate and reach what Ryan was looking for.

A minute passed.

Then, as expected, the single beep sounded. That meant that, whoever the engineer was who Caitlin had worked with had made sure that a microelectromechanical system, i.e. a MEMS microphone, was buried inside the pendant.

Caitlin wasn't only watching, she was listening.

As someone else might be.

Ryan turned off BUGGY. He had to handle this next part subtly and effectively. Caitlin had to understand—loud and clear—what he needed from her. Conversely, he couldn't alert any eavesdropper to the same.

Which meant using verbal code words, words that would be meaningless to anyone other than Caitlin.

He thought for one long minute, before a self-satisfied grin curved his lips.

Holding the pendant the appropriate distance away, and with the front of it averted so no one could see he was sitting right in front of it, he said, "I'm heading home now, Mom. I'm beat. After working round-the-clock for days, I could sure use a pick-me-up. How about when I visit Kennedy tomorrow afternoon, you surprise me with my favorite dessert?"

15

Claire's Apartment
East Village
Manhattan, New York
Wednesday, March 15, 6:05 a.m.

After tossing and turning all night, Ryan had given it up and was now sitting, coffee mug in hand, at the breakfast nook in Claire's one-bedroom apartment.

Taking a gulp of the dark brew, Ryan glanced idly about. Given all the months the two of them had been together, he now felt surprisingly at home here, even though it was the complete opposite of his tech-friendly loft. The muted pastels and a cluster of wicker furniture, complete with a few paintings depicting sweeping landscapes, brought a sense of peace to the apartment. It was Claire, through and through, lovely and ethereal.

They were still spending half the time here and half the time at Ryan's place. That solution had grown less and less palatable to Ryan as time had passed. He had plans to change it, and soon. The minute this case was solved, he and Claire would be having a different conversation, one he'd been pondering for a while now.

But first, he needed to put things to rest, and to bring peace to himself and to his family.

"Good morning." Claire interrupted his thoughts, walking into the kitchen wearing her pale blue nightshirt with the words *yoga maven* on it. "I didn't hear you get up."

"Hey." A corner of Ryan's mouth lifted. "You were pretty much out for the count. I guess I wore you out."

"Temporarily." Claire gave him a teasing look, and then headed over to brew herself a cup of herbal tea. "Did you get any sleep—after you wore me out, that is."

Ryan shrugged. "Not really. Maybe a couple of hours."

Claire nodded, putting two oatmeal-raisin muffins on a plate and bringing them over with her tea. She placed the plate on the counter, then slid onto the stool beside him. "You had a lot of heavy things on your mind. For that matter, so did I." She gestured at the muffins. "Eat. They're homemade with all natural, good stuff in them."

"Sold." Ryan picked up a muffin and took a bite. "Mmm. You might not bake often, but when you do—hey, maybe I'll give up my day job and be a kept man."

That made Claire laugh. "You'd be totally bored and starving to death. Neither would work for you."

Ryan couldn't argue away that one. "You're right. But I could live with being a sex slave in between working and eating."

"I'll remember that." Claire grew serious, placed a gentle hand on his forearm. "When are you planning on driving to your parents' house?"

Ryan put down his muffin and coffee mug. "Agent Barkley is showing up to interview my mom at two. I want to get there well before that so I can take care of a few things, and then get Kennedy out of the house with plenty of time to spare until Barkley arrives. Before I head to the Bronx, I want to bring the team up to speed." He turned to Claire. "And so do you."

A definitive nod. "As I told you, last night I got such strong flashes of insight when I held the Washes' towels again. Shane and Caitlin behind closed doors. The two of them talking about existing danger and the man who was inciting it—a man who's important and powerful. It feels like something more personal than just a police or FBI case. But not completely personal. A threat that started with Caitlin and Shane, and has now widened to include Kennedy. That's been since Caitlin ran. Maybe this man thinks Kennedy knows something, or maybe he thinks Caitlin's been in contact with her. I'm not sure. What I am sure of is that I'm very relieved that Patrick put extra security on Kennedy."

"So am I. *Very* relieved." Ryan frowned. "You and I have managed to give her some hope. But I want to take it a step further. I have an idea, but it hinges on what Caitlin does next and on my racing the clock to do a ton of finely detailed—and extraordinarily brilliant—work, followed by an enactment worthy of Hollywood."

Claire's brows rose. "Wow, have you piqued my interest. Let's shower and get into the office. I'm willing to bet that, after a night off, everyone will be in for a morning catch-up. After which you'll drive straight to your parents' house."

Ryan picked up his cell phone. "Let's not leave it to chance," he said. He Slacked the whole team, told them that he and Claire would be in before eight, complete with updates. He made sure to stipulate that, with Casey's okay, everyone had to be there for an eight o'clock meeting, and that he had to leave the brownstone by eleven.

The replies ranged from Casey's "Meeting approved" to Emma and Angela's "I'll be there" to Patrick's "Already in" to Marc's "Halfway there."

"Good," Ryan said. "Yeses across the board."

Quickly, Claire drank down her tea, while Ryan polished off his coffee and muffin.

"C'mon, Mr. Mysterious," Claire said. "Let's shower and get moving."

***

Offices of Forensic Instincts
Main Conference Room, Second Floor
Tribeca, Manhattan, New York
Wednesday, March 15, 7:48 a.m.

Emma was the final team member to arrive. She looked puzzled as she walked into the impressive room and stared at the entire group gathered around the sweeping oval table, iPads poised and ready. They were currently all sipping at their coffee mugs and nibbling on bagels and cream cheese.

"Am I late?" she asked with a glance at her Apple Watch.

"Nope," Ryan assured her. "Early by twelve minutes."

"Okay, then I'm confused. I stopped at the first-floor conference room as soon as I walked in. I thought we were waiting for next week to move back up here."

In her seat at the head of the table, Casey leaned forward, interlacing her fingers in front of her. "We changed our minds."

Emma turned her palms up in question. “Did everyone know this except me?”

Marc grabbed this bull by the horns, making sure it wasn’t going to turn into one of Emma’s unintentional poke-the-bear moments. “Nope. Just our esteemed leader, who says she’s feeling more than able to climb one flight of stairs. So grab a cup of coffee and a bagel, and join us—without asking Casey any more questions.”

Emma heard the pointed note in Marc’s voice and shot off a mock salute. “Got it. And thank you to whoever supplied breakfast.”

“That would be me,” Angela said. “The subway was actually on time today. So I got here with forty minutes to spare. And I figured we all needed sustenance.”

Quickly, Emma got her coffee and bagel, and then slid into her seat. “All set.”

Casey opened the meeting. “I hope everyone managed to eat dinner and get a decent night’s sleep. As you all know, that doesn’t happen often.”

She didn’t wait for responses, but continued. “To recap, Claire and I interviewed all the McKays yesterday. John met with more of his police contacts and utilized Yoda’s refined list to expand his questioning. And Marc shared Aidan’s findings about Shane’s and Caitlin’s blood both being at the crime scene with the team, after which he and Patrick called as many medical facilities as possible to see if Caitlin had been treated for her injuries. So we have lots to tell each other. But, once again, Ryan called this meeting, so we’ll let him go first.”

She glanced at Ryan. “Your Slack message sounded just as urgent this time as the last.”

"It was." Ryan was barely able to sit still. "I've got something major to report. And Claire should go after me. She made some great headway, too—headway that will give us valuable insight and might even alter our course a bit."

"Okay, go," Casey urged.

Ryan told the team everything, from his suspicions about Kennedy's pendant, to Fiona's confirmation of the same, to the microphone on a chip that BUGGY had picked up, to the seeds he'd planted for Caitlin, and to the fact that, should those seeds bear fruit, he had a monumental task ahead of him—as did the team.

"Are you planning on telling us what this monumental task is?" Patrick asked.

"Yeah. As soon as Caitlin responds. My fingers are crossed that she'll be sending me a lunchtime dessert with enough of a message for me to act. When that happens, I'll tell you guys everything. Because, even though I'll be doing the work, every single one of us is going to be on high alert, ready to take on the end result. But it's a complex explanation with specifics we need to plan as a team, so I want to make sure we have what we need before I dive right in. If Caitlin comes through—and I really believe she will—we'll have another meeting at the end of the day, I'll give you all the specifics, and we'll chart our course, so to speak."

"Fair enough," Casey accepted, although she looked as puzzled and curious as Patrick. "Most of all, amazing work on your part, Ryan. Truly impressive."

"Thanks, boss."

"How much did you tell Fiona?"

"Nothing," Ryan replied. "Obviously, she knows there's something weird about the pendant. But I let her know our call was confidential. So there won't be any leaks."

Casey nodded again. The team had formed a tight friendship with Ryan's sister, especially after they'd saved her life. So there were no doubts about her integrity where FI was concerned.

"Cool." Emma was still processing Ryan's findings. "So Caitlin's been watching everything Kennedy does. Not so cool that she has to watch the pain she's in, see how much she cries."

Ryan waved away Emma's assessment. "I was pretty upset about the last part of what you just said. Then I realized that Caitlin can't view much of Kennedy's physical reactions. The only time she can see her is when Kennedy's either gazing at herself in the mirror or staring at the pendant when she takes it off."

Marc looked intrigued. "Good point. The pendant is around Kennedy's neck, facing outward. So, for the most part, Caitlin is watching everyone else, not Kennedy."

"Yup. Exactly." Ryan swallowed. "It's not very uplifting, but at least it eases my angst a little. Caitlin must be going through hell. The last thing she needs is to be haunted by Kennedy's pale, tear-streaked little face."

"I agree one hundred percent," Casey concurred, choking up as she spoke. "Just watching Kennedy grieving yesterday broke my heart."

She cleared her throat, brought herself under control. "On to you, Claire. Obviously, I was with you at Ryan's parents' house, as well as with our interviews of the rest of the McKays—which yielded no new information—so no need to restate that. But none of us knows anything after that. So tell the team about what took place when we were with Kennedy, and then fill us all in about the rest of the day. The floor is yours."

Claire explained her talk with Kennedy, as well as the perceptions that had steered it in the right direction. Then, she went on to tell them everything about her interaction with Shane's and Caitlin's personal items, and what she'd deduced from that.

John spoke up first. "Are you suggesting we back away from our NYPD interviews?"

Claire shook her head. "No. I'm not suggesting we back away from anything. I'm definitely not ready to rule out Shane's law enforcement connections as part of the puzzle. Not until I can zero in on what the exact threat is and who it's coming from. It's just that I keep getting the sense that this atrocity was personal as well as—" She broke off, her gaze growing faraway.

"Claire?" Casey asked at once. "What is it?"

Claire gave a slight shake of her head. "I'm not sure. But I'm getting the oddest sensations. Caitlin's aura is growing stronger, clearer. Her presence is intercepting my other sensory perceptions—even those involving Shane. It's like she's fighting to get through…" Abruptly, Claire turned to Ryan. "Arrangements are in the process."

"She's sending me what I asked for," Ryan deduced, gazing steadily at Claire, who he'd quickly filled in on his plan. "Which means it will show up earlier than expected. I'll be out of here by ten thirty, and arriving an hour later. I'll tell my mom to expect me for an early lunch."

***

The McKay Residence
East 236th Street
Woodlawn, Bronx, New York
Wednesday, March 15, 11:55 a.m.

Ryan jumped out of his Corvette and slammed the door, locking it as he did. He'd hit traffic and he was ripping. He'd called his mom three times from the road to make sure no package had arrived for him. She'd assured him the answer was no. He'd cut off her questions until she'd wisely stopped asking them.

No one else on the team had had crucial recaps. There was no word from any hospitals of someone matching Caitlin's description who had required treatment, and no significant forward motion on the NYPD. So Ryan had taken off, only to be stuck behind one asshole after another.

Finally, he was here.

He strode up to the front door, his sharp gaze sweeping the steps. Nothing. Not that he expected there to be. Someone would have to be home to receive the package. Caitlin couldn't use a credit card, so it would be COD.

Ryan rang the bell, turning to look up and down the street. No van of any kind in the vicinity. If Caitlin was doing as he asked—and, after what Claire had said, he had no doubt that she was—her tasty gift had yet to arrive.

Maureen opened the door. "Lunch is on the table," she said without preliminaries. She could sense that Ryan was practically vibrating.

"Thanks, Mom." He glanced past her. "Where's Kennedy?"

"In the den." Maureen pointed. "Watching some martial arts movie while she waits for you." A quick once-over. "Are you okay?"

"Yes," Ryan replied. "Just follow my lead. I'll fill you in later."

"Ryan!" Kennedy rushed into the hall and hugged him as if she hadn't just seen him the night before.

"Hey, sunshine." He gave her a hard squeeze. "I hope the movie is good—but not too good. You'll have to put it on pause. Aunt Maureen is worried that you and I are both starved and withering away."

A hint of a smile. "No chance of that. I had bacon and eggs for breakfast."

Maureen scowled. "And left over more than half of it. Lovey…" She stroked Kennedy's head. "You must eat. For my sake, if not for yours."

Kennedy gave a reluctant nod. "Okay, I will."

"You sure will—but not too much," Ryan stipulated. "Don't forget our upcoming contest. After lunch, we'll be heading over to the Old Ice Cream Shop."

"Where I'll humiliate you," Kennedy fired back.

"That's what I'm afraid of."

"Ryan—you're a bad influence," Maureen retorted, gesturing for them to take their seats at the table. "Time for a good meal. Hot potato soup. It'll stick to your ribs and warm your insides enough to brace you for mounds of ice cream."

Kennedy and Ryan caught the twinkle in her eye, and they both laughed, heading for the table while Maureen hurried into the kitchen to dole out the portions of soup.

While they ate, Ryan and Kennedy continued their bantering, even though he could feel the tension emanating from her—a tension that exploded when the doorbell rang.

"Is that Agent Barkley?" she asked, nearly leaping out of her seat and running off. "Do you think he's here early?"

Ryan shook his head, then rose, heading for the front door. "That's not the FBI's style," he reassured her. "More likely, it's the postal carrier with something that wouldn't fit in the mailbox. I'll check."

Mentally, he crossed his fingers, and went to find out.

Sheer relief flowed through him when he opened the door. A brightly decorated van was in the driveway, motor running, and a lanky teenage boy stood on the front step. As soon as Ryan appeared in the doorway, the kid held out a pastry-sized box.

"Ryan McKay?" he asked.

"That's me." Ryan dug in his pocket. "How much do I owe you?" As he pulled out the requisite cash plus a generous tip, he noted that the box looked larger than expected. But most important, there was a small white card-sized envelope tucked in the red and white wrapping strings.

Heart racing, Ryan thanked the kid and pocketed the card—which he'd read later—before turning to shut the door behind him and carrying in the box.

Kennedy's expression turned from frightened to curious. "What is it?"

"I don't know." Ryan winked at his mother as if she knew exactly what the delivery was, despite the fact that he was aware she was clueless. "Let's take a look."

Kennedy caught Ryan's wink. "Is it a surprise?" she asked. She watched as he cut the strings and opened the box.

Inside were three pastries: a huge Guinness brownie, which was Ryan's sweet-tooth downfall; a sugar-drizzled cream puff, which he recognized as his mother's dessert of choice; and an enormous chocolate chip cookie, Kennedy's most cherished snack.

Bless you, Caitlin, Ryan thought. *You thought of everything.*

Kennedy was squealing and snatching the cookie from the box. "Thank you, Aunt Maureen!" she exclaimed, hugging her aunt before rushing back to her chair. "How did you remember how much I love these, especially when they're straight from the bakery all warm and gooey?"

Ryan shot his mom a purposeful look—one she acted on right away.

"I'm like an elephant," she replied to Kennedy, playing her part to perfection. "I never forget." Her brows knit. "But I didn't expect these to arrive until late this afternoon."

"That's okay, Mom," Ryan said. "There's no time like the present."

"Not this time." His mother folded her arms across her breasts. "Not until every bit of lunch is gone."

Kennedy shifted impatiently in her seat and Ryan's lips twitched.

"We'd better listen, sunshine," he advised Kennedy. "Besides, we don't have a leg to stand on since we're having two desserts this afternoon."

"Correction: one and a half," Maureen countered. "It's the rest of lunch and then half a cookie. If you still have room after your ice cream fiesta, you can eat the other half after dinner."

It wasn't a suggestion. It was a command.

"Okay, Aunt Maureen." Clearly, Kennedy knew when to stop pushing. She picked up her spoon and resumed eating her potato soup.

Ryan was torn between roaring with laughter and excusing himself so he could read the card.

His curiosity won that war.

"I'll be right back." He pushed back his chair. "Then I promise to finish off every spoonful of my soup."

He walked to the bathroom, flipped on the light, and shut and locked the door.

There he pulled the card out of his pocket, and read:

Bean—dessert, debris, pat's, late four.

Ryan reread the coded words three times until he had them memorized in order, complete with punctuation.

Then he stuffed the card back into his pocket.

The decoding process was going to have to wait.

16

Offices of Forensic Instincts
Ryan's Lair
Tribeca, Manhattan, New York
Wednesday, March 15, 5:30 p.m.

Ryan had gotten back a half hour ago. Thankfully, Agent Barkley had gone easy on both his mom and on Kennedy, making Ryan's goodbyes that much easier. He needed to get back, to his lair and to Yoda.

So, after huge hugs and promises to return as soon as he could break away again—not to mention withstanding a boatload of bragging by Kennedy, who'd won the ice cream contest by a landslide—he'd packed up his Guinness brownie and headed back to the office.

Now, he was hunched over his computer, and he and Yoda were hard at work, decoding Caitlin's message.

"The Bean part is easy," Ryan began. "Caitlin is telling us she's in Boston, which we already suspected."

"I agree, Ryan," Yoda responded. "'Dessert' is challenging. She's certainly not telling you about your brownie, which you already knew.

Nor, do I believe, about either your mother's or Kennedy's treats. However, if we follow the logical sequence of her wording, 'dessert' would signify the place in Boston where she's telling you to go."

Impatiently, Ryan nodded. "You're right. But why 'dessert'?" What place would that equate with? A bakery? Which one?" He broke off, his forehead creased in thought. "And where is there a Boston bakery that makes great Guinness brownies? I went to MIT in Cambridge—until I dropped out—and spent a shitload of time in Boston. Believe me, I'd know if there was a place that did."

"Excuse me, Ryan, but I believe you're being too literal."

Ryan's head came up. "Meaning?"

"Meaning, I just performed a destination search in Boston, specifically seeking out locations where college-aged students flock to. It appears there's a street in Boston where there are several highly frequented night spots. The street is called Guinness Way. Does that hold any memories for you?"

Ryan shot up like an arrow. "Yes. Yoda, you're brilliant and so am I for creating you." He rushed on. "There was a bar on Guinness Way where I used to hang out at when I didn't want to study or cram for my exams—which was most of the time. The bar was called Mickey's Tavern. Great beer. Great burgers. Great music. Caitlin and Shane went there with me two or three times when they visited."

"Mickey's Tavern." A brief pause as Yoda tapped into his data banks. "The bar is still there," he confirmed. "Number 101. I just confirmed that with an aerial sweep."

"Yesss!" Ryan punched the air. "So we have our place. Now we need specifics." He calmed down, muttering, "The problem is that Caitlin would never arrange an in-person meeting. Not after taking such great pains to remain in hiding."

"I agree. Caitlin would not want to appear in public—either inside or outside of a tavern. So how would she connect with you?"

"The exact way I planned—a drop site. So there has to be a spot near Mickey's where she would expect me to leave her—" Ryan broke off and began to laugh. "'Debris.' Of course. The second time Shane, Caitlin, and I went to the tavern together, we all left more than a little drunk. Shane tripped over the trash can just outside the bar. He fell and broke his big toe. His toe of all things. Not exactly a macho accident. We busted his chops about it for a week. That's an event Caitlin wouldn't forget—nor would I."

"Therefore, she wants you to leave her something in that trash can?" Yoda inquired.

"Yup. And that means she has a pretty good idea what I have in mind. Like I said, Caitlin is one smart woman. She and I are on the exact same wavelength. I know what to do."

Ryan stared at the words on the page and let out a groan. "She's either got a lot of faith in me or she's crazy. Paddy. St. Patrick's Day, which is on Friday. She's expecting my package in two days."

"At four o'clock," Yoda finished up.

"Yeah, which doesn't give me much time." Ryan was already Slacking the team for an immediate meeting. "'Late four.' I guess I should be grateful. She's giving me until four p.m., rather than four in the morning. That gives me a couple of hours overnight, all day tomorrow, and a few hours on the seventeenth. It takes four plus hours to get from Tribeca to Boston by car. Personal cars. We can't leave a paper trail—no train or plane tickets, and no car rental agreements."

"I quite agree, Ryan."

Ryan was already out of his seat. "Call Josh at System76. They're in Denver, which is Mountain Time, so he'll still be there. Tell him to get me two Lemur Pro laptops. Whatever they have in stock. Configuration doesn't matter. Money doesn't matter. I need it messengered to me now. The fastest service that can fly it here. I don't care if it arrives at three in the morning. I'll be waiting."

***

Offices of Forensic Instincts
Main Conference Room
Second Floor
Tribeca, Manhattan, New York
Wednesday, March 15, 6:40 p.m.

Ryan barely waited for everyone to be seated before turning to Casey. "I need to talk stat. The clock is ticking."

"Understood," she replied. "Go."

Succinctly, Ryan told the team about the Guinness brownie's arrival and what the accompanying card said.

"Yoda and I just finished decoding the message Caitlin was sending." Not even pausing to boast about his accomplishment, Ryan went on to tell them where and when the drop had to be made.

"How can we assist?" Marc asked.

Ryan's expression was intense as he looked from one teammate to another. "I need you to help me pick out seven convincing destinations—on top of the obvious one—and then to figure out who's going where on Friday."

Claire's shoulders lifted. "Sorry, Ryan. But I think you've just lost us all. I don't even know what it is we're 'dropping.'"

"Sorry. My mind is all over the place. Here's what's going down: I'm going to be customizing two identical System76 laptops—one for

Caitlin and one for me. They'll each have a built-in satellite phone. The communication will have a proprietary end-to-end encryption that makes it impossible to snoop on the communication. To mask the end points from anyone who could be tracking it, it'll be bounced through hundreds of different servers."

Patrick's brow furrowed, although he was accustomed by now to the extent of Ryan's capabilities. "So, if I understand you correctly, you're saying that based upon your magic laptops, you and Caitlin can be in contact with each other via text, telephone, or video undetected?"

"Nice interpreting skills," Ryan praised him. "That's exactly what I'm saying. The laptops will be here sometime in the middle of the night." His features tightened. "I want to give Kennedy the surprise of her life. A St. Patrick's Day face-to-face talk with her mommy."

"The timing of all this sounds awfully tight," Emma said. "I don't understand computer jargon, but creating two highly customized laptops in less than two days sounds like an overwhelming task, even for you. Can you pull it off?"

"I'll pull it off," Ryan stated. "I have to. Caitlin and I will make this virtual meeting with Kennedy happen. Frankly, I think that talking to her daughter is what she had in mind when she determined the date and time of the drop."

"Hutch's agents are still watching us like hawks," Marc reminded him. "You think they won't notice if you take off for Boston?"

"Of course they will. That's why I won't be going there. And that's where the fun part of this plan comes."

Ryan lit up like a Christmas tree as he explained. "Friday morning, all of us will drive our personal cars to work and park in the garage on Duane Street. We'll walk straight here since the FI offices will be everyone's starting point. At ten thirty—leaving ample time for traffic—we'll all march out single file en route to the garage. We'll collect our cars, after which we'll scatter like cockroaches. Each one of us will be carrying a laptop bag or a briefcase. All but one will be stuffed with a shirt box filled with enough magazines to weigh as much as a laptop—which, given my skills, will be the FBI's natural assumption as to what we're toting around. The other bag will hold the real laptop in it. We'll each be going to a specific destination; we'll pick those now."

Casey had listened intently and was now nodding, brows drawn together in thought. "Personal cars mean no paper trail. All we have to do is avoid tolls or pay cash." A smug grin tugged at her lips. "We'll drive the Bureau crazy."

"Brilliant strategy." Marc was clearly enjoying this, as well. "We're the good guys, but we get to do a mob impersonation. To ease this along, we have boxes and boxes of those black poly bubble mailers, each laptop size, in the storage room. We'll use those to hold the magazine-filled shirt boxes, and, in one case, the laptop. Then, we'll pull them out of our bags and leave them at our respective drop sites."

"Oh yeah." Ryan was at the edge of his seat, loving how the momentum was building.

For the first time, Angela spoke up. "I'm the best choice for the actual Boston drop. Not only am I the least likely to be on the FBI's radar, but I have a sister in Brookline, which is directly adjacent to Boston. I'll drive straight to the tavern and make the drop. Then I'll spend the night at my sister's and drive back on Saturday. Does that work?" Her lips twitched. "Because I'm dying to push the FBI's buttons."

This time Casey laughed aloud. "Uh-oh. I fear we've created a monster."

Angela shot her a look. "Remember, I was a defense attorney for high-profile clients who did lots of bad shit. Driving law enforcement—and prosecutors—crazy is in my blood."

"Yes," Casey said dryly, thinking of a time when FI and Angela were not such good friends. "I more than recall. Fine. The real delivery is yours. Time to discuss where the rest of us are going."

"You're not going anywhere," Marc said quietly. "First of all, you're not up for traveling. And second of all, Hutch will really come down hard on you on this one—and he'll be right." A pause. "That's not disrespect, Case. It's caring. If you can think of a way around it—one that doesn't involve you traveling a distance and tipping Hutch off in the process—I'm all ears."

Casey was quiet for a moment, dealing with the internal struggle.

Claire saved her. "I have an idea. Open spaces make great drop sites. I've watched enough kidnapping movies over Ryan's shoulder to know that. How about if you and I go to Central Park? You'll be brought here in the morning by car service—business as usual these days while you recoup your strength—and we'll take my car on our jaunt. It'll get some much-needed exercise, since I rarely drive. We'll do a bunch of trips around the park. Then, it'll take hours just to find a spot to double or triple park. As for the weather, it'll be a little chilly, but we'll stay close to the park entrance and find a trash can to dump our package in. The trip will be easy, and you'll be right here in Manhattan. Plus, I'll be with you if you need a little help. How's that?"

Casey gave Claire a grateful look. "It sounds ideal. Your compassion mixed with Ryan's logic and strategizing. Clearly, he's rubbing off on you."

Now *that* brought a smug grin to Ryan's lips. "Rubbing off on her, huh? Nice image. Very hot."

Claire rolled her eyes. "Even given the intense pressure we're under, that ego never quits."

"Nope. Not the ego, and not the libido."

"Ryan, cut it out," Claire instructed. "We've got more locations to pick out."

Immediately, he sobered. "Right. With regard to me, I've given this a ton of thought. From the Bureau's—and Hutch's—perspective, I'm the most likely suspect, so to speak. I'm smack in the middle of this investigation, and also the only team member with the tech skills sharp enough to tamper with what is obviously a laptop. So I'll take another scene out of those spy thrillers. An airport. Specifically, JFK. What's better than one of the country's busiest airports for a missing person to pick up an anonymous drop?"

The rest of the team gave Ryan the thumbs-up.

"Now we need to cover due north, due south, due east, and due west," Patrick said. "It'll throw off the authorities even more, since they'll have to follow us every which way. How about if I handle due north—specifically Lake George? There's a little inn where Adele and I frequent when we visit. I'll do my drop, then we'll have dinner and stay over. We'll drive back early Saturday. And it goes without saying that Adele will ask no questions and I'll supply no explanations."

Ryan was starting to look like the proverbial cat who swallowed the canary. "Great. Now Marc, what about you?"

"I'll handle due south," Marc replied. "Atlantic City and the boardwalk. It's only a few hours away, precluding an overnight, which is essential for me these days. Maddy obviously can't join me and I won't be far away from home for too long."

Casey gave him a sympathetic look. "Of course not. And your suggestion is excellent. That takes care of north and south."

"I'll drive east to the farthest tip of Long Island," John announced. "I love the view of the Atlantic from Montauk Point State Park. I'll do my drop there with pleasure."

"Great," Casey agreed. "So we're all covered except Emma."

Emma waved away any suggestions before they could be offered. "I know I have to go due west. But if I'm doing this, I might as well get a few hours of fun out of it. Is that okay, Casey?"

Casey inclined her head. "What did you have in mind?"

"Something cool…like a concert. I can find one that's west of here. I'll crash at a hotel and be back by Saturday, no problem."

Seeing Emma's hopeful look, Casey relented. "Why not? Who do you want to see? And whoever it is, they can't be performing halfway across the country."

Emma sighed. "Who I'd really love to see is—"

"Your favorite performer is Rebecca Merland, as I've heard you say countless times," Yoda interrupted her. "Alternative rock. Well, she'll be in concert at the Pennsylvania State College at University Park this weekend, which I assume you knew."

Emma started. "You're right, Yoda. She will be at Penn State. Does that big brain of yours also tell you that Friday night's event has been sold out for months?" A deep sigh. "Ah, the impossible dream."

"That does seem to be an impasse," he replied.

"Not impossible at all." Angela stepped in with a solution. "I'll get you a seat. I know Rebecca from an old lawsuit my firm and I were fighting for her—a fight we won. I'll give her manager a call. How about a backstage VIP pass?"

Emma blinked. "Just like that?"

"Just like that." Angela's lips curved. "Had I known you were a fan of hers, I would have offered this sooner."

"Oh, thank you, thank you! I knew right away that I would love you." Emma waved her arms in the air, as if the concert was already underway. "Can I take one of my roommates? It's a long drive—not to mention she's also a huge fan."

"Go for it," Casey replied with a wave of her hand. "Just be innovative about what you tell her. No giveaways."

"Of course not. I'll tell Brynn that I accidentally brought my office's recyclables home with me. I'll throw the bag into a recycling container on campus. She'll be too excited about the concert to even hear my explanation, much less see what I'm doing." Emma's eyes were still glowing. "Wow, she and I are going to have a blast!"

"I'm sure you will." Yoda spoke up again. "Since this is your first stay near the campus, I've compiled a list of appropriate and safe hotels where you and your friend can stay."

Ryan chortled at that one. "See how protective Yoda is about you, Emma?" he teased. "I'm not your only FI big brother. And, by the way, do you even know how to drive?"

Emma made a face at him. "Yes, I can drive—in my cool secondhand Mazda3, which is jet black and in near-mint condition. I've also got long-term parking a couple of blocks away from my apartment in Chinatown, which I can now afford. When I'm in the city, I take mass transit. When I travel outside the city, I drive. I'm a damn good driver, too. And I don't need a red Corvette to do it in, like some showoffs I know."

"Burn!" Claire was openly laughing. "She's got you there. Any snide comeback?"

"I'm sure I'd have one." Ryan was pushing back his chair. "But duty calls and the clock is ticking. So it's back to the lair for me. Yoda? Are my laptops en route?"

"Indeed, Ryan. Josh was most cooperative. He did say you owe him one, though."

"Okay, no problem. He and I will figure that out another time. Meanwhile, I need you to monitor the laptops' delivery progress. Send me a message if any time deviations occur en route."

"Understood."

Ryan beamed. "Excellent. When the laptops arrive, I'll shove one of them in a black bubble mailer, then inside my laptop duffel, and weigh it. I'll give the weight specs to Emma. She'll prepare identical black bubble mailers for everyone. Then, you can start putting magazines in them, stuffing it all into your bags or briefcases, and gassing up your cars."

17

Offices of Forensic Instincts
Ryan's Lair
Tribeca, Manhattan, New York
Thursday, March 16, 7:10 a.m.

The timer on Ryan's cell phone sounded.

He dragged his gaze away from the System76 that he'd been hard at work programming since two thirty a.m. For one moment, he stared stupidly at the phone, wondering why it was bugging him. Then, he remembered. Time to call his mom, to let her know he wouldn't be able to get away from his lair today, and to give her time to break that news to Kennedy. Because he knew his sunshine. Even though his promise as to when he'd be returning had been vague, she'd be expecting him sometime today. And, because of what was about to go down, there was no way he could indulge her.

His mom would ask why he couldn't come.

He'd dodge the question.

She'd get the picture.

But Kennedy wouldn't.

Shutting off the annoying alarm, Ryan dragged both hands through his hair, rising only to stretch, and then to pour himself yet another cup of crappy coffee from his own mediocre coffeemaker. He didn't have time to go upstairs and get himself a pot of the good stuff—even though Yoda had brewed one. Maybe later. Now, he was flying on adrenaline and on a roll, working his butt off to achieve his goal.

Thanks to Claire, he had a great alternative to pass along to his mom, who would, in turn, pass it along to Kennedy.

Claire had presented the idea to him sometime around four thirty a.m.—the first and only time she'd interrupted his work. She'd eased into the lair, waiting patiently to be noticed.

When Ryan sensed her presence, turned his head, and peered at her through red-rimmed eyes, she'd shoved a mug of the A+ coffee brewed upstairs at their Jura station into his hands, and plopped a steaming box of pizza on the nearby table.

"Hey, thanks," he'd said, his mind still on the software he was writing and installing. "I skipped dinner. You probably just saved my life."

Claire had nodded. "No problem. But that's not the only reason I'm here. It occurred to me that Kennedy is going to expect you to visit. If not tomorrow—sorry, I mean today—then Friday, since it's St. Patrick's Day. I know you'll get there by evening, but she doesn't. So I wanted to run a suggestion by you. Since Kennedy and your mom will be hanging out alone today, I thought I'd go over and keep them company. Your whole family will be there tomorrow. But today might be lonely. I've finished my pressing work, plus all I need to get ready for Casey's and my trip to Central Park tomorrow. So, after I go home, grab a shower, and get a few more hours' sleep, I have plenty of time to fill the void."

An expression of sheer gratitude and relief crossed Ryan's face. "That would be awesome. You really wouldn't mind?"

"Of course not," Claire replied with a soft smile. "I'm really beginning to treasure my time with Kennedy. And your mom and I have developed a great rapport. We'll have a lovely day." A twinkle. "And if we run out of conversation, we can always discuss you. I'm sure I still have lots to learn."

That had made Ryan laugh, and he'd taken a gulp of coffee and reached for a slice of pizza. "From what I understand, you've already made a dent in that with Kennedy." As he spoke, his restless gaze shifted back to the computer.

"Go back to your magic-making," Claire had urged him. She walked over only long enough to give him a tender kiss. "If anyone can make this happen, it's you."

Two and a half hours later, and with the way things were clicking, Ryan was starting to believe Claire was right.

He grabbed his cell phone, saw that it was now nearing seven thirty, and—after downing another slice of cold pizza and swallowing two more gulps of now-cold coffee—he called his mom's home line.

"Hello?" Maureen sounded guarded, and more than a little beat.

"Hey, Mom, it's me."

His mother sighed. "Yes, I've been expecting your call."

"Huh?"

"Claire beat you to the punch. She called a little before seven, told me you were inundated, and asked if Kennedy and I would enjoy a visit from her."

Ryan blew out a breath. "When it comes to people and feelings, she thinks of everything." A pause. "Do you think Kennedy will be okay with that?"

"We'll make sure she's okay," Maureen replied. "She knows you're intently trying to bring her mother back, and to investigate who killed her father. Yesterday, you told her that you might not be able to get back here right away. She'll understand why. And, other than you, Claire is the best medicine for her. Not to mention, I think Fiona will be dropping by, as well. You know what good friends she and Claire have become. And they both care deeply for Kennedy. So we ladies will have a very pleasant day. We'll also do some planning. We want to try to make it an as-close-to-festive-as-possible St. Patrick's Day for Kennedy. She obviously can't attend a parade, the way she ritually did with Caitlin and Shane, but we'll think of acceptable substitutes. We'll bake. We'll do some crafts. So don't worry. We're fine."

"Thanks, Mom," Ryan replied. "The three of you are making me feel a little less guilty."

"Don't feel guilty," Maureen said. "Just do what's necessary." A pause. "What about tomorrow? Nolan, Garret, Fiona, and your dad and I will be here for St. Patrick's Day itself. Will you be able to join us?"

Once again, Ryan hedged. "Yes, and no," he finally said, watching his words very carefully. "I'll have to miss most of the day's festivities, but I'll be there in time to dig into your famous corn beef and cabbage. Oh, and tell Dad to save me some Guinness straight from his kegerator; I'll need it. I'll also bring Claire; I'll even make her wear green." His voice broke a bit. "I know that's not ideal, but can we make it work? I wouldn't do this to you—to any of us—if it weren't urgent."

Maureen didn't miss a beat. "You're on to something, something significant. And you can't tell me what it is."

She was greeted by silence.

"That's the only answer I need," she said. "Do what you must. And may God guide you and help you answer Kennedy's prayers."

***

The McKay Residence
East 236th Street
Woodlawn, Bronx, New York
Thursday, March 16, 2:15 p.m.

Maureen sat back on the sofa, watching Fiona sitting cross-legged on the carpet, showing Kennedy how to make a shamrock charm bracelet. Claire was seated on the sofa next to Maureen, smiling as she watched Kennedy's intent expression as she followed Fiona's instructions.

"She's got talent," Claire noted. "Maybe Fiona will have a junior partner one day."

Maureen chuckled. "Given how busy Fiona is, I'm sure she'd welcome an artistic addition. Soon—but not too soon. Childhood lasts for so brief a time. Kennedy should enjoy it…" Her voice trailed off, a shadow of pain crossing her face. "I don't know what I'm saying. Kennedy's happy childhood is gone. A cold-blooded killer shattered it, took away the foundation of her life. How can she ever—?" Maureen broke off, blinking away the tears that had formed in her eyes.

Claire covered Maureen's hand with her own. "No, things won't ever be the same for Kennedy. But we're going to do all we can to restore a portion of that childhood."

Maureen shot Claire a quick glance. "Ryan is working on that right now."

Claire didn't respond to that. But she did tackle another area. "Mrs. McKay…"

"Maureen," Ryan's mom corrected her. "I think we've more than arrived at that informality."

A nod. "Thank you. Maureen, I've found a professional who I think is the ideal child psychologist for Kennedy to see. Her name is Dr. Melissa Zitter. She's trained in childhood trauma, and has dozens of exceptional reviews. Several of the psychologists I've worked with in my pre-FI life recommend her highly. If you'd like I can contact her myself to initiate the process and tell her to expect your call. Or you can just dive right in, use the professional reference names I'll give you, and do it yourself." A slight pause. "But even after Caitlin is back at home, Kennedy will need some counseling. As you said, she needs as much of her childhood back as possible."

Maureen squeezed Claire's forearm. "I truly appreciate what you've done, and I agree with you. I'm not a mushy sort of person, but I want you to know how lucky I feel to have you, not only in Ryan's life, but in ours, as well."

"The feeling is mutual," Claire replied. "Being an only child, and not one who comes from a close-knit and loving family, I feel privileged to be so much a part of yours. Thank you."

Their emotional moment was interrupted by Kennedy, who called out: "Look! I did it!" She proudly held up her new charm bracelet.

Maureen beamed. "That's excellent, lovey. Fiona, you'd best get Kennedy on board quickly. Otherwise, the competition might steal her away."

"You're right." Fiona shoved waves of black hair off her face. "I'll draw up an employment contract right away."

Kennedy giggled, for once holding another piece of jewelry other than her pendant. "I probably won't understand the legal stuff. So I'll let Nolan and Garret read it over."

Fiona grinned. "Smart girl."

Maureen clapped her hands. "Movie time. And, instead of zombies, spies, and martial arts, why don't we choose a classic? That way, we can all enjoy it."

Kennedy didn't look the least bit upset. Instead, she gave an eager nod. "A musical," she announced. "I love those. So do you, Aunt Maureen."

"I certainly do." Rising, Maureen gestured toward the den. "Let's get settled and choose."

"I'll make the popcorn," Fiona offered, already on her way to the kitchen. "But I vote for *My Fair Lady.* Let me know if I win. There's no one like Audrey Hepburn, especially in those gorgeous diamonds she wears to the ball."

"No, there's not," Maureen agreed. "She's in a class by herself." Abruptly, she sucked in her breath, pausing as Kennedy headed into the den.

Claire heard her slight gasp, and somehow knew to lag behind. "What is it?" she asked.

"Audrey," Maureen replied. "That's the friend of Caitlin's I couldn't think of, the one who calls herself @mimosagirl121. I remember Caitlin telling me that she was her oldest, if not closest, friend, and that every January 21 they got together for a delicious buffet of some kind."

"Just like the amazing brunch in the photo Casey showed you." Claire's heart was pounding. "Did Caitlin ever mention Audrey's last name? Or anything else about her? A spouse? Children?"

Maureen slowly shook her head. "No. But I am sure that Caitlin brought her up to meet me one day when we had lunch." Her brow furrowed. "It seems to me that they went to school together—grade school through high school. Then, they went their separate way for college, and afterward."

"Did Audrey move away?" Claire pressed. "Because Caitlin pretty much stayed put."

"I'm not sure." A frustrated shrug. "But somehow...I did get the feeling that Audrey lived elsewhere, but not so far that they couldn't make their annual buffet happen."

"Was January 21 one of their birthdays? Is that why they had the celebration?"

A small smile touched Maureen's lips. "Funny how things come back to you. Caitlin told me they chose that date because January felt so depressing that they wanted to reprise the holidays." A pause, accompanied by an irritated sigh. "I wish I could remember more."

Claire had already whipped out her cell phone. "You've already given me more than I ever hoped for. Go in and start the movie. I need to call the office."

One of Maureen's brows rose. "Say hello to my son for me." She turned and followed Kennedy into the den.

Excitement pumped through Claire's veins as she called Ryan's cell. As expected, it took five rings for him to answer.

"Claire?" He sounded disoriented and surprised.

"Sorry, but this couldn't wait," she replied. Quickly, she recapped everything Ryan's mother had said. "Can Yoda help?"

"He sure as shit can." Ryan sounded excited now, too. "I'll have him find every Audrey in Caitlin's high school yearbook. She and Shane went to the same school, but she graduated a year after him. Once we zero in on the right Audrey, we'll track her, see if she's using a married name, etc. But this is just what we needed."

"And, Ryan, Boston is driving distance from New Rochelle, at least for an annual get-together. And every one of my instincts is screaming that that's no coincidence. I—" Claire broke off, images flashing through her head. "A cobblestone walkway. Stone structure. White shingles. Soft gray shutters. Trees all around…"

"You're describing Audrey's house," Ryan clarified. "Can you sense where it is?"

"A relatively high-end suburb." Claire frowned. "I keep seeing figs."

"Figs?" Ryan asked. "Like the fruit?"

Yoda inserted himself to clarify. "Actually, Ryan, a fig is technically an aggregate fruit lined with tiny flowers inside it."

Ryan made an impatient sound. "Fine. It doesn't matter. As long as I'm visualizing the right thing. Figs…" He sounded as confused as Claire. "Is that part of the town's name?"

"I don't think so," Claire murmured. "It's more intangible. I just don't know in what way."

"Intangible figs." Ryan tapped his fingers on the desk. "Okay, Yoda, you have another task to tackle when you track this Audrey."

"I've already begun the process," Yoda replied. "You continue to work. It is now three thirty-two on the sixteenth of March. Your time is running short. And my sensors tell me you're low on energy. May I suggest sending out for more food? You've finished your subtemperature pizza."

"Yeah, okay. Just research Audrey and figs. Right now, I'm working solo anyway…" Ryan was already back on task, not even hearing the part about food.

"I'll make the call for takeout, Yoda," Claire said through the phone. "Sustenance will be arriving shortly—and without breaking Ryan's concentration. Talk to you both later."

"If you think of anything..." Ryan murmured.

"I'll let you know."

***

Offices of Forensic Instincts
Ryan's Lair
Tribeca, Manhattan, New York
Thursday, March 16, 6:30 p.m.

Ryan was tweaking a crucial piece of software code when Yoda spoke up again.

"I apologize for interrupting, Ryan. But I have the information you were seeking regarding the specific Audrey in question."

Ryan's head shot up. "Go on, Yoda. I'm all ears."

Yoda complied. "A young woman named Audrey Melnick graduated high school with Caitlin. She met and married her husband, Douglas Harrington, after getting an engineering degree at Tufts University. The couple and their two young children reside in Newton, Massachusetts, which is an affluent suburb of Boston."

"That holds promise. Did you find anything to indicate that Caitlin and Audrey were more than just classmates?"

"I did indeed," Yoda replied. "I accessed Audrey Harrington's Instagram presence and determined that her handle is indeed @ mimosagirl121. I located the identical photo and caption that Claire described as being on Caitlin Walsh's page. Audrey's entry was more detailed, and designated January 21 as the annual date that they met—and I quote: 'to revive the holiday festivities that were lost during the January doldrums.'"

Ryan's adrenaline was running high. "Makes sense. What about Claire's visions about figs? Anything on that?"

"Indeed there is. My research indicates that the Fig Newton was the first commercially baked cookie in the United States. It originated in the late nineteenth century from the work of a Philadelphia baker and a Massachusetts-based bakery, and was named after the location Newton, Massachusetts. It became a staple in American households from then until this very day, and even has its own holiday. National Fig Newton Day is celebrated annually on January 16."

"Yess!" Ryan pumped his fist in the air. "Given what Claire told us, this information points to Newton as the suburb where Audrey lives." He paused, pursing his lips. "Although I doubt Caitlin is staying at Audrey's house. That would be too hard to explain and too disruptive for her family. Audrey would put Caitlin nearby, but in a more generic location."

"I agree," Yoda said. "So I checked further. There are two motels that are within a comfortable driving distance from Audrey's house." Yoda supplied Ryan with the names, addresses, and phone numbers of both places, as well as a list of registered guests at each.

"Great work." Ryan leaned back in his chair. "I'll take a hard look at that list. But I'd be willing to bet a month's income that Caitlin is staying at one of those places, under an assumed name."

"I'm certain you're correct. Still, I'd be negligent if I didn't point out that a bet of that caliber isn't wise. Your income here has reached a substantial level. Should you choose to share that wager with the team, I would choose something less extreme to bet."

Ryan chuckled. "You make a good point. So, even though I'm as sure as you are, I'll protect my interests by betting something smaller. However, once I make my case, I doubt anyone will take the bet. So I'll keep the original wager between you and me. This way, I can still be smug." Smile vanishing, Ryan looked back at the computer. "I can't take a break now. But I'll share this information with the team before all of us head out in the morning."

18

Offices of Forensic Instincts
Entranceway
Tribeca, Manhattan, New York
Friday, March 17, 10:30 a.m.

The FI team was clustered together, laptop cases looped over their shoulders as they waited for Casey to give the word and send them on their way.

Casey didn't have to count to know they were all there.

"Any last-minute questions or concerns?" she asked. "Cars all fueled up?"

"Nope. And yup," Marc replied. "Fortunately, we're leaving after rush hour. That gave Ryan enough time to finish and us less traffic to battle."

"Finish? Yeah, by a hair," Ryan agreed. He looked like hell, his eyes bright red and narrowed into slits after three sleepless nights, and days of concentrated hours writing software, after which he'd updated the team on Yoda's latest findings.

Claire eyed him with concern. "You're sure you can manage this part? I can do your drop after Casey and I get back from ours."

"Not on your life. This is my baby. I'm seeing it through. And I want the agents to see me at JFK. Not anyone else. Me." He managed a half smile. "But thanks, Claire-voyant. I appreciate the offer."

Emma shifted a little, frowning at her bag, which was bulging at the seams. "I didn't expect these magazines to be so heavy. There aren't that many of them."

Patrick's brows lifted. "The magazines aren't the problem. It's the two changes of clothes, the hair straightener, and the exploding makeup case I saw you cram in there that's weighing you down."

Emma made a face. "I'm female. And I'm going to the coolest of concerts. I only took the necessities—and the magazines."

Patrick's smile was nostalgic. "The necessities. Right. How many times have I heard my daughter say the same thing?"

"Well," Emma defended. "She's right."

Angela rolled her eyes. "I'm female. I'm traveling overnight. And I have the real laptop in here." She wiggled her bag. "Yet somehow I don't look like I'm heading off to fill the room at my college dorm." She gave a tolerant shrug. "Then again, I'm not in my twenties, and dancing 'til I drop at a concert."

The whole team chuckled at that one.

"Where is your roommate meeting you?" John asked Emma.

"Outside the Starbucks on Chambers Street," she replied. "This way the Feds will see me driving off from here alone. I told Brynn to put in a mobile order for two lattes and to pick them up for us both."

"Time to get moving," Ryan interrupted. "Remember, some of us have long trips and others much shorter ones. Like JFK is only a half hour from here, without traffic. And Central Park is around the corner. Those of us who have those destinations have the sheer joy of leading the BU on a wild goose chase before they reach their drop sites. Claire, you and Casey go out for a nice long brunch—carrying your cases with you. Do some boutique shopping if Casey has the strength. I'll stop at a bunch of high-tech stores to check out the latest and the greatest equipment. Then, I'll grab some food and dessert along the way, maybe even hang out at the airport long enough to study upcoming flights. Who knows where I might be traveling to? Inquiring minds will want to know."

That last statement seemed to amuse him.

"Men never grow up," Claire muttered.

"Maybe. But this man is creative, right?" Ryan winked at her, then grew serious. "Just remember, we'll all be doing our drops at four o'clock on the dot. That's what's important. Even though we're all creating smokescreens, I need Angela to reach the bar at the precise appointed hour."

"And I will," Angela replied. As she spoke, she eased her way to the front door, then turned to face the whole team. "Now for the job I joined FI to do. Each of you will place a dollar in my hand as you walk out. You'll then be covered by attorney-client privilege in the event the FBI gets snarky and pushes you for answers. I've already met with our outside counsel and provided them with my own dollar bill. So all holes are officially closed up."

The entire team stared at her, then threw back their heads in laughter.

"Resourceful, as well as brilliant," Casey said, pulling a dollar bill out of her laptop bag and pressing it into Angela's palm. "I knew you'd be a great addition to the team. Glad I listened to my instincts."

"Me, too." Angela grinned. "You wanted the best? Well, you got her."

Emma made a whining sound. "I don't do cash. Can I Venmo you instead?"

Casey rolled her eyes, pulled out another single, and handed it to Emma to officially present to Angela. "Here, Emma, I've got it. You can owe me toward my next cup of coffee."

Utter relief flashed across Emma's face. "Thanks so much. I'll do one better than a partial coffee. I'll buy you the whole cup—make that a latte. And a croissant, too."

"Sweet," Ryan said as he and the others—Emma included—gave their singles over to Angela. "How do I score that deal?"

"You don't," Emma replied with a smug smile. "It's for VIPs only."

Chuckling, Angela waited until everyone's single was in her hand. Then, she stuffed the money into the front pocket of her laptop case. "Okay then, we're all set—and fully protected."

With a lingering grin, Casey opened the front door. "Let's hit the road."

***

Mickey's Tavern
101 Guinness Way
Boston, Massachusetts
Friday, March 17, 3:56 p.m.

Angela walked the half block from the parking garage where she'd left her car, down Guinness Way, and to her destination. Rather than her customary upscale attire, she was dressed to fit into the crowd, wearing jeans and a cable-knit sweater, with a down jacket on top to keep out the winter cold. And no fast-paced Manhattan stride; just a casual step.

There were a fair number of people—mostly under twenty-five—strolling along the sidewalk, but not nearly as many as would show up later, when the masses of college kids descended to party hearty. That was fine. She'd be long gone and eating dinner with her sister by then.

Slinging her laptop bag higher on her shoulder, she approached the brick building with the tall windows and the wood shingle hanging overhead with an illuminated sign that read "Mickey's." She paused two buildings away, subtly scanning the area to see if any law enforcement was hanging around, and also to make sure there were enough people near the bar to hide her from view, but not so many as to make her stand out.

All good. She could even see the requisite trash can—now a decorative piece of pottery with flowers lining the rim.

She stifled her grin, along with the urge to stop directly in front of the bar and take a photo for Ryan. Definitely not the dumpster he'd remembered.

Sensing the minutes pass, she wriggled the sleeve of her jacket high up enough so she could check her Apple Watch. Three fifty-nine. She waited patiently until the numbers moved to four-zero-zero.

Then she moved.

She unzipped her bag as she walked, easing the black bubble mailing envelope out and into her hand. Never slowing or stopping, she walked past the tavern, letting the package drop into the trash can and continuing on her way. She paused once—at the street corner—to see if there was any sign she'd been noticed.

Everything continued to unfold as it had been, without a single pair of eyes looking her way.

Job successfully completed.

She couldn't help herself. She took out her cell phone, pretending to scan her email like everyone else was doing. Subtly, she aimed her phone and took a quick photo of the trash can.

She'd send it to Ryan when she got back to her car.

***

JFK Airport
Queens, New York
Friday, March 17, 4:10 p.m.

Ryan had been intently studying the computerized flight schedule on the wall in front of him for the past ten minutes—ever since he'd dropped his parcel into a nearby trash can. Now, he turned, brow furrowed as if contemplating where he'd be flying to next. But not today. Today he was ready to go collect his Corvette and head back to the FI brownstone.

The trill of an arriving text message sounded.

Praying that there'd been no problems, he pulled out his cell and opened the message as he walked:

> *A souvenir of the modern-day version of your oldie but goodie. Very classy. Now very full.*
> *See you tomorrow.*

Eyeing the photo, Ryan threw back his head and laughed.

***

Mickey's Tavern
101 Guinness Way
Boston, Massachusetts
Friday, March 17, 4:12 p.m.

Her hood pulled over her head, she carried her purse out of the bar, where she'd spent less than five minutes. She gulped down the remainder of her beer, then crushed the empty can she'd requested. Rather than tossing it into the trash, she leaned over, dropped both her purse and the empty can inside, muttering a curse under her breath as if the purse had fallen by accident. With utter distaste, she bent over, and groped inside the trash, shuddering with revulsion as she did.

A moment later, she straightened with a relieved smile, having retrieved both her purse and the bubble-wrapped envelope that had been waiting for her.

No one had so much as looked her way.

Satisfied, she walked off.

19

The McKay Residence
East 236th Street
Woodlawn, Bronx, New York
Friday, March 17, 5:24 p.m.

Inside the house, a rousing game of charades was taking place.

Kennedy was winning the Irish performers segment of the game, while Colin had cleaned up on the Irish history part, and the rest of the family—other than Maureen, who was busily cooking—was clamoring for a change in topic.

"How about Celtic jewelry?" Fiona suggested.

Her brothers rolled their eyes.

"Yeah, right," Nolan said. "I wonder who that topic would give the edge to. I vote for Irish laws enacted in the current century."

"Great idea," Garret concurred.

"No it's not," Maureen called out from the kitchen. "Let Kennedy choose. At least she'll play fair. Something that puts you all on even footing. Like Irish cooking through the ages."

The whole family threw back their heads and howled with laughter.

***

Friday, March 17, 5:35 p.m.

Six blocks away from the McKay residence, the stolen Con Edison truck drove down the street and parked alongside a utility pole. A black sedan with two passengers passed by. The driver of the sedan stuck his hand out the window and gave a mock salute to the two guys in the truck. After that, he made a turn, and he and his partner continued on their way toward the McKay house—passing it and going on to park on a back street behind their house, so as not to be spotted. Although they'd checked beforehand, as had their counterparts. There were no security cameras in the vicinity. And the clusters of trees hid them from view.

The guy in the passenger seat pulled out his walkie-talkie, pressed the button, and said: "We're in position."

The guys in the utility truck acted on cue. While one of them stayed put as a lookout, the driver got out, opened the back of the truck, and removed the requisite traffic cones, placing them in front and back of the vehicle. It looked like a normal utility emergency.

Except it wasn't.

He climbed up on top of the truck, got into the bucket, and manipulated the hydraulics to raise himself up to the transformer. That done, he placed the small explosive device with a remote detonator next to the transformer and took some black electrical tape, strapping it into place.

Job completed, he lowered the bucket and locked the mechanism into place. He climbed down to the pavement, and while his associate collected the traffic cones, he examined the transmitter to make sure communication was properly established with the explosive device.

Success.

He turned and called out to his colleague, "We're finished here." Both men jumped into the car. The driver maneuvered the truck slowly down the street away from the booby-trapped transformer—and in the opposite direction of the McKay house.

When he was a far enough distance away, he pressed the triggering button.

The transformer exploded, plunging the neighborhood into an eerie darkness.

***

Inside the McKay house, everyone reacted at once.

The family abandoned the St. Patrick's Day charades, Maureen hurried out of the kitchen, and Kennedy ran to her.

Purposely retaining his composure, Colin rose. "It's just a power outage," he assured all of them.

"But there's no storm or wind," Maureen protested, drawing Kennedy close.

"I know." Colin shrugged offhandedly. "But an electrical wire might have gone down. Or it could be half a dozen other explanations I'm not qualified to make. I'm sure ConEd will fix it and the power will come on soon."

"I hope so," Kennedy murmured, her eyes huge. "I hate blackouts."

Maureen's arms closed around her great-niece. "I know, lovey. I hate them, too. But the good news is that the whole family is together and we still have some daylight, not to mention lots of flashlights, to help keep the celebration going."

Kennedy's eyes teared up. "But we're not all together. Ryan hasn't gotten here yet."

"He's on his way; I'm sure of it." Maureen spoke with utter conviction. "He promised he'd be here by dinner. And he will be."

A knock at the door broke into the conversation.

"Mrs. McKay?" a male voice called. "It's Agent Winston. Is everything in there all right?"

Garret walked over and opened the door to one of the agents who'd been assigned to safeguard Kennedy. "We're fine. Thanks for checking."

"No problem." On instinct, the agent glanced quickly at Kennedy and, satisfied that she was safe, spoke to the adults in the room. "I've called Con Edison. Apparently, a whole section of your neighborhood is affected by this outage. They're on their way to find out what caused it. Stay calm and this should be cleared up quickly. I'll remain inside with you, just as a precaution."

"We'd appreciate that, sir," Nolan said.

***

As Special Agent Winston was assuring the McKays of their safety, the final part of the intruders' plan was unfolding.

The passenger from the idling black sedan pulled on his gloves and slid out of the car, his few supplies packed in a small duffel bag. He slung the bag over his shoulder and, squatting low, he made his way to Maureen's backyard. There, he cut a hole in the backyard chain-link fence, pulled back the wire, and, gripping his duffel, crawled into the backyard and up toward the back door. He continued to stay down so no one inside—including the FBI agent who'd run in to make sure all was well during the blackout—would see him.

He reached the porch.

There, he worked quickly and silently. He unpacked the contents of his bag, which included a mason jar with homemade napalm in it and a gasoline-soaked rag. He was a pro. He knew that napalm made a great incendiary device because it was like a gel and stuck to the surface it struck.

He yanked a lighter out of his pocket, lit the rag, and stuffed it into the mason jar. He then threw the jar against the house. The jar broke, shattering glass across the porch and all over the back of the house. Both the wood porch and the clapboard siding burst into flames.

Leaving the place in a blaze, he took off before he could be seen. As he ran, once again squatting low, he used his burner phone to call the great-aunt's cell. Even from outside, he could see mass pandemonium breaking out inside the house.

It took a long time before the woman answered. "Hello?" She sounded quite hysterical, and he could hear the FBI's voices as they ushered the family out of the house through the front door. "Is this the fire department? Are you on your way?"

"Just a reminder that we can get to the little girl" was all he said before disconnecting the burner and flinging it as far as he could into the woods.

***

Maureen let out a scream, dropping her cell phone and falling to her knees.

"Come on, ma'am," SA Winston said, urging her to her feet and leading her outside to the front lawn. "We've got to evacuate." By now, his counterpart had joined him in his task, as had the FI security team, who'd notified the fire department, and the EMTs, and was helping the FBI make sure that no one was severely burned or had endured extreme smoke inhalation.

On the front lawn, Colin reached his wife's side as sirens of all kinds began to screech toward the house.

"Maureen?" He wrapped an arm around her shoulders as she wept uncontrollably, her hands covering her face, and her whole body shaking. "My God, what is it? Are you hurt?"

"That phone call… Kennedy…" Her head came up and she frantically searched for her great-niece, her eyes closing in relief when she saw that Kennedy was wrapped in Fiona's arms. Thank God her daughter understood that a conversation was being held that Kennedy should not be exposed to.

"Tell me," Colin commanded. "Why did you scream like that? Who was on the phone?"

Maureen repeated what the man had said. "I should have known…the fire department wouldn't have called my cell phone…"

Colin's jaw tightened so much it looked as if it might snap.

He turned, summoning Agent Winston with a wave of his hand.

"Yes, sir." Winston was by their sides in an instant. "Is your wife hurt?"

"Not physically." Maureen spoke for herself, although her voice kept breaking. "But that phone call…"

"I saw your reaction. Who was it and what did they say?"

Maureen told him, conveying what had occurred to both him and to Garrison Miles, the Forensic Instincts security expert who'd also reached her side.

"We'll have many questions," Agent Winston said. "But they can wait until things calm down. One of our agents is already searching the area to see if there is any suspicious activity going on." He stopped short of elaborating.

But Maureen understood. "Thank you," she whispered. "This nightmare never ends. It just keeps getting worse."

As she spoke, Garrison turned to one of his FI counterparts. "Stay with Kennedy," he instructed him as another FBI agent strode over to do the same. "Let's let the firefighters and medical professionals come through."

The fire truck had already stopped, and firefighters were leaping out, rushing around to the back of the house to extinguish the blaze before it could rage out of control. EMTs were climbing out of their mini ambulance, going from person to person to help in any way they were needed.

Ryan's Corvette screeched to a halt at the curb, and he and Claire were out of the car almost before it stopped moving.

"What the fuck?" he exploded, shoving his way onto the scene and trying to take everything—and everyone—in all at once.

"Ryan!" It was Kennedy who spotted him first. She was shaking and weeping, cringing in Fiona's arms. But when she saw Ryan, she leaped to her feet and practically flew over to him. "The flames were tall. I was so scared. First the blackout. Then the crash. And then the fire."

Ryan held her to him, then squatted down, scrutinizing every inch of her. "Sunshine, are you hurt?" He'd heard every detail she'd provided. "Did you get burned or inhale lots of smoke?"

She shook her head, gripping his forearms. "I think the agents and your security guys got us all out in time. And the fire is back there." She pointed. "We were in the front of the house when it started."

An EMT appeared beside them. "Sweetie, I need to check you out," he told Kennedy. "Just for a minute."

Kennedy refused to release Ryan. "This is my uncle. He has to come with me."

"No problem." The EMT gestured for Ryan to follow and guided Kennedy over to the medical van, where he did a few routine tests. "All good," he said with a smile. "You were stronger than the fire."

Ryan was gazing around, like a wolf scenting danger. At the same time, he heaved a sigh of relief when he saw Claire at his mother's side. His mom was weeping and gesturing about, obviously filling Claire in on what had occurred. Well, there was no one better to confide in.

Turning, he grabbed his brother Garret's arm as he exited the mini ambulance with a clean bill of health.

"Can you tell me if everyone is safe?" Ryan asked.

"We sure are." Garret squeezed Ryan's shoulder, speaking guardedly since Kennedy was hanging on to his every word. "We McKays are a tough bunch. It takes a lot more than a porch fire to bring us down."

"Thanks," Ryan said, once again, awash with relief. "You go take it easy."

Holding Kennedy's hand, Ryan went over to his parents, opening his mouth to speak just as the firefighters came around front, their equipment turned off.

"We used chemical fire extinguishers to put out the fire," one of them said, looking troubled as he spoke—probably because he guessed what the fire marshal would determine, given the absolute evidence of an incendiary device. A broken glass jar. A gel that stuck to the siding of the house that was obviously napalm. There was no explanation other than arson.

He continued speaking. “The fire ate up the entire porch, and the back of the house and roof overhang have severe fire damage. The rest of the house is fine.” He cleared his throat. “The fire marshal has been notified and is on his way.”

“We understand,” Colin replied, knowing full well what the firefighter was implying.

The firefighter was looking about, taking in the number of family members assembled on the lawn. “You and your family are going to need major construction for the repairs. It’ll be tough to live here. It’s your choice whether you do or whether you stay elsewhere while it’s done.”

Ryan didn’t miss a beat. “Dad, you, Mom, and Kennedy are coming with Claire and me to Forensic Instincts. There’s more than enough room at the brownstone for all of you. You’ll be comfortable, and you’ll be safe.”

Neither of the FBI agents protested, although Ryan was sure they wanted to. A nice motel would be more to their liking than moving in with the pain-in-the-ass investigators.

Well, tough.

Maureen clearly agreed. “We can come back for our things when it’s safe,” she said. “For now, we’ll go with you.”

Nolan was standing nearby. “I’ll drive everyone but Claire and Ryan, who came on their own. Besides, a toothpick could barely squeeze its way into Ryan’s Corvette.”

“Good.” Ryan nodded. This was the best possible solution. Everyone safe and accounted for. And the reunion between Kennedy and Caitlin could take place in his lair. “Nolan, your CRV has a hell of a lot more room in it. Plus, there's a spare booster seat for Kennedy stored in your trunk. Claire and I will lead the way."

With that, Ryan turned to SA Winston. "You're welcome to call and arrange a visit to the FI brownstone, where you can ask any questions of my family you need to. But that will have to wait. They're shaken and in shock. We're leaving now."

He didn't wait for a reply.

20

Offices of Forensic Instincts
First Floor, Library
Tribeca, Manhattan, New York
Friday, March 17, 6:15 p.m.

Casey wasn't surprised when she heard the pounding at the door. She'd been expecting it. After what FI had pulled today, in conjunction with the fire at the McKays' that Claire had called and filled her in on, this scene was going to be ugly.

Thankfully, there was no one at the office other than her to deal with the explosion when it came—her and Hero, who was stretched out on the library floor beside the sofa where Casey had been relaxing. Given how long the team knew this day was going to be, and how insistent Casey was about staying in her office, she and Claire had stopped at Casey and Hutch's apartment after their drop and brought Hero back to the brownstone so he could have company and spend the remainder of the day with Casey.

With a slight wince, Casey rose from the library sofa. She'd pushed herself to the max, and she was feeling it. Silencing Claire's protests, she'd carried her laptop case throughout their brunch and boutique shopping—right up to the moment when they dropped it in the Central Park trash bin. And, after all that walking and carrying, man, was she feeling it now.

Keeping her gait as normal as possible, she walked to the front door—Hero by her side—unlocked it, and pulled it open.

"Hello," she said to her husband.

Hutch blew by her, a vein throbbing at his temple, the blazing look in his eyes one he never used on her—not until now.

"What the fuck did you think you were doing?" he blasted, staring straight into Casey's eyes. "Something illegal? Something you should have told us about? Because I've reached my limit."

Casey raised her chin, refusing to back down. "We had errands to run," she replied. "I'm sorry if that offended you."

Hutch sucked in a breath, visibly trying to bring himself under control. "I'm not laughing, Casey. In fact, I'm dead serious. So answer me. Why did you and your team all march out of here with laptop cases, only to split up and head for parts unknown?"

"Your agents are following us? I suppose I should be flattered."

Hutch's entire body went rigid. "Don't bait me. It will only backfire. And you don't want that. Now answer me."

"Not without my attorney present," she replied.

"Your attorney?" Hutch sounded incredulous. "Angela? Who's in just as much trouble as the rest of you are? Not a wise contact; you're only digging yourself in deeper."

"I'm just protecting myself and my team."

"Speaking of your team..." Hutch glanced around. "Anyone back yet? Other than you, and Ryan and Claire, who I know are at the McKay house dealing with a suspicious fire that you'd better not be poking around about. Goddammit, we're trying to solve two serious interconnected crimes. And you're undercutting us at every turn, blatantly impeding a federal investigation. Well, that's over now."

Casey went very still. "Is that a threat of some kind?"

"You're damn right it is—one I'm prepared to carry out." Hutch's lips thinned into a tight, angry line. "As of this moment, Forensic Instincts is restricted from any investigation into the murder of Shane Walsh, or the disappearance of Caitlin Walsh. If I have reason to believe you're ignoring my directive, I won't hesitate to go to the US attorney's office and have them bring you up on charges. *All* of you, Angela included. So be prepared."

Casey actually did a double-take. "What did you say?"

Hutch's expression didn't change. "You heard me. And you shouldn't be surprised. I warned you it would come to this if you kept walking the path you were headed down. You ignored me. Time for consequences."

Casey's strength was ebbing, and fast. Her head was throbbing, her abdomen was hurting, and her body was shaky and weak. As subtly as she could, she leaned against the wall for support. She couldn't give in to weakness, not now. She had to defuse this situation before her team and her company were in real trouble.

She should have realized Hutch's eagle eye wouldn't miss a thing.

It was as if the red haze abruptly cleared from his head. He frowned, eyeing Casey in an entirely different way. "You're white as a ghost. You're also weaving on your feet and in visible pain, that's how much this marathon day took out of you. The car service is outside. Go home. Now. Take Hero. I'll be working at the field office all night anyway."

"No thanks." Casey fought with her last ounce of strength. "I'll stay here in my old bedroom. You've issued your edict. Now, please leave."

"Casey, your old bedroom is four flights up. You're in no condition to tackle that." Instinctively, he reached for her.

Casey backed away. "Don't even bother playing the devoted husband," she said. "I'm not interested. I want my privacy. And I do need to eat something and lie down. I'll pass your directive on to my team tonight, as soon as I wake up. *Good night*, SSA Hutchinson."

***

Offices of Forensic Instincts
Tribeca, Manhattan, New York
Friday, March 17, 8:05 p.m.

Casey had walked back to the library, where she'd sunk down onto the leather sofa, swallowed one of the sandwiches she'd ordered, and then forced herself to lie down.

She'd rested her body, but her mind was wide awake. Hutch had been distracted by her physical discomfort. But he wasn't finished with his interrogation. He'd want to know more about the laptop cases—what was in them and where they were going. And there was just so long she could put him off before supplying answers.

Rather than fighting her anger, she'd spent her resting time tamping down on it, and ordering herself to think rationally, to work through what had to be done next.

Unfortunately, she knew just what that had to be. She wouldn't jeopardize her company or her team, and she couldn't count on Angela being able to defend this away. It was impossible.

Time to back off, work behind the scenes, and achieve their goal through channels only they knew about. She was still playing with fire, and she knew it. But there was no other way.

"Our guests have arrived," Yoda broke the silence to announce.

"Thanks, Yoda."

Rising, Casey fought a wave of dizziness, determined to push through the rest of this night's drama before dragging herself up to bed. A lot had happened, and there was still a lot more to come.

She waited for the lightheadedness to pass, collected her strength, and made her way into the foyer, watching as Ryan opened the door and stepped inside, empty laptop case in tow.

"Hey, boss," he greeted her, looking on the verge of collapse himself. He led Maureen, Colin, Kennedy, and Nolan inside.

"Hey back." With that, Casey turned and walked over to Maureen, grasped the older woman's hands in hers. "I'm so sorry for what you went through. I readied everything for the three of you to settle in. We've got a guest room on the third floor with a queen-size sofa bed and more than enough room for a foldaway." She gave Kennedy a gentle smile. "Hi, sweetie."

The little girl was huddled between Maureen and Claire, her face streaked with tears, her eyes wide with shock. "Hi," she managed. "Thank you for not making us stay at the house."

"Of course not. We want all of you here."

Colin stepped forward, extended his hand to shake hers. "Ms. Woods, I'm Colin McKay. I can't tell you how much we appreciate your hospitality. Under the circumstances…" His voice broke. "Just thank you."

Casey shook his hand. "Don't thank me. And please call me Casey. As I'm sure you've guessed, we're very informal here." A slight smile curved her lips. "Ryan resembles you. So does Fiona."

Colin smiled back. "I'll take the credit for their coloring and Ryan's height. But, thankfully, Fiona is a lot prettier than I am. And call me Colin; we're also informal."

"Consider it done," Casey replied.

"Hi," Nolan said, stepping forward and introducing himself. He also had his father's height and striking features, but his coloring was more like his mom's. "I'm just the chauffeur tonight. But I also appreciate your kindness. I'm the eldest of the McKay kids, and tonight I'm feeling my age."

They all chuckled—a tense chuckle, but one that felt good after all that had happened.

Casey gestured toward the library. "I'm sure you're all exhausted. But you have to eat. So I ordered in a tray of sandwiches, there's coffee and tea in the kitchen, and our fridge is stocked with beer, soda, and bottled water." Her eyes twinkled as she directed her gaze at Kennedy. "And, as it happens, a tray of cookies arrived with the sandwiches. They need to be eaten. Do I have any volunteers?"

This time, Kennedy smiled. "I'll volunteer. Thank you very much."

Claire was studying Casey intently, clearly disturbed by what she saw. She moved forward to take charge.

"Food sounds great, Casey," she said, urging everyone into the library. "I'll do the serving. As things stand, we didn't have the chance to enjoy Maureen's famous corn beef and cabbage."

"But you will," Maureen assured her as they all sat down. "I'll pick up the ingredients locally and make tomorrow night's dinner right here."

"If that doesn't lift our spirits, I don't know what will," Colin said, squeezing his wife's shoulder.

Ryan was already reaching for the tray of sandwiches. "I'm eating," he announced. "After all that drama, I'm starved."

His mother's brows rose. "Aren't you always?"

Nolan helped himself to a sandwich, as well. "It runs in the family," he announced, chuckling as Hero adhered himself to his side and waited until Nolan gave him a slice of fresh bread.

"This is Hero, by the way," Ryan introduced him. "He's a former FBI human scent evidence dog with the best olfactory sense ever. He's an official member of the FI team."

Kennedy approached shyly. "Is he friendly?"

"When he's not on duty, he's a big baby," Ryan replied. "He loves belly rubs. So feel free to pet him."

Kennedy went over and did just that. Within minutes, she and Hero were fast friends, and Ryan was grateful to divert her anxiety for a while.

They all ate and chatted, purposely avoiding any talk of the disaster they'd left behind.

Ryan was clearly restless. Even as he wolfed down food, he kept glancing at his watch, and shifting around in his chair.

"I hate to be rude," Casey said to the entire room. "But may I borrow Ryan for a few minutes?"

Maureen didn't look surprised. "As long as you return him, help yourself."

Another shared laugh.

Casey led Ryan into the first-floor conference room. As Ryan crossed the threshold, his cell phone buzzed, and he looked down at it to see a Slack message from Casey to the entire team, calling for a midnight Zoom meeting.

He gazed at her quizzically, perching at the edge of a tub chair while Casey shut the door behind them.

"What's going on? Something else is clearly wrong."

Casey blew out a breath, then spilled out the whole situation.

"Shit," Ryan said when she'd finished. "What do we do now? I have to take Kennedy down to my lair and let her talk to Caitlin. But if I do, I'll be blatantly defying Hutch's orders."

"Technically not. Remember, you programmed the laptops and we made the drops before Hutch reined us in," Casey responded.

"That's true. But we're not stopping now. There's no fucking way I'm letting the Bureau know about the laptops, or worse, surrendering them—not after all I did to make this happen." Ryan gave a defiant shake of his head. "We're talking to Caitlin—hopefully on a regular basis—and solving this case, all of which is taking place *after* Hutch shut us down. So what do you suggest?"

Casey perched at the edge of the settee. "As you just saw, I set up a full-team Zoom meeting for midnight. We all need to get on the same page. But before that, you and I need to talk—and it's got to be before you take Kennedy down to your lair to connect up with Caitlin."

Ryan nodded. "I'm listening."

"Bottom line? We have to get as much information out of Caitlin as we can, while warning her *not* to tell us her exact location. That way we still won't know for certain where she's hiding. So at least we're not withholding that crucial piece of information from the FBI."

"Nuances. I get it. Iffy, but okay." Ryan's mind was still racing. "Problem is, we're not calling a halt to things. So we'll still be keeping major investigative findings from Hutch."

"So we have to make sure he doesn't know that." Casey paused. "We're walking a fine line and I know it. One wrong move and we're history. I'm calling our outside counsel in the morning. But, that aside, this puts you in the shittiest position. Because you'll be the only one who actually speaks to Caitlin."

Ryan waved that away. "Yeah, but the whole team will act on what she tells me—even if it is behind closed doors. So we're all taking a huge risk." He didn't miss a beat. "If you're asking, I'm willing if you are."

"I'll do whatever is necessary to solve this case," Casey replied. "Personally, for you, and, professionally, for FI. We see the cases that are brought to us to a successful conclusion, and we don't back down. Period."

"I hear you." Ryan still looked troubled. "But what about tonight's call between Kennedy and Caitlin? Kennedy is going to have a million questions—and she's going to beg to talk to her mom again. Caitlin will be smart about what she tells her. Still, there's the FBI. How do we protect Kennedy from them?"

Casey had been prepared for this complication. "The FBI has already interviewed Kennedy. They won't put her through that again. And we're sure as hell not going to tip our hand. It's up to you to make Kennedy understand the need for secrecy, and for keeping conversation with the agents vague and brief. Claire will help you find a way. You'll keep her close to your mom and to you. She can't be left alone with them at all, and their focus should be on protecting her, not questioning her."

"And now? How do Caitlin and I get into what's really going down with Kennedy there?"

"Let Kennedy and Caitlin have their reunion. Then, just explain to Kennedy that there's some investigative stuff you have to talk to her mommy about alone. Kennedy's a very bright child. She'll get it, and she'll accept it. As long as she knows she can talk to Caitlin again, she'll be fine. I'll send Claire down to the lair to bring her upstairs while you and Caitlin talk details."

Casey glanced at her watch. "It's almost nine o'clock. You'd better get moving. Poor Kennedy is falling off her feet and you owe it to her to give her the St. Patrick's Day surprise she's praying for."

Ryan nodded, hesitated, and then spoke up. "I don't mean to butt in, but you're falling off your feet, too, boss. Not to mention I can see you're in pain. Stay in here and rest. Claire's got the hostess routine down pat. I'll text her when it's time to collect Kennedy. But for now, I'm bringing her downstairs for a reunion with her mommy." His lips curved. "Yoda will wake you up at eleven forty-five—enough time for me to catch you up on what happened, and then to have our team Zoom meeting. Right, Yoda?"

"Duly noted, Ryan," Yoda replied. "Eleven forty-five on the dot."

Reluctantly, Casey nodded, sinking back against the cushions of the settee. "You're right." Her eyes were half-closed. "My reserves are shot. But, Yoda, you'd better wake me."

"I intend to, Casey. Like Ryan, I'm not interested in losing my job."

Ryan chuckled as he shut the door behind him.

21

Offices of Forensic Instincts
Library, First Floor
Tribeca, Manhattan, New York
Friday, March 17, 9:05 p.m.

Everyone looked up when Ryan reentered the room.

"Where's Casey?" his mother asked.

"She's out for the count," Ryan responded with total candor. "She pushed herself pretty hard today. I talked her into taking a nap. Claire and I will take over as host and hostess."

"That's nonsense." Maureen stood, wrapping an arm around Kennedy's shoulders as the little girl rose, as well. "Poor Casey went through a near-death experience, one she's still recovering from. I feel terrible that we're imposing."

"You're not," Claire jumped in quickly. "I'll show you to the guest room upstairs, and bring in that cot for Kennedy. It's been a draining night, to say the least. Everyone needs sleep."

With that, Nolan downed the rest of his Diet Coke, set down the empty can, and shrugged back into his parka. "I've got to get going myself. I want to check in with the NYFD and law enforcement, and then head home for some shut-eye. But I'll call you guys tomorrow," he told his parents.

"See that you do." Maureen assessed him with a mother's eye. "I want to hear that you're safe, and anything you find out from the fire department, the police, or the FBI."

Nolan shot off a salute. "You got it, Mom." He gave Claire a grateful look and ruffled Kennedy's hair. "Good night, all."

As Nolan headed for the door, Ryan and Claire exchanged a quick glance.

"Maureen, is it okay if Kennedy stays up for just a little while longer?" Claire asked. "Ryan needs to spend a bit more time with her. I promise to bring her upstairs to bed the minute they're done."

Maureen pursed her lips, glancing from Claire to Ryan, to Kennedy's curious face.

"No questions and no answers, Mom," Ryan said quietly. "Not yet."

Hope filled Maureen's eyes, and she gave him a quick nod. "That's fine. Dad and I will go upstairs with Claire and settle in." She gave Kennedy a hug. "Are you okay with that, lovey?"

Kennedy nodded. "I'm not sure I understand, but as long as Ryan is with me, I'll be fine."

"Great." Ryan walked over and slung his arm around Kennedy's shoulders. "Let's go downstairs and talk in my lair."

Her nose wrinkled up. "Aren't lairs for lions?"

Ryan grinned. "Yeah, and for guys who need a private man cave to work in."

"So you hibernate. That makes you more like a bear than a lion," she pointed out.

Laughter rumbled in Ryan's chest. "Nice analysis. Pretty accurate, too." He eased Kennedy toward the stairwell leading downstairs. "Okay, sunshine, let's make this happen."

They climbed down the flight of stairs, and Ryan led Kennedy into his private work arena.

"This is where your genius uncle makes things happen," he informed her, opening his arms wide to let her into his world.

Kennedy's eyes were huge as her gaze swept the room. "Wow. So much—stuff. Computer stuff. Gym stuff. A cool wobbly chair. A comfy couch. And a pile of weird thingies in the middle."

Ryan chuckled. "Those 'thingies' are my experiments. Different-sized and different-programmed robots that could end up being awesome or end up being trashed."

Kennedy wrinkled her nose. "You might be a genius, but you're also a hoarder." She turned her insightful gaze up to his. "Why are we down here? I mean the real reason?"

Ryan grew serious, and he squatted down in front of Kennedy, placing both hands on her shoulders.

"I have a surprise for you. A wonderful surprise. But you must, *must* promise to keep it between us. No one—not even the rest of our family—can know about it. It's crucial that you follow that rule, otherwise the surprise can be taken away, and the situation can blow up in our faces. Okay?"

Kennedy had paled, but she didn't question him, only nodded.

"Good." With that, Ryan rose, taking Kennedy's hand and leading her over to his desk, where his own laptop had been shoved to a side, and a different, brand-new-looking laptop sat in its place. "Sit," he said gently, waiting until Kennedy had complied before he pulled over a second chair, took a seat beside her.

Kennedy seemed to sense that something meaningful was about to happen, because her shoulders straightened and her breathing got faster.

"It's okay," Ryan assured her. "It's all good—I promise."

"Okay." Kennedy nodded again.

Ryan reached past her and turned on the System76. He waited for it to whir to life and the screen to light up. Then, he logged in and began pressing a whole series of keys.

Finally, he relaxed his shoulders, ruffled Kennedy's hair, and hit one final key.

"For you, sunshine," he said, sitting back in his chair.

The screen went dark for an instant, and when it came on again, Caitlin was sitting on the opposite side of the screen. At the sight of her daughter, she pressed her hand to her heart, and her eyes filled with tears. "Hi, baby," she managed.

Kennedy gasped, her hands flying to her mouth. "Mommy?" she whispered. Then a loud, deeply emotional sob. "Mommy!"

Both of them were crying now, and Kennedy reached out to touch the screen. "Is that really you?"

Caitlin placed her own hand on her screen, touching Kennedy's as if they were truly together. "Only if it's really you."

Not only was Kennedy sobbing, she was shaking to the point where Ryan got up and wrapped a blanket around her shoulders.

Kennedy glanced at her uncle, as if suddenly remembering he was in the room. "You did this."

"Not without your mommy's help, I didn't."

Kennedy nodded, visibly still in shock as she turned back to her mother. She sucked in a harsh breath. "You're alive. You're okay. Why aren't you home? Did that monster hurt you? Threaten you enough to scare you away?" She inhaled sharply again, not even pausing for an answer. "Mommy, he killed Daddy."

For a brief instant, Caitlin's eyes squeezed shut. Just as quickly, they reopened, tears wetting her lashes. "I know, baby. And I'm so, so sorry. Daddy loved you so much. I love you so much. We're going to miss Daddy forever. But we're also going to make it. You'll see." Her gaze shifted to Ryan. "From the bottom of my heart, thank you. There aren't words…"

"No need to search for any." Ryan's eyes were also damp. "Besides, as I said to Kennedy, I didn't do this on my own. You made it possible." He forced a smile. "Your genius might even rival mine."

Still standing, he shifted away from the screen, speaking softly to Kennedy. "I'm going to head over to my bench to work out so I keep in shape. While I'm doing that, you can talk to your mommy alone. But, sunshine, afterward I'm going to need some talk time with her, too. When that happens, Claire will bring you up to bed. It's late and you must get some sleep. Aunt Maureen and Uncle Colin will be right there in the room with you."

He saw Kennedy's terrified expression, and, correctly interpreting it, he squeezed her hands. "You'll be able to talk to Mommy again, and not just once. You have my word. All I ask is that you follow her lead. Don't ask her where she is, because she can't tell you. And let her set the boundaries—for all our sakes. Promise?"

"Promise." Kennedy was still staring at Caitlin's face. "How did you know we'd be in Uncle Ryan's workroom now to talk to you?" she asked her.

"I didn't." Caitlin dashed the tears off her cheeks. "But I knew we'd talk tonight. So I sat here and waited. This way, you and I wouldn't miss a minute together."

"Oh, Mommy..." Kennedy couldn't stop saying her name or stem her tears.

Gently, Ryan brushed his thumbs over her cheeks, stroking away the wetness. "Have a great reunion."

He headed off to bench press and to give them time and space.

***

Still staring at Caitlin as if she might somehow vanish, Kennedy couldn't help but ask the fundamental questions, even though she was desperate to savor every single minute of their time together.

"Why?" Her lips trembled. "Why is all this happening? Why did—"

"Listen to me, sweetie," Caitlin interrupted. "Like Uncle Ryan said, I can't answer most of your questions—not yet. But he and his team are amazing. They'll figure this out. And once the animals responsible for this are caught, I'll be home in the blink of an eye, and we'll be together."

Animal*s*. Kennedy didn't miss her mommy's use of the plural.

"More than one person did this?"

"Yes," Caitlin said honestly. "Only one of them shot Daddy. But there are others. That's why I'm not home yet and why you need to be protected." An anxious pause as Caitlin scrutinized her daughter's face. "You're okay, right? Ryan's company has security watching you?"

Kennedy nodded. "Yes, tons of it. So does the FBI. And Aunt Maureen is always there with me. The rest of the family—especially Uncle Ryan—are over a lot. I'm never alone." She hesitated, visibly torn, trying not to upset her mother.

Leaning forward slightly, Caitlin asked, "What is it, baby?"

The dam burst. “I’m staying at Uncle Ryan’s office tonight. So are Aunt Maureen and Uncle Colin. There was a fire at their house a few hours ago. Uncle Ryan brought us here.”

Caitlin paled, although she didn’t looked shocked. She’d seen and heard enough via Kennedy’s locket, even if what she’d heard had been muddied by activity. “What kind of fire? A kitchen fire?”

Kennedy shook her head. “No. A backyard fire. The porch. The back of the house. I heard the firefighters talking. I got the feeling they didn’t think it was an accident. But we’re all fine,” she hurried on to say.

“Oh, God.” Again, Caitlin squeezed her eyes shut, then opened them. “Were you burned? Did you get smoke in your nose and throat?”

Again, Kennedy shook her head. “No one was hurt. But there are extra guards now posted here and at Aunt Maureen’s. More FBI agents, too. I’ll be okay.”

Caitlin forced a smile. “I always wonder which of us is really the mommy and which is the little girl. You’re so mature and brave. I’m very, very proud of you.”

“I love you, Mommy.”

Caitlin swallowed, hard. “And I love you. More than anything or anyone else in the world.” Her gaze darted over Kennedy’s shoulder for a fraction of a moment.

Again, Kennedy’s wisdom and insights took over. “You need to talk to Uncle Ryan now, don’t you?”

“Yes, baby, I do.”

“Do you promise we can talk tomorrow? I won’t ask where you are or any more questions. And I won’t breathe a word about this to anyone. I just need to see you, to talk to you." Again, Kennedy broke down. "Please?"

"You never have to ask," Caitlin replied. "Thanks to Uncle Ryan, we can talk every day until I'm home. I promise. Now I need you to listen to him, and to follow all his instructions. Okay?"

"I understand. You want me safe. Whatever you and Daddy found out puts me in danger, too, right?"

Caitlin blinked. "You're incredibly smart. Yes, baby, it does."

Kennedy nodded, as exhausted as she was scared. "I'll do whatever Uncle Ryan says. I'll be okay if you will."

"It's a deal." Caitlin held up her pinkie. "Pinkie swear."

Kennedy did the same. "Pinkie swear."

Caitlin kissed her own finger then pressed it to the screen. "Sleep tight, my amazing little girl. I'll talk to you tomorrow, and I love you."

Kennedy repeated her mother's motion, then pressed her own pinkie to the screen. "I love you, too." She sniffed, and then forced a smile. "Maybe we can read together tomorrow."

"It's a date."

At that moment, Claire walked down the stairs, extending her hand to Kennedy. "Come on, sweetie. Bedtime." She leaned over the screen for a moment. "Hi, Caitlin, I'm Claire. I'm so grateful you're safe. We'll bring you home."

Caitlin blinked back her tears. "Thank you, Claire." A hint of a smile. "It will be great to get to know the woman who stole Ryan's heart."

Smiling back, Claire gripped Kennedy's hand and led her out the door of the lair and to the stairs.

She shut the door behind them.

***

Caitlin was quiet as Ryan seated himself behind the computer. Still, the tears continued to slide down her cheeks.

"Shane's gone, Ryan," she whispered, her bravado gone, her shoulders shaking as she wept. "We'll never have him back again."

Ryan gave a hard swallow, knowing now was the time for him to be strong.

"I know, Caity," he said with more than a touch of emotion. "There are no words—"

"They don't exist. So let's not even try to find them," she interrupted him, dashing the tears off her cheeks.

Ryan's jaw tightened. "We're going to get the bastards who did this. I swear. But I'm going to need your help. Whatever Shane uncovered, whether it involved the Bureau or the NYPD, whoever—"

"It wasn't the Bureau or the NYPD," Caitlin interrupted. "It was Scott Security. And Shane wasn't the target. I was."

22

Ryan's jaw dropped. A long moment of silence followed Caitlin's reveal.

When he spoke, his tone was incredulous. "*You*?" he managed.

Caitlin nodded. "Yes. My employer, not Shane's. I stumbled into hell, and I couldn't escape. Shane was investigating for me. For our family. Because the danger spread to all of us. He was trying to protect us. And it got him killed." This time, she fought back her tears, knowing that the only way to help Ryan was to provide him with as many facts as she had—and she had plenty.

Ryan was still recovering from the shock, and his mind was racing. Caitlin was an intelligence analyst at Scott Security, Inc. Ryan didn't know a lot about the company or its CEO, Charles Scott. He knew that they were an international company based in White Plains, New York, and that the clients they safeguarded were high-profile—the rich, famous, and powerful, from Hollywood celebrities to business moguls. Their motto was: We protect our clients and what's important to them.

The company operated under the radar, but as far as Ryan knew, there'd never been any lawsuits associated with it. Just a stellar reputation and quiet, privileged clients. He wasn't naïve; he was sure payoffs and confidentiality agreements were the tools Scott Security deployed with a vengeance to make bad situations disappear without a trace. But no scandals involving their clients had made their way into the media. Ryan did vaguely remember that, at one time, Emma's recording idol, Rebecca Merland, had been followed and threatened by a stalker, and law enforcement had come up empty. Scott Security had stepped in, ferreted out the offender, and made sure the guy was found guilty and had to endure a disproportionately punitive jail sentence. Scott Security had resources and connections at their beck and call.

Were they slimy? Most likely. Companies like Scott didn't keep their hands squeaky clean. But slimy and illegal were two different things. How well Ryan knew that after his years working for FI. And like FI, Scott Security's success rate was sky-high and they were in high demand. But in Scott Security's case—had they crossed the line for criminal reasons?

Ryan was about to find out.

"Talk to me about the company," he instructed Caitlin. "I remember the Rebecca Merland stalker. Oh, and that supermodel, Alison Madding, whose über-valuable blue-ribbon-winning Brussels Griffon was kidnapped while she was walking him on Rodeo Drive. Scott Security recovered the dog when the Beverley Hills Police Department came up empty-handed. That rescue was splashed all over the news."

Caitlin gave a shaky nod. "The rescue was public but the investigation was not. Scott was careful to always keep those under wraps."

"That's not a surprise. Did you have a role in that investigation?"

"Yes, just as I did in many other projects. My job was to analyze all aspects of Alison's life, video appearances, video surveillance, alarm system data, GPS car tracking, social media accounts, press releases, public media—every potential vulnerability in her life. That was typical of what my role at Scott Security entailed."

Ryan was, once again, reminded of the breadth of Caitlin's abilities. "And in doing your job, you tripped on something you weren't supposed to find?"

"Not then. But recently, yes."

"How?"

Caitlin sucked in her breath. "On my own time, I developed a new security operations screening process—an untried approach to penetration testing. It's good, really good. So I decided to test it out on Scott itself, to see if the company systems were vulnerable. Obviously, I used an external network to probe the security systems."

"That makes sense. Just like a real hacker would."

"Exactly. So I went to my local Starbucks with my personal laptop, connected to their Wi-Fi, and did my thing. To say I got more than I bargained for would be the understatement of all time. I accidentally found the existence of"—Caitlin paused, using her fingers to make air quotes—"an 'off-book' division of Scott that only a tight group of people were privy to and a part of."

"How high up did this go?"

"To the top. The division is headed up by Charles Scott himself, and it's far-reaching. I saw evidence of clandestine activities all over the world. Criminal activities that included horrific things like killings. I saw cryptic email exchanges, reports, even evidence that Scott himself had hired a contractor to terminate someone who was a threat to one of their clients. And when I say far-reaching—he also has contacts in various government organizations." Again Caitlin paused, this time to suck in a breath. "I panicked. I was way out of my league, unsure of what to do, and scared to death."

"So you went to Shane."

"Yes. I wish to God I hadn't. Because he started his own investigation, which, for all I know, made him a mark, as well. I have no way of knowing what they knew or how they found out I had discovered their secret division."

Caitlin's supposition triggered a realization in Ryan's mind. "How many times did you probe your company from that same Starbucks?"

"Three. I didn't find the 'off-book' division until that last time. And I quit right then."

"Not soon enough," Ryan replied. "Your poking around must have raised a red flag to the IT security team, and whoever got the report went directly to Scott himself. Scott then ordered one of his trusted operatives to eliminate the problem. They conducted an investigation and zeroed in on the IP address of the New Rochelle Starbucks."

Caitlin's eyes widened. "After which, they must have sent someone to surveil that Starbucks. I go there every day, including the mornings I go into the office. They must have connected the network infiltration to me and that's when they decided to eliminate me."

"Did they know your husband was an FBI agent?"

Caitlin gave a shaky shrug. "At first? I don't know. They knew I was married. Shane is the beneficiary of the group life insurance I receive as a company benefit. When they targeted me, they must have dug up that information. After that, they have enough resources, not only to know all about Shane, but to figure out he was poking around. And Kennedy..." Caitlin's voice broke. "She's old enough for them to suspect she might have overheard something. And they're ruthless enough to kill an innocent child. If I doubted that before, I no longer do. The fire and the phone call I heard your mother describing was, at the very least, a warning, and at worst, attempted murder. It's my fault." Caitlin covered her face and began to weep. "Everything that's happening. It's all on me."

"No." Ryan gave an adamant shake of his head, his tone decisive. "Caity, stop. You're as much a victim as Shane and Kennedy."

He waited until she'd calmed down, lowered her hands, and had gotten herself under control. Then, he continued. "Blaming yourself is not only wrong, it's counterproductive. Let's put our heads together and get at some basics we can work with. For example, did you see Shane's killer? Did he see you? Clearly, you were on the scene at some point. Your blood was found on the floor, along with Shane's. How did it get there? Are you injured? And if you did see the killer, can you describe him to me?"

Caitlin digested all Ryan's questions, unsurprised by any of them.

"For starters, I'm fine. I cut myself on an edge of Shane's shattered cell phone. No big deal. And, yeah, I saw the killer, although he was covered in black from head to toe. Plus, I didn't see him up close. He didn't see me. I hid under the staircase near the hallway. I guess that makes me a coward." Caitlin's voice cracked again, and fresh tears began to flow.

"It doesn't make you a coward, it makes you smart," Ryan replied. "Sweetie, there was nothing you could do to stop what happened. And it would have destroyed Shane if you got hurt or killed. Not to mention what it would do to Kennedy."

Caitlin gave a shaky nod. "It was over in seconds, but it felt like slow motion playing out. I heard the shot even before I ducked under the staircase. After the SOB ran, I checked Shane's vitals a half dozen times. It was too late. I operated on autopilot. I'm sure you know the rest."

"Tell me what you remember about him."

"He was tall. Lean and light on his feet." She pressed her fingers to her temples. "That's all I remember. I've thought about it nonstop, but nothing else is coming."

"You were in shock." Ryan pursed his lips. "Listen, Caity, let me talk to the rest of my team. This investigation just made a one-eighty. We need to figure out a strategy. Our key goals will be to expose Scott and his people, get them thrown in jail without a key, and, most important of all, to bring you home."

"How are you going to do that?"

"Give me time, just a little. Now get some sleep. We'll talk tomorrow."

***

Offices of Forensic Instincts
Second Floor
Tribeca, Manhattan, New York
Saturday, March 18, Midnight

Casey began the Zoom meeting on time, with the entire team ready to get started. Most of them were Zooming either from home or a hotel room, other than Ryan and Claire, who were at FI, along with Casey. Casey was alone in the conference room, and Claire and Ryan were in Ryan's lair.

All eyes were on Casey.

"Sorry to screw up everyone's plans, but this is urgent," Casey began. "I'll start by telling you that Hutch is on the warpath. He exploded in here earlier this evening, and it wasn't pretty. He's not flexing, not this time. We've been warned to stay off these investigations or he'll get a court order forcing us to do so. I'm not sure how far he'd take this—he even threatened to have charges brought against us—but I'm not willing to find out."

"Shit," Marc muttered. "This is going to limit us, big-time." He paused, eyeing Casey. "We'll tackle our strategy in a minute. First, are you okay? No prying, but I'm guessing you're not going home tonight. And it's been a brutally long day."

Casey's lips thinned into a grim line. "I'm fine. I even took a nap a little while ago. And I plan to sleep in my old bedroom, at least for tonight. Other than that, it'll be business as usual."

"And what will that entail?" Patrick tactfully avoided asking any personal questions about Casey and Hutch, instead focusing on his ofttimes worry when FI pushed the legal boundaries just a little too far. "The Bureau has our hands tied. If we blatantly ignore Hutch's command, we can wind up arrested and in jail, with FI shut down—undoubtedly for good."

"I realize that." Casey's jaw was set. "So we're going to have to get very insular and very creative. We'll bandy ideas around in a few minutes. First, you have to hear Ryan's update. A lot has happened since we last spoke. Everything's changed. Our entire focus has to change with it. Ryan, go ahead. Fill them in on the bomb you dropped on me right before this Zoom meeting."

Ryan nodded. "Steel yourselves, guys. We're going to be making a one-eighty." Without pause, he told the team everything: from the suspicious fire at his parents' house, to the threat to Kennedy, finally leading into his talk with Caitlin and everything she had revealed.

Marc let out a low whistle. "So we've been chasing our tails, looking in all the wrong places for all the wrong reasons."

"Wow," Emma breathed. "This is terrifying stuff—in some ways bigger than our original suspicions."

"Yes, and the FBI knows nothing about it," Patrick felt obligated to add.

"Nor are they going to," Casey responded adamantly to Patrick's second pointed comment. "Patrick, I know this is going to go against the grain for you. It won't be the first time. But remember, you're part of FI. If you want to be our kite strings, go ahead. But we're seeing this investigation through, Bureau or no Bureau. Do you want to sit this part out, or are you in?"

He didn't hesitate. "You know I'm in."

"Good. So let's get into it. Ideas, anyone?"

Ryan cleared his throat. "I've had more time than the rest of you to think about this. We know we're on the FBI's radar, and by now we're on Scott Security's, too—just by virtue of the fact that we've visited my parents' house repeatedly, especially me, and the fact that my folks and Kennedy are now staying here, obviously for safety purposes. We're in everyone's sights, and that sucks."

"So we're further limited," Casey said.

Ryan nodded. "Yeah, we are. Add to that the fact that Scott Security has tentacles all over the world—an international reach. So maybe we're better off lying low and letting a different expert handle this—an expert we know and trust."

Marc didn't have to think. "Aidan," he said.

"Absolutely, and, in this case, Terri, too," Ryan added.

Terri Underwood was Aidan's right-hand at the Zermatt Group. She was also a former NSA analyst and now a sought-after computer security consultant. Anything IT-related she could handle. Further, she and Ryan had worked together on previous cases, international as well as domestic, when FI and Zermatt had joined forces. She was brilliant, which was the highest of compliments coming from Ryan.

Casey's nod was enthusiastic. "That would be the ideal solution. We'd be off the radar, and hiring a team who are far more experienced than we are about handling international spy cases." She glanced at Marc. "Do you think Aidan will do it?"

Marc grinned. "A chance to break open a criminal organization using Zermatt's own creative methods and, in the process, paying for their efforts with the bad guys' money? Hell, yeah. Zermatt is as good as in."

"Is Aidan still in New York City?" Casey asked. "Because I want this to be an in-person, one-on-one talk between you two."

"Yup," Marc replied. "Aidan's in Manhattan and, actually, so is Terri. Whatever they're working on can obviously be run from Zermatt's home base. So it's no problem for me to set up a one-on-one meeting with my brother."

Ryan's brow furrowed, telling the team he was deep in thought. "All our in-house FI communications are encrypted, as I'm sure Zermatt's are," he said. "But we need to ensure complete encryption between our teams, not to mention giving Zermatt a way to connect with Caitlin." A quick glance at Marc, then at Casey. "I'll find a way to get another System76 overnighted to me. It's after midnight, so it'll take some arm-twisting and a shit ton of money. Is that okay, boss?"

"Use whatever resources you need," Casey replied.

"Great. Then I'll handle it. Marc, give me the okay after you talk to Aidan. Once the computer arrives, I'll need less than a day. I'll clone the new System76 so it's identical to the ones I programmed for Caitlin and for me. We'll communicate solely through that channel."

“Done.” Marc glanced at his Apple Watch. “Not quite one a.m. Aidan is like the city—he never sleeps. I’ll make arrangements as soon as we end this Zoom meeting.”

Business concluded, Casey turned her gaze to Ryan, who, despite his on-point ideas, looked haggard. “How was Kennedy’s reunion with her mom?” she asked gently.

Ryan swallowed hard, a muscle working in his jaw. “Incredible. Emotional. Exuberant. Painful.” His eyes misted over. “They shared the pain of losing Shane and the joy of being together. I got pretty choked up. I stepped away, because they needed time alone. To keep busy, I did some weight-lifting while they talked. And afterward, when Caitlin and I were through and she signed off, I went upstairs. Kennedy was waiting, sitting in the kitchen with Claire. She sobbed in my arms for a long time. The entire experience pretty much gutted me.” He broke off at that.

“I’m sure it did.” Casey’s expression was rife with empathy. “What about your parents? How much did they overhear?”

“Nothing, as planned. Kennedy stayed in the kitchen. It was just her, Claire, and me.”

“I’m glad Claire was there.”

A shaky nod as Ryan squeezed Claire’s hand. “So am I. She helps me stay centered, to use her words. Plus, she and Kennedy have a great rapport.”

“It all worked out,” Claire assured Casey. “Kennedy finally went to sleep, a lot more peaceful than she has been. I talked briefly to Maureen, who somehow contained herself from blurting out the dozens of questions she was dying to ask.” A small smile. “But I’d be lying if I said she didn’t look both eager and curious.”

“She’ll handle the rest of the family,” Ryan assured them.

"All good news," Casey said. "In which case, I suggest we all catch some sleep." Her gaze shifted to Marc. "Not quite yet for you. You have a meeting to set up."

***

Ryan's Apartment
Park Slope, Brooklyn, New York
Saturday, March 18, 2:30 a.m.

Ryan lay on his side on the bed, his arms wrapped around Claire, holding her tight as he listened to the even sound of her breathing that told him she'd fallen asleep. After the endlessly long day—and the two hours they'd spent making love—it was no wonder she was wiped.

So was he. But, despite how depleted he was physically and how much Claire had taken him down mentally, he was on major sensory overload.

And that sensory overload stemmed not just from the investigation, but from the beautiful woman lying in his arms—the woman who, over the past hellish week, had stepped up to give him her strength, to be his support and his constant since this nightmare had begun.

Ryan's mind returned to his previous thoughts for the future—thoughts that tonight had only intensified.

Loving Claire was a given. Since the day they'd committed to each other, spoken those three life-altering words aloud, their relationship had deepened, grown. It wasn't just explosive sex anymore, nor was it only playful banter, biting debates, bouncing things off of each other, and tender moments. It was something bigger, richer, and definitely more all-encompassing. And that reality had struck him like a blow to the chest tonight, in a more powerful way than it ever had.

Claire was his perfect counterpart, ethereal and instinctive to his grounded and scientific. Yet through this tragedy, the roles had subtly reversed. She'd been his rock, strong and take-charge as she guided him through the pain, the loss, and the solutions. She'd also become part of his family, and, most of all, she'd come to be his other half.

Which changed everything.

This was no longer just about his objections to their separate living arrangements. Not anymore. It was more than that. Much more.

He'd wait until this case was solved and the healing was underway. But after that, he and Claire were going to have a very different and life-altering conversation.

23

Marc and Madeleine's Duplex
Upper East Side
Manhattan, New York
Saturday, March 18, 11:15 a.m.

Marc opened the door and let his brother in. The two men looked much alike—tall, dark, and broodingly handsome, as Emma always like to describe them. But where Marc's eyes were dark and slightly narrowed at the edges—favoring their mother's Asian heritage—Aidan's eyes were rounder and midnight blue, indicative of their father's European blood.

Now, Marc shook his brother's hand and shut the door behind him. "Thanks for coming so quickly."

"I aim to please." Aidan strolled into the living room, his lips curving into a smile as he saw Maddy propped up on sofa cushions, a blanket covering her lap and a snack tray filled with a plate of French toast and a cup of tea beside her. "Hi, Maddy. How are you feeling?"

"Starting my third trimester, and getting big," she said, putting down the novel she'd been reading and placing a palm on her growing belly. "But I have no complaints. The baby and I are doing great." She glanced behind Aidan, looking disappointed. "You didn't bring Abby with you? I would have happily watched her while you and Marc talked."

Aidan chuckled at the image of his wild, precocious six-and-a-half-year-old daughter taking it easy on Maddy. "You're on bed rest, remember? Abby would have you doing gymnastics in no time. That would be a big no-no for you and for the baby. Besides, my little princess is on the verge of winning a popularity contest. She's at yet another play date with one of her school friends, and I was not invited. They're polishing each other's nails. Both her friend's parents are there, as is Joyce, who'll be with her all weekend."

Aidan was referring to Joyce Reynolds, Abby's middle-aged nanny, who took care of Abby on weekdays—and on weekends when work required his full attention, plus whenever Aidan had to travel or work overtime. She spent many an overnight or a late night in Aidan's guest room. She also cooked, straightened up the apartment, and took Abby to school, as well as to her afterschool activities and play dates. She had twenty years of experience, an enormously long fuse, and a genuine fondness for her little charge. She was a lifesaver.

"The deal I made with Abby was to behave with Joyce," Aidan continued. "In return, I had to promise to play nail salon with her tonight. I'm sure I'll have neon nails by bedtime."

Marc barked out a laugh at that image.

"Laugh while you can," Aidan informed him. "In six-plus years that will be you."

"I'll survive—with pleasure." Marc was gearing up for the joys of fatherhood, something he'd been wanting for a long time. He and Maddy knew they were having a girl, and he was over the moon about it.

"Besides, Abby gets practice sessions in on me, too. So far, I've escaped being made-up, but I'm sure that will come." He sobered. "Much as I love talking about our girls, you and I need to have that meeting."

Aidan also grew serious. "Ready when you are."

Marc walked over to the sofa and gave Maddy a tender kiss. "Aidan and I will be in my office. Text if you need me."

"Promise," she replied. "But I'll be just fine. Brunch. Reading material. I'm all set." She waved her hand in the direction of Marc's office. "Go have your meeting."

***

Marc and Aidan settled themselves in the two club chairs in Marc's office.

"Shoot," Aidan said.

Quickly and succinctly, Marc filled Aidan in on their case, where things stood, and what the FI team needed from him and from Zermatt.

Aidan let out a low whistle. "FI has really backed itself into a brick wall," he said. "You're walking targets, both to the FBI and to Scott Security. Any move you make will be a bad one."

"Yeah, that much I knew."

A corner of Aidan's mouth lifted. "Fortunately for you, Zermatt has no such problem. We're totally off the grid. No law enforcement agency has crossed paths with us—at least to their knowledge. And none of the scummy companies we deal with has any idea who screwed them over."

"We need the works—everything about Scott Security, who exactly is part of the criminal arm of the company, how far their reach is, specifics on what they have and what they're doing, how they're getting their money—"

"This isn't my first rodeo, frogman," Aidan cut in, looking amused. "I'll get it all, and then some—and do what has to be done. And, before you ask, I'll be bringing Terri on board." His grin widened. "She'll jump at the chance to bring these bastards down."

Marc nodded. "Good. Ryan already programmed two computers—one for him and one for Caitlin Walsh—both with the ultimate levels of security. He's waiting for the go-ahead from me to program a third computer for you, so you can communicate with him, and also with Caitlin."

Aidan folded his arms across his chest. "Give it to him. I need that computer yesterday. We need to jog Caitlin's memory enough to get more specifics about Shane's killer. That'll be your job, former BAU agent. You'll do the talking. Terri and I will do the listening and move on whatever you learn." A frown. "When can we realistically expect Ryan to finish programming the computer and get it to us?"

"Less than a day. I'll hand-deliver it to you tomorrow at your place and we can make that call. I'll tell Ryan to let Caitlin know about our arrangement so there won't be any surprises."

Aidan rose to his feet. "And Terri and I will get started today. We'll already have a shitload of information by the time we talk to Caitlin."

Marc nodded. "I never doubted it." He gripped Aidan's shoulder. "Thanks."

"For what? You know what Zermatt is about. This will be a labor of love."

***

Offices of Forensic Instincts
Main Conference Room, Second Floor
Tribeca, Manhattan, New York
Saturday, March 18, 1:45 p.m.

Casey frowned as she hung up the phone with John Nickels. John had used his NYPD connections to get a lowdown from the NYFD on the status of the fire at the McKays' residence.

No surprise that it was being investigated as arson. The guy who'd started the fire had all but left his calling card at the house. Even so, Casey's gut told her that the incident hadn't been done to kill or to cause maximum structural damage, as much as it had been done to scare the crap out of everyone, Maureen in particular. Scott's goal had doubtless been to push Maureen to her limit, to the point where she'd contact Caitlin and get her out in the open—assuming she knew where Caitlin was.

Well, that plan had backfired. Maureen had no clue where Caitlin was, although Casey was sure that despite Ryan's mom's reluctant lack of questions, she was well aware that both Kennedy and Ryan had spoken to Caitlin.

No one but the team, and of course, Kennedy, was certain of that.

The fact that the McKays were now staying at FI kept them safe, plus it allowed Kennedy to talk to her mommy daily. It also kept the specialized computer safe in Ryan's lair, and eliminated Ryan's need to commute to the Bronx. Less time away. Less risk by not having to move the computer back and forth. It was a win-win.

Meanwhile, Ryan was in his lair now, working at the speed of light to clone the third computer so it would be ready to turn over to

Marc early tomorrow morning, where it would then be transferred into Aidan's and Terri's capable hands.

With a hard wince of pain, Casey leaned back in her chair and massaged her temples. She knew damn well that FI had to stop in its tracks after that, at least where it came to overt action. It didn't take a scholar to know that Hutch was watching them like a hawk, and that if they so much as dug deeper into the arson investigation, he'd be taking legal action against them in the blink of an eye.

Damn the man.

And not only because of the existing threat he represented, but because everything he'd said to her about her health had been right.

Her physical condition was deteriorating.

At this point her entire body ached from a day of toting around a backpack and walking blocks of Fifth Avenue—despite Claire's protests and frequent offers to help. She'd also climbed up and down three flights of stairs numerous times as she'd put in ungodly hours for the past two days. She was shaky and bone-weary, and the sharp internal flashes of pain she was experiencing, along with the rawness and pain near the site of her incision, were bad enough to red-flag her. She'd lost her spleen and a hell of a lot of blood to that shooting. No time to be a martyr. She had to make a call to her surgeon. Stoic or not, she wasn't going to play Russian roulette with her body, not after three months of fighting to get back to herself.

Disgusted and a little afraid, she picked up her cell phone and called her surgeon, who, fortunately, was in his office at the hospital. As she'd dreaded, he instructed her to get to the ER pronto. He had one more virtual appointment, after which he'd meet her there.

So much for resting. She'd call the car service now, then text Marc from the car saying only that she had to go out. There wasn't a prayer that she was sharing this situation with the team, or even with Hutch, for that matter. And not because she was angry. She just didn't want to make a huge deal out of this. It was probably nothing more than her body's protest at being overworked.

With that, she made the phone call to the car service, then rose, unsteady and with a bout of internal chills.

Not good.

***

Offices of the Zermatt Group
West Seventy-Fifth Street, Seventh Floor
Manhattan, New York
Saturday, March 18, 3:45 p.m.

Aidan had gone out to grab two sandwiches for himself and Terri. Now, he headed directly for the windowless room at the rear of his apartment—the room that served as the strategic command center for himself and Terri, the two key members of the New York City–based Zermatt Group who resided in Manhattan, rather than abroad.

He and Terri dubbed this space "the Cage" because the entire room was encased inside a Faraday cage. It blocked electromagnetic waves from entering, and thereby protected all the sensitive electronic devices within its walls from surveillance. All communications to the outside world were hardwired, heavily monitored, encrypted, and protected with multiple firewalls. When someone tried to reach either Aidan or Terri on their cell phone when inside the Cage, the call would be routed instead to the desk phone in the room.

Aidan barely paused in front of the solid steel door and the Hirsh keypad that controlled access to it. Adjacent to the keypad was a small red light that, when glowing, meant that either Terri or himself was inside, hard at work.

He punched in the code and stepped inside, sealing himself from the world. The entire long wall of the Cage was a panorama of LED monitors partitioned into smaller screens that displayed everything from international news broadcasts to PRISM to computers monitoring events all over the world.

He deposited the sandwiches on the desk where Terri was frowning in concentration, staring at her monitor.

"What have you found?" Aidan asked, knowing he'd get a solid answer. He'd left her digging into Scott Security and Charles Scott himself.

Terri Underwood lifted her gaze from the laptop screen, where she'd been concentrating as her fingers flew across the keys. She was nearly six feet tall and well-toned, with long, wavy dark hair and piercing brown eyes. Emma claimed she looked like Wonder Woman, and, other than her darker skin tone, Aidan had to admit that Emma was right.

"I inputted everything you gave me courtesy of Ryan," Terri now reported to Aidan as he unpacked the sandwiches and handed one to her.

She nodded her thanks, opened the wrapper, and took a bite of her ham and cheese sub. "I reached out to our network of people and asked about Charles Scott and Scott Security," she continued through bites. "The data matches what Caitlin Walsh provided. On the surface, Scott Security appears to be comprised of public relations fixers—people who solve various issues for rich, high-profile people. They have offices all over the world, in places where the rich people hang out, and an extensive network of contractors who extend their reach in places where needed. When the problems can't be solved through the usual methods of nondisclosure agreements, payoffs, etcetera, they have a less visible organization that makes the problems vanish—an organization headed up by Charles Scott himself. Some of those problems have been known to take flying leaps off of balconies or vanish into thin air. Scott has a reputation of hiring psychopaths for this criminal arm of his business and paying them well for their services."

"A wholesome arrangement," Aidan said dryly, munching on his own chicken parm sub.

Terri nodded. "With regard to Charles Scott himself, he's a dream come true on paper. The best private schools, the highest IQ, an avid sportsman and philanthropist—I think I'm going to puke. In reality, he's the scum of the earth, a pro at running the dark side of his company. Scary high-level contacts, crimes like homicide—at some flunky's hands, of course—littering his well-secreted path. No point in going on. You get the drift."

"I do. Bringing him down will be one of the pleasures of this assignment." Aidan put down his food. "Moving on to specifics of this investigation, do we have anything on Scott's hire to kill Shane Walsh?"

"That's what I'm working on now," Terri replied. "I'm peeling back layers. It's going to take some time. But, since we don't yet have facts, I'm starting with suppositions that are damn close to hardcore facts. For example, there's no doubt that after dispatching Shane Walsh, the killer's orders from Scott would be to disappear, relocating to a country with no extradition treaty. That would take place either on the day of the murder or the day after—as soon as the right flight was available."

"March 10 or March 11," Aidan murmured. "That's a weekend, which might mean fewer flights to bog us down."

"Right. That'll play in our favor. With regard to destination, I eliminated hostile countries like China and Russia, since it would be a major pain in the ass to gain permanent residency there, not to mention an unfriendly environment to live in. I did the same with other nations that are highly unlikely to be attractive to someone fleeing the US with the intent of making his destination a permanent home. The description we have thus far tells us only that the killer is male, and that he's tall and lean—an unexceptional physicality that gives us very little to go on. It's imperative that tomorrow's interview with Caitlin Walsh yields additional clues to help fine-tune our search."

Aidan nodded his agreement. "That will be Marc's job. He'll gently extract a more in-depth description from Caitlin—specifics she doesn't even realize she knows. We'll combine that with whatever you uncover in your research." A thoughtful pause. "What you've just given me is enough of a start to get Simone involved. She'll recruit the necessary Zermatt contacts and brief them. I want them leaving right after we speak to Caitlin Walsh. At that point, we'll have a leaner list to pursue."

"Do you want me to reach out to Simone?" Terri asked.

"No. I'll handle that while you work."

Simone Martin was the third core member of the Zermatt team, the fourth being former MI6 operative Philip Banks, who was based in London. Simone and Aidan had a very hot, very long-distance relationship, but her professional abilities were independent of that. Based out of Lyon, France, she spoke five languages fluently. In her "real job" as a managing partner for McKinsey and Company, she was head of recruiting. Her role was to find the best people in the world and convince them to join the firm. As the Zermatt Group's human capital expert, she applied the same skills in recruiting talent for them.

Aidan relied on Simone, not only to find new talent, but when a project presented itself, to scan their talent pool and develop a short list of professionals with the skills and team chemistry to be successful.

With Simone's expertise, the Zermatt team would be assembled and ready in a heartbeat.

That's when the fun would begin.

24

FBI New York Field Office
26 Federal Plaza
Manhattan, New York
Saturday, March 18, 4:15 p.m.

Hutch was cranky as hell, just as he had been since his altercation with Casey yesterday. He'd sequestered himself in his office, had worked straight through the night, and was up to his ass in investigative follow-up. Sometimes paperwork just plain sucked.

Still, he kept pausing, struck by a niggling feeling that something was off. He didn't know what, but it was eating away at him. His every instinct told him that his presence was needed. Was it case-related? He didn't think so.

He sat up in his chair, rubbed his eyes, and took a healthy swallow of his now-cold, shitty coffee.

He hadn't heard from Casey since he'd left FI headquarters, having blasted her. He felt no guilt about what he'd said, because it was necessary and it was the truth. But he hadn't liked the way she'd looked—so drained, so tired, and in more pain than usual.

He picked up his cell phone and pressed the key for her private line.

Ring. Ring. Voice mail.

Dammit. He wasn't leaving a message. He was aware that his wife was furious at him, but not so furious that she'd be childish enough to avoid his call. So what the hell was going on? Was this why he was so off-center?

He called Marc, hoping to make some progress there.

"Hey, Hutch." Marc sounded troubled.

"Is Casey in the office?" Hutch demanded without prelude.

"Nope. She texted me a while ago saying she had to leave. Hopefully, she went home. Frankly, she looked like shit."

Hutch squeezed his eyes shut. "Yeah. I know. And, so far, she's not answering her phone. But I'm trying her again."

He tried several times and was on the verge of panic when his cell phone rang. Seeing Casey's private number unblocked, he blew out a breath of relief.

"You okay?" he demanded.

Casey's voice was shaky and slightly slurred. "Not really… I'm at the hospital… My surgeon met me in the ER. The staff ran some tests and took some X-rays, which he read on the spot… Turns out I have an infection and some abdominal inflammation from overexertion after the splenectomy… They just gave me some pretty strong antibiotics and painkillers—I can't remember what." She paused, obviously trying to gather strength and clear her head. "If home treatment doesn't work…or if the infection worsens…I'll have to be readmitted to the hospital. And now…they won't release me on my own. Hutch…" She swallowed hard. "I'm scared."

Hutch swore under his breath. "Don't be scared, sweetheart. We'll fix this." He was already in motion. "I'm on my way."

***

Casey and Hutch's Apartment
Battery Park City, Manhattan, New York
Saturday, March 18, 5:45 p.m.

Hutch carried Casey into their apartment and into the bedroom, where he placed her gently on the bed.

She'd been completely out of it on the drive home. Now she was shivering. Twice she shuddered and once she actually whimpered in pain.

That was *not* Casey.

"If I undress you, can you get into bed?" Hutch asked, a huge knot twisting his stomach.

She nodded, white-faced.

"Okay." He gently slid her out of her clothes, leaving her in just her bra and her thong, murmuring soothing words as he did. "The IV medication they gave you will last another six hours. Then we'll start you on the oral doses of antibiotic and pain meds the surgeon prescribed." As he spoke, he eased her beneath the covers and grabbed a second blanket, which he laid over the first to help stop the shaking.

"Thank you," she mumbled.

Swallowing hard, Hutch sat gingerly at the edge of the bed beside her.

"Prescriptions at…pharmacy," Casey managed.

"I know," Hutch reassured her. "They're being delivered. I'm also hiring a full-time nurse. I want a professional with you at all times to make sure you follow your surgeon's instructions." Hutch heard his own voice quaver. "I also don't want you left alone at any time."

For once, she didn't argue.

Just seeing her so depleted brought back memories Hutch tried daily to forget. They forced out his next outburst, even though he'd promised himself he'd stay calm.

"Goddammit, Casey. Do I have to tie you to the bed and burn all your devices?"

Casey gave him the barest hint of a smile. "That's…extreme."

"Is it? Do I need to remind you how close you came to dying? How close I came to losing you?" His voice cracked a little at the end, and he reached out, running his fingers through her hair and then cupping her face. "I was never so frightened in my life. Do you know how much I love you? I don't think so. Because if you did, you wouldn't break me this way."

Tears filled Casey's eyes, and she visibly struggled for coherency. "I'm…sorry. I love you. It's so hard. Giving in." She waved her hand. "To weakness… Physical… Emotional."

"You're not weak. You're the strongest person I know. But you're human. And right now you need to get well. For me."

"I will."

Hutch kissed her, then rose. "Once I've hired the nurse, I'll call your team—not in any professional capacity. As your husband. You're going to sleep the rest of the night, and hopefully, half of tomorrow. After that, you'll stay in bed doing nothing but resting. When you're feeling stronger—and by that, I mean not for a few days—you can set up a Zoom meeting with your team, since they're idle anyway. Right?" He wasn't waiting for a response. His words were pointed and his gaze challenged her. "And Case, I'm not asking you. I'm telling you."

Feeling weak as a kitten, Casey nodded. Her eyelids were already drooping from the narcotics. "Ev'n though you're a hard-ass, you make it hard t'stay mad at you," she murmured.

An instant later, she was asleep.

***

Offices of the Zermatt Group
West Seventy-Fifth Street, Seventh Floor
Manhattan, New York
Sunday, March 19, 10:25 a.m.

Marc strode out of the elevator and down the hall to Aidan's apartment. The cloned laptop was in a computer bag slung over his shoulder.

Aidan was waiting for him in the open doorway.

Wordlessly, he let Marc in and shut the door behind them, tipping his head toward the fortress in the rear of the apartment after double-locking his front door.

Marc glanced around the silent apartment as he walked. "Abby?" he asked.

"Out with Joyce, meeting up with friends at her favorite playground," Aidan responded. "They'll be gone for a good portion of the day. Obviously, I didn't tell her that her uncle Marc was coming over. She'd never have left your side and we wouldn't get a thing done. You can play with our little princess next time."

"I can't wait," Marc said with a hint of a smile. It was no secret that he adored Abby and that the feeling was mutual.

Aidan punched in the key code, and he and Marc stepped inside the Cage. Marc had never been in this room, and he looked around, visibly fascinated.

"Wow," he said. "Pretty impressive."

"We like to think so," Aidan said, his lips quirking in a grin.

Terri rose from behind the desk and extended her hand. “Good to see you, Marc.”

“Likewise.” Marc shook Terri’s hand, then waited as she shifted her computer to the side, then offered him her chair and went to sit on his right, in one of the two other chairs that were grouped around the desk. Aidan seated himself in the chair on Marc’s left, indicating that Marc was center stage and captaining this particular ship.

Settling in behind the desk, Marc unzipped the computer case, and then placed the laptop directly in front of him. “Programmed and ready,” he said.

“Is Caitlin expecting this meeting?” Aidan asked.

Marc nodded. “Ryan filled her in. She’s ready and eager to help. She knows only that we have two other professionals working with us and that I’ll be handling the interview.” He glanced from Aidan to Terri. “No mention of Zermatt.”

“Never expected otherwise,” Aidan replied. He bent his knee and crossed one long leg over the other. “Let’s get started.”

Marc opened the laptop, turned it on, and tapped the keys that Ryan had instructed him to press.

It took a minute or two, and then a woman appeared on the screen. She was attractive, alert yet anxious, and Marc could see the resemblance to Kennedy.

“Hi, Caitlin,” he began. “I’m Marc Devereaux, as I know Ryan told you. Let me begin by saying how terribly sorry I am for your loss.”

She drew in a slow breath. “Nice to meet you, Marc. And thank you. Ryan speaks very highly of you. He says you’re as good as they come and that you used to work for the FBI.”

“I did. First as a supervisory special agent in the Violent Crimes division. Then in the Behavioral Analysis Unit. Now I’m part of

Forensic Instincts. And these"—he pointed to Aidan and Terri—"are two of my professional contacts. Aidan and Terri. They're working alongside Forensic Instincts in this investigation."

They all acknowledged each other politely.

"So how does this work?" Caitlin asked with an attempt at humor. "Do you hypnotize me?"

Marc chuckled. "No, nothing like that. We just talk. I'll lead you through what we already know about Shane's killer, and see if together we can deepen that knowledge." His smile faded. "I know how difficult this is for you, and I apologize in advance for adding to that pain."

"Don't." Caitlin gave a firm shake of her head. "I want this bastard caught and punished. And I want to come home to my little girl. I'll help in any way that I can."

"Good." Marc's expression didn't change. "Let's begin with what we know." He ran through what Ryan had told them. "Is that all accurate?" he concluded.

"Yes."

"Okay, so you had a limited view of the killer, and he was dressed from head to toe in black. Are you certain he was male?"

Caitlin blinked. "Yes. His body type. His stance. His gait. The way he moved. I'm certain."

"Good. Now let's discuss what you said about him being light on his feet. How so?"

"The way he stepped toward Shane. The way he made his escape. He was like a cat burglar only with muscles."

"So he was well-muscled?"

Caitlin narrowed her eyes in thought. "Actually, yes. Lean, but with muscles."

"And the way he moved—would you say he was a young man?"

Her brows drew together as she continued to search her memory. "Not teenager young, but in his twenties or thirties." She gave a mirthless laugh. "I guess people like Charles Scott don't hire middle-aged hitmen. Certainly not paunchy ones."

Marc gave her a faint smile. "Think hard about the crime scene you witnessed. Then take me through it."

"Ryan told you that I hid under the stairwell." It wasn't a question. It was a reiteration of that part of Marc's recap.

Marc nodded, realizing how agonizing it was for Caitlin to recall these memories. She needed the reassurance of repetition. So he gave it to her.

"He did. So you obviously had a decent enough view. Did you actually see Shane get shot?"

"Only the immediate aftermath and the killer's escape," Caitlin replied. "I heard the shot. I hid. I looked up. The killer was lowering his left arm, but he was still holding the gun in his hand. I remember because..." She gasped in sudden recall. "Because I saw a bit of his arm at the wrist, between the edge of his shirt and his glove. Only for a few seconds, before he pulled the sleeve down. Marc, he was white. I'd forgotten until now."

Marc digested all Caitlin had said. "Not only was he white, he was left-handed. Those are two huge recalls. Only one out of every ten white males is left-handed. You've just helped us narrow down the search significantly."

She blew out a relieved breath. "Thank God. Now what?"

Marc glanced from Aidan to Terri, waiting to see if they had more questions they needed answered. He wasn't surprised to see that Terri had leaned forward and was busily typing on her own computer.

Pausing, she said, "Caitlin, in many ways my skill set mirrors Ryan's, and yours. From what Ryan conveyed to me, you developed a new security operations screening process—an untried approach to penetration testing."

"I did. I'm sure Ryan also told you that I tested it out on Scott Security to see if the company systems were vulnerable. I wish I'd never done that. If I hadn't, Shane would be alive today."

Compassion flashed in Terri's eyes. "I understand. So let's get him the justice he deserves and end Charles Scott's career and his freedom."

A hard nod.

"You accidentally stumbled onto the dark side of Scott Security," Terri continued. "I need to follow this through. Can you help me determine the best way to hack into the dark side of their database? I'm quite sure they're deleting compromising information. I need to look for old backups."

Caitlin looked thoughtful as her mind raced through the scenario. "I think so." She went on to supply Terri with a complex explanation that seemed to make sense to her.

It made sense to Terri, as well.

"That's just what I was looking for," she said. "And I'll follow through on it to extract what I need."

"I hope it works," Caitlin said.

"I'll make it work."

Caitlin looked from Terri to Aidan to Marc. "How else can I help you?"

"We're good for now," Aidan told her. "I'm sure you'll be hearing from us as the need for more information arises."

The mother in Caitlin kicked in again, and her hands gripped the table in front of her. "Wait. Do you have a sense of how long this will take?"

Again, Marc and Aidan exchanged glances. "Not yet," Marc replied frankly. "We have a fair amount of territory to cover."

"But we work fast," Aidan said. "Trust us. You'll soon be reunited with Kennedy, the threat to your lives will be over, and Shane's killer will be dealt with—as will Charles Scott."

25

Casey and Hutch's Apartment
Battery Park City
Manhattan, New York
Monday, March 20, 5:05 p.m.

Hutch's command-and-control voice boomed out, bouncing off the walls of the bedroom. "Don't even think about it."

Startled, Casey paused in her efforts to wriggle her way to the edge of the bed.

She froze, a guilty look crossing her face.

"There's no need to blow me away. You scared the hell out of me," she told her husband, who was hovering in the open doorway.

"The important thing is that I stopped you."

Casey squinted at the wall clock. "It's early. Why are you home? And where's Sophia?" She was referring to Sophia Ramirez, the lovely, experienced nurse Hutch had hired to take care of her.

Hutch folded his arms across his chest. "I left early and brought work home. I gave Sophia the evening off. I took over. Now, where was it you were headed?"

Casey blinked, clearing the medication-induced cobwebs from her head. "To the bathroom?"

"Try again. Sophia keeps a thorough chart. I know when you ate, when you took your meds, and when you last used the bathroom."

With a cranky grunt, Casey reached around to plump up her pillows.

Hutch crossed over and completed the task, then eased Casey back so she was comfortable. "In case I didn't mention it, your cell phone and iPad are locked away in my desk drawer in our office. So don't waste your time."

She rolled her eyes. "I was only going to quickly check in with my team."

"And we agreed that wasn't going to happen until after tomorrow's follow-up appointment with your surgeon." Hutch lowered himself to the edge of the bed, his eyes boring into her. "Besides, there's no great urgency for you to connect with your team, considering the fact that FI is no longer working on the Walshes' cases. Right?"

Casey didn't miss a beat. "You ordered us to back off. So that's what we're doing."

"Why do I find that hard to believe?"

A shrug. "Because you're a born skeptic?"

"Or because I know you too well."

"My company is pretty renowned at this point, which means we're very busy. Maybe we took on a new client."

Hutch arched a brow. "Uh-huh. And maybe the sun turned cold. New investigations aren't even addressed, much less taken on, without you there, either in person or via Zoom. Not to mention, we've seen no new comings and goings at FI. So no recent clients and no new investigations."

"You're surveilling the brownstone."

"Sure are. Any more questions? Because now I have a few."

Casey sighed. "I'm surprised you waited this long."

"I wanted you strong and clear-headed enough. Which, considering your feistiness, it seems you are. So, let's get started. I'll keep it brief and to the point, so I don't tax your strength."

Casey gritted her teeth. SSA Hutchinson was back. And he knew her too damn well. The fire at Ryan's parents' house. The FI team filing out of the brownstone, splitting up, and making obscure drops in trash cans. Half-truths that still hung between them.

"Do you know where Caitlin Walsh is?" Hutch demanded, going straight in for the kill.

"No." An honest reply.

"But you're actively looking for her—everywhere from New York and New Jersey to New England."

"We were. We stopped when you threatened to shut us down."

"What about the company she works for—Scott Security? I'm sure you've checked them out. Found anything?"

"Probably the same things you found. They're sketchy. So are their business practices. But nothing overtly illegal."

"Overtly illegal," Hutch repeated. "Good choice of words. So, tell me, have any methods FI used for information-gathering into Scott Security been either overtly or covertly illegal?"

Casey sighed. "I don't know what you're implying. So I'm going to choose not to respond. Why? Has the FBI uncovered something of import?"

"Nice try. But I'm the one asking the questions. And you're not going to divert me or con me into filling you in on our investigation."

"Then I guess we're at a dead end," Casey replied with a shrug.

Hutch's eyes narrowed. "Let's try another subject—the fire at Ryan's parents' house. Any thoughts about that?"

Casey met her husband's gaze directly. "My guess? It was someone's attempt to draw Caitlin out in the hopes that she'd run straight to Kennedy to ensure her safety. To my knowledge, that hasn't happened. I'm aware that the entire incident is now being treated as an active arson investigation. But that's all I know."

Hutch didn't avert his gaze. "I could demand you tell me what was in the laptop cases you marched out of here with."

"If you did, I'd tell you they held mostly magazines. Anything more, and I'd have to meet with my team before I elaborated."

"I'll let it go for the time being," Hutch responded. "But only because the Bureau is making some significant progress of our own. I might be coming back to you on this, though."

Casey wanted to press him, but her eyelids were starting to droop. "I'm sure you will."

Hutch rose, ran gentle fingers through her hair. "You're damned good at evading my questions, even when you're half out of it and in pain. Enough for now. You get some sleep. I'll wake you when it's time to take your meds."

A hint of a smile curved Casey's lips. "Or when you decide it's time for round two." She yawned. "Don't expect better results the second time around. G'night."

***

Offices of the Zermatt Group
West Seventy-Fifth Street, Seventh Floor

Manhattan, New York
Tuesday, March 21, 7:45 p.m.

Terri sat straight up in her chair, fisting her hands in triumph. "Gotcha," she announced to Aidan, who'd just wrapped up a call to Simone.

He recognized the tone of Terri's voice and swiveled around to face her.

"What do you have?"

"With the insights Caitlin shared on Sunday about Scott Security, combined with my own knowledge and tools, I pried open the lid on the dark side of Scott Security's backup personnel files. I cross-matched the names, time frame, and physical description we're focusing on."

"And, clearly, you got a hit."

"Not *a* hit. *The* hit." Terri angled her computer so Aidan could see it. "Meet Owen Willard, now Milos Popovic. He was scrubbed from the dark side of Scott Security three hours after Shane Walsh's murder. Just after that, his one-stop flight to Podgorica, Montenegro, departed. It came complete with a new identity and a new bank account. An anonymous source wired ten thousand euros to Popovic's account that same day."

"Not much for a paid killer." Aidan propped his hip on the edge of the desk. "But not a surprise, given he fucked up his assignment. Shane's dead, but Caitlin is still alive and in hiding. Willard is probably hoping it's a down payment until he flushes Caitlin out. Well, he can forget about that happening. It's been too many days, and too many failed attempts. Instead of money, he'll be getting a visit from Scott's goons, who'll fly into Montenegro to take care of him."

Aidan strode across the room as he spoke. "Do you have Willard's new address?"

"Of course."

"Text that and his new ID to Simone. I'm calling her back now." He grabbed the telephone.

Simone answered on the first ring.

"You missed me, *chérie*?" she inquired lightly. "It's only been ten minutes."

"The situation just got urgent." Aidan's voice told her all she needed to know.

"I'm listening."

Succinctly, Aidan relayed everything Terri had found. "Scott is doubtless in the process of sending men to eliminate Willard, since he's outlived his usefulness and is now a huge liability instead of an asset. Terri just texted you his new name and address. I need a Tiger Team dispatched there to land before dawn. We need the cover of darkness. Use the Zermatt jet. We'll be exfiltrating Willard from Montenegro and bringing him back to the US—alive."

***

Podgorica, Montenegro
Wednesday, March 22, 3:25 a.m. CET

Owen Willard—now Milos Popovic—paced around the kitchen of his third-floor apartment, swallowing another glass of whiskey—his third in the past hour. Maybe if he drank enough he'd pass out and forget the sense of doom that was knotting his gut.

He'd checked his online bank account twice yesterday and once an hour ago. No new funds had been wired to him. And the two calls he'd made to Scott Security had been interrupted by a computer-generated voice that informed him his call could not be completed as dialed.

What the hell did that mean?

It meant Scott was cutting him off.

Abruptly, reality dawned. What an asshole he was being. He hadn't just fucked up, he was a dangerous loose end. He wasn't being cut off. He was being cut down.

Swept with panic, Owen felt his self-preservation instincts kick in.

Slamming down his glass, he dashed into the bedroom, grabbing his duffel bag and shoving all his essential things inside. Money. Passports. Weapons.

He wiped his cell phone and threw it into the garbage. He'd get a new one, find a new place to live—somewhere Scott wouldn't find him.

He'd barely reached the living room when his apartment door flew off its hinges, and the terrace's sliding glass door exploded into a thousand shards of glass.

Three men dressed in black, wearing ski masks and goggles and carrying MP5s, burst into the room, tossing a flashbang grenade inside.

Explosive noise. Blinding light.

Owen screamed, squeezing his eyes shut and clapping his hands over his ears.

The Zermatt team moved like a well-oiled machine. Before Owen could regain his bearings, his arms and legs were bound with black zip ties, and his cries of pain were silenced by the duct tape that was slapped over his mouth.

The Tiger Team had just prepped the portable stretcher they'd brought to ready him for transport, when, out of nowhere, two separate men burst in through the entrance door, pistols raised.

Scott's goons.

They barely got into the apartment.

As they blinked to clear the smoke burning their eyes, the Tiger Team whipped around and took them out. They raised their MP5s and double-tapped each of Scott's men, then sent single bullets through their heads.

The men fell like stones.

"You're lucky we got here first," one of the Zermatt guys muttered to Owen, just as he felt the prick at his neck. "Nighty night."

With their drugged captive out cold, the Tiger Team strapped him to the stretcher. Swiftly, they donned fake vests that made them appear to be Montenegro emergency services. Then, lifting the stretcher, they stepped over the two dead bodies and headed toward the stolen ambulance that would take them to the Zermatt jet.

26

FBI New York Field Office
26 Federal Plaza
Manhattan, New York
Wednesday, March 22, 7:45 p.m.

Hutch sat at his desk, irked and on edge. He hadn't been particularly productive all day, not after spending a frustrating, sleepless night—the first since Casey had reinjured herself—back in their bed.

She hadn't told him a thing. She'd been too wiped out for another interrogation. Instead, clad in an oversize nightshirt, she'd curled up against him, her face buried in his chest, her sleepy voice murmuring her pleasure at having him beside her. He wholeheartedly agreed, grateful that she'd healed enough to make this possible. But even though he'd kissed her until she dozed, then wrapped his arms around her, he was terrified he'd aggravate her inflammation by falling asleep and pressing too close or squeezing too hard.

Not to mention, his noncompliant body was throbbing for hers, uncaring of the fact that a longer wait was on the horizon. And he was ripping pissed at himself. Dammit, he was in his late thirties, certainly not a kid anymore. Yet he felt like a horny teenager, desperate for sexual relief from the woman he loved.

By dawn, he couldn't take it anymore.

He'd gotten up, taken an unpleasantly cold shower, and then called Sophie as he dressed. Fortunately she'd been available to arrive and take care of Casey by six a.m., and could remain with her until her replacement, Brenda Hill, arrived at five p.m. to take over.

Which meant that Hutch was able to get a jump start on the workday and delve further into his investigation for however long it took.

Unfortunately, none of his or SA Barkley and his team's leads were panning out. It was as if they were all banging their heads against the wall. Hutch's already sour mood was evolving into outright anger. He was starting to actually envy Forensic Instincts, who were happy to color outside the lines. Being restricted by using only legal methods was frustrating as hell. And his questioning session with Casey had only reinforced what he already suspected: he might have curtailed FI, but that didn't mean they weren't finding subtle ways to circumvent his orders.

He was just about to get himself a cup of shitty coffee when his cell phone sounded, indicating that a text had come through. He glanced at the unknown number and frowned. Normally, he wiped messages from anonymous sources like this without even sparing them a glance.

Something told him not to do so this time.

He clicked into the message, his eyes narrowing as he read:

We're gifting the offender in the Shane Walsh murder case to you. You can find him inside hangar #33 at the northwest corner of

Teterboro Airport. You already have the 9mm Glock that was the murder weapon. Now you have the killer to go with it.

You're welcome.

Lips pursed, Hutch reread the text, understanding the meaning behind it. The Bureau hadn't released any information on the murder weapon. Yet this sender knew what it was and was verifying their legitimacy by supplying it.

Which was proof that this text wasn't one to ignore.

***

Teterboro Airport
111 Industrial Avenue
Teterboro, New Jersey
Wednesday, March 22, 10:15 p.m.

Everything was in place.

Hutch had gone through proper channels to make this happen. He'd made his case to his assistant director in charge, claiming that, while he didn't have probable cause, there were exigent circumstances to explore the contents of the text. Technically, the guy inside that hangar could be injured or dying.

He'd gotten the okay. The ADIC would allow Hutch to bring SA Barkley and a two-man SWAT team when they closed in. The field office's SWAT coordinator was brought on board, organizing the raid. In-house research was expediently done on the location in question, only to find that it was indeed a seldom-used maintenance facility.

Now, Hutch's team waited a few blocks away as the drones they'd flown over the hangar did their job before the team approached. A good visual was obtained, confirming that there was no ambush in the vicinity. Also confirmed was that the hangar had two doors—a wide entry/exit door and an emergency door.

That was all the information they needed to move in.

The agents left their black SUV and made their way slowly and carefully down the far side of the runways. Their bulletproof vests were in place and their weapons were loaded, gripped, and ready.

Hangar #33 was a large single-story corrugated metal building in the corner of the airport, its wide, tall doors there to provide easy entry and exit for heavy snow removal equipment.

The team of agents crept forward and surrounded the door.

Hutch signaled Barkley that the two of them should hold back and let the SWAT guys take the lead. Barkley nodded.

SWAT moved forward. One of them removed the hinges, then stepped back to blast the top and bottom of the door.

The door teetered, then crashed to the ground.

"FBI," one SWAT guy shouted as they both barreled inside, sweeping every section of the room.

It didn't take long before Hutch heard them call out: "All clear!"

That was Hutch's cue to act.

He led Barkley inside, pistol raised, and was greeted by concrete floors, equipment from snow plows, dump trucks, and bulldozers, all parked and ready to go.

And in the center of the hangar, sitting atop a pallet containing bags of ice melt was a man—a struggling man whose eyes were wild with fear. His hands and legs were immobilized with black zip ties, and his mouth was sealed with a piece of duct tape. He was secured to the pallet with additional zip ties, clearly to prevent him from taking off.

Around his neck was a clear document pouch with papers inside and a Post-it slapped on top of it.

Hutch was there in a heartbeat. He snatched both the Post-it and the pouch, simultaneously glancing over the guy before announcing, "He seems intact, but summon the paramedics."

With that, he turned his full attention on the Post-it, which read:

Name: Owen Willard. Former employee of Scott Security, assigned by Charles Scott to kill Shane and Caitlin Walsh. Given the full assignment was never completed, Willard is now on Scott's hit list. With minor persuasion on your part, he'll tell all. Re: the attached papers: a composite of all Scott's illegal alliances and activities.

Act quickly. Make arrests. Get Caitlin Walsh home.

You don't know us, but now you owe us.

No signature.

Without pause, Hutch opened the file and skimmed the pages, his mind racing. Physical evidence that implicated Scott in the most heinous of crimes, carefully organized with names, dates, places, and specifics. Too precise to be fabricated. Illegally obtained, but handed over freely and anonymously, so legally usable.

Handed over by whom?

This work was beyond FI's skill set.

So who had engineered this? And why? A vendetta?

Hutch knew he'd probably never get those answers. And right now he didn't give a damn. He'd take his gift and run with it.

He leaned forward and tore the duct tape from Willard's mouth.

***

Offices of the Zermatt Group
West Seventy-Fifth Street, Seventh Floor
Manhattan, New York
Wednesday, March 22, 10:50 p.m.

Aidan ended the call with his on-the-scene Zermatt operative and hung up the phone.

"Hutchinson and his team took Willard," he announced. "They put him in their SUV, and transported him to the New York field office. I'd bet the bank that he waived his rights in order to get as lenient a sentence as possible and is spilling his guts to the Bureau as we speak. And every word will match the details in that file and put another nail in Charles Scott's coffin."

Terri nodded, her brow furrowed as she focused on her computer screen. "Willard knows that Scott sent a team to kill him, and he'll do whatever he has to in order to stay alive, and to get Scott's ass behind bars. From what Forensic Instincts has told us, Hutchinson is sharp as a tack. He'll bring this investigation to a close in record time."

"Yup," Aidan agreed with the sense of satisfaction he always felt when Zermatt's brand of justice was served. "So that's a wrap."

Terri clicked a few final keys on her keyboard, scanned her screen, and then sat back with a broad grin. "No, *this* is a wrap," she corrected him. "I drilled around Scott Security's finances, and drained a substantial amount from their illegitimate accounts. Same for Charles Scott's personal offshore accounts. All of those funds have been moved to the Zermatt coffers. So we've now officially been paid for our work."

Aidan's lips curved. "Nice to be handsomely compensated and to break that bastard. He won't be reporting his losses to law enforcement; I can assure you of that."

"No, he'll be vacationing in a supermax prison cell." Terri folded her arms behind her head.

Aidan picked up the phone again. "Time to advise Marc that they can contact Caitlin Walsh. I'm guessing that, in the blink of an eye, she'll be coming home to her daughter."

27

One Week Later

Hutch had moved mountains over the past seven days, knowing that there was a nine-year-old girl who needed to be reunited with her mommy.

For starters, he'd taken the time on the drive back to the field office with Willard to contact an assistant US attorney he knew well and ask her for a favor: to expedite things by meeting Hutch at the field office ASAP.

As a result of that meeting—and with the anonymous file of damning information courtesy of Zermatt—Hutch got the immediate okay for search warrants for Charles Scott and his company's financials, as well as the go-ahead to search his house, his office, and to seize all his electronic devices.

The wheels of justice spun at a breakneck pace. With all the incriminating data now being uncovered by the joint efforts of the FBI, the Bureau had enough for a long line of arrest warrants within days. Not only was Scott cut off at the knees, so was his entire criminal enterprise. The evidence was irrefutable, and the entirety of his alliances were now either in FBI custody or, where it came to moles inside government agencies, being ferreted out and taken in. As for Scott, it came as no surprise that his high-powered lawyers advised their client to stay silent, even after the courts deemed him a flight risk and he was remanded without bail.

What neither Scott nor his attorneys had counted on was Owen Willard being there, alive, and ready to testify.

So much for Scott's final safety net.

He was going nowhere except behind bars.

And that meant it was finally safe for Caitlin Walsh to come home.

Zermatt had come through big-time.

And the Forensic Instincts team was elated.

Ryan had been the one to contact Caitlin and tell her the good news. She'd wept and wept for joy, and then followed his instructions to call Hutch and reveal her location.

FI's policy was consistent: let the FBI take the credit. All Casey and her team wanted was Caitlin at home where she belonged.

EPILOGUE

The McKay Residence
East 236th Street
Woodlawn, Bronx, New York
Thursday, March 30, 6:35 p.m.

The entire Forensic Instincts team—including a still-weak Casey, who had been permitted this one short momentous visit by her surgeon—plus the entire McKay family were sandwiched in the entranceway of Maureen and Colin's house immediately after SA Barkley's text to Maureen.

Maureen's eyes had filled with joyous tears as she peeked out the window. "They're here!"

The words were barely out of her mouth when Kennedy shoved her way past everyone, flung open the front door, and raced outside.

"Mommy!" She bypassed Barkley and leaped into Caitlin's arms, sobbing the word over and over and shaking violently as she held tight to her.

"Oh, baby." Caitlin squatted down to hug Kennedy closer, tears coursing down her cheeks as she rocked her child to and fro. "Oh my God, I can't believe I'm holding you again."

Kennedy nodded fervently, finally leaning back to study her mother's face. "You're really okay?"

"Thanks to Special Agent Barkley and the FBI, I am." As instructed, Caitlin omitted any mention of FI, Aidan, or Terri. Instead, she dashed the tears off her face, trying hard to bring herself under control. "And so are you. Aunt Maureen obviously took wonderful care of you. You look tired, but otherwise great."

As Caitlin spoke, Maureen hurried forward to embrace her, closely followed by the entire McKay family, most especially Ryan, who hugged her tightly and murmured something touching about Shane in her ear. The rest of the FI team hung back, aware that, ostensibly, they'd never met or spoken to Caitlin.

Caitlin followed their instructions, focusing completely on her family, pausing only to thank SA Barkley again. "I can't begin to tell you how grateful I am," she said to him.

Barkley smiled. "That's my job, Mrs. Walsh. I'm so very glad the Bureau could make this reunion a reality."

Casey stifled a grin. Barkley might be content with the way things had played out, but Hutch had definitely not been. At home last night, he'd plagued Casey with questions about FI's behind-the-scenes activities, including who they'd worked with to "help" the Bureau solve this case, as well as how they knew where Caitlin had been hiding.

But this was one secret that would remain as such. The Zermatt Group would continue to exist under a veil of secrecy.

Casey had given her husband a sunny smile and assured him that the team had no idea where Caitlin had been hiding. And that whatever assistance the FBI had received, it hadn't come from Forensic Instincts.

As angry and frustrated as he was, a hint of admiration flickered in Hutch's eyes. "You know what, beautiful? I'll deny it if you repeat that I said this, but you and your team managed us quite nicely. You pulled off this coup. No one else knows that, but I do. Granted it was definitely done illegally. But you covered your asses and got the desired results. You're good. *Very* good."

Casey had closed the subject by showing him just how good she was—not professionally, but personally.

And all was right with the world.

***

Ryan waited until the celebration had moved to the living room, where Kennedy was sitting close to Caitlin on the sofa, and everyone was talking, laughing, and chowing down on his mother's numerous desserts.

Then, he put his long-awaited plan in motion.

He came up behind Claire, who was standing to bring in the next tray of goodies.

"Go ahead and deliver that," he said. "And then come with me."

Claire shot him a puzzled look, but she did as he asked.

Ryan seized her hand and pulled her out of the room and into the empty den, shutting the door behind him.

"Ry?" Claire inclined her head. "Is everything okay?"

"You tell me," he replied.

With that, he dropped to one knee and pulled a small square velvet box out of his pocket.

"It seems like I've waited forever for this moment," he began. "I even prepared a speech for it—me of all people." His gaze locked with Claire's as she stared, a fine mist of tears dampening her eyes. "What we have is incredible, Claire. But it's no longer enough. I want it all. I want you in every way there is. Emotionally, physically, legally. You're my other half, and I love you. You've changed me forever, and I never want to go back." He drew in a shaky breath. "I can't believe this is me, but it is. It's what you helped me become. Please, let's make it official—marriage, kids, maybe a house in the suburbs. Whatever you want."

He snapped open the box, and a moonstone with shades of blues and browns subtly blended in with the creamy ivory color, the entire ring surrounded by tiny diamonds glistening back at them. Claire gasped, her hand covering her mouth.

"The moonstone symbolizes feminine energy, intuition, and emotional balance, not to mention being linked to love, nurturing, and enhanced psychic abilities," Ryan continued. "What could be more perfect for you? And it's the stone for new beginnings—that's us. Marry me, Claire. Share your life with me. Please."

Ryan reached for her left hand, watching, waiting.

Claire took a deep breath and swallowed her tears. "I love you, Ryan. I have no speech to offer. So I'll just say yes. Yes to everything you just said. Yes to all you want. Yes."

"Thank God," Ryan murmured, sliding the ring on her finger, then rising to take her in his arms, kissing her with tenderness and awe.

Claire kissed him back. “I can’t believe this is for real,” she said.

“Believe it. Because it is. Do you think you can handle being an official part of the overwhelming McKay clan?”

Claire’s eyes sparkled. “With pleasure.”

He drew back, a triumphant Ryan-like grin on his face. “Good. Then let’s go out there and make my mom’s day.”

ACKNOWLEDGMENTS

With many thanks to:

James McNamara, Captain of Marines, Supervisory Special Agent, Behavioral Analysis Unit, FBI (ret.).

Laura M. Zartman, Esquire, attorney extraordinaire, and top-notch FBI Special Agent, former senior team leader of Evidence Response Team, Newark Division (ret.).

The FBI's Office of Public Affairs

The FBI's Victim Services Division and Victim Specialist Brandon Becker

FBI Nashville

LP, my one-of-a-kind editor, who knows just what's missing and helps me find it

Beth Attwood, a miss-nothing copy editor who smooths out the rough edges

And, as always, Brad Kane, Wendi Kane-Millard, and Laci Millard—the heart of every page I write and the foundation of my life.

We hope you enjoyed this book from Bonnie Meadow Publishing.

Connect with us on BonnieMeadowPublishing.com for more information on our new releases!

Other ways to keep in touch with Andrea Kane:

andreakane.com

facebook.com/AuthorAndreaKane/

@andrea_kane

goodreads.com/AKane